Path to Promise

Path to Promise

Sherryle Kiser Jackson

www.urbanchristianonline.com

Urban Books, LLC
97 N18th Street
Wyandanch, NY 11798

ISBN 13: 978-1-60162-772-8
ISBN 10: 1-60162-772-6

First Printing November 2013
Printed in the United States of America

10 9 8 7 6 5 4 3 2 1

Distributed by Kensington Corp.
Submit Wholesale Orders to:
Kensington Publishing Corp.
C/O Penguin Group (USA) Inc.
Attention: Order Processing
405 Murray Hill Parkway
East Rutherford, NJ 07073-2316
Phone: 1-800-526-0275
Fax: 1-800-227-9604

To Erica Dixon, who I know is on the path.

Acknowledgments

I'm happy to be on the path with my husband, Arvell Jackson. We give and take, and I truly believe our begging, stealing, and borrowing from one another balances out. For any debt outstanding, God grants a grace expense account.

To anyone who knows me, you may have heard me say, "I am practically placed as a teacher, but passionately preserved as a writer." That is a lot of p's. Add to them the path to promise. There are a lot of people to thank when you are on a path that's rugged and winding. The path to promise, I'm coming to understand, is not always a lateral move to the side, and to the side again, but is a perilously steep climb, with God's promotion to the next level. I am on the path, and I would like to thank the following people.

My gratitude goes to fellow authors of the Christian Authors on Tour, including A'ndrea J. Wilson, Lynn Pinder, and Joy Elizabeth Turner; and to Urban Christian and Faith and Fiction Retreat authors Joylynn Ross, Rhonda McKnight, Shelia Lipsey, Pat Simmons, Tiffany Warren, and Norma Jarrett for continuing to let your voices be heard among the rhetoric of the day.

And I'd like to extend my heartfelt thanks to all the readers and reviewers, especially Janette Malcom, Michelle Rawls, TaNisha Webb of KC Girlfriends Book Club and the editor in chief of *Book Club 101 Magazine*, Monique "The Delta Reviewer" Bruner, and

Crystal Gamble-Nolden from OOSA Book Club, who will make time in their massive reading schedules for one of my books. I appreciate you.

Thanks go to my sorors of Delta Sigma Theta, who in 2013 are keeping it a hundred and have shown a dedication to continuing the legacy of service of our founders. You are dynamic and awe-inspiring.

As always, I needed legal counsel from my line sister Crystal Flournoy and my literary friend Norma Jarrett. In the end, I did my own interpretations. I do not hold you liable, just dependable. That law stuff is no joke and is taxing on the brain.

Chapter 1

Will had never liked board meetings, whether on the job or at church. Just like the term suggested, they were stiff and impersonal. He looked around at the three members on the executive board of Grace Apostle Methodist Church, who served under his father as pastor, and found the air particularly tense. He'd rather be at home in his jeans and tennis shoes than in a suit and tie, but his father had reminded him that his casual attire was not always appropriate for Kingdom business. If this meeting was called to do damage control for some kind of drama, he'd much rather be crammed in a crowded mall with all the gift returners and gift card redeemers and be reminded that he didn't have anyone special to celebrate his holidays with. He had broken up with his longtime girlfriend in hopes of pursuing a relationship with his best friend, Rebecca Lucas. She had literally left him in the trail of her taillights and exhaust fumes.

"Anyone know what this is about?" Will asked as he casually banged his empty water bottle against his knee, trying to rid his mind of fleeting thoughts of her—the second or third time today.

"We'd prefer to wait until your father gets here," Deacon Contee replied.

"Wait, my father didn't call this meeting?" Will asked, tugging at his right earlobe.

Silence was his answer. Will took a chance on tossing his bottle, in hopes of making the wastebasket a few feet away. He had risen slightly to have better odds and had unbuttoned his suit jacket in the process. He looked around to see if anyone else was as stunned as he was when he banked the bottle on the first try. He didn't have a good feeling about this.

His dad's seat was reserved on the opposite side of the desk, and Will reflected on the month and a half he had filled in for his father. He'd rate his time a C-. He got a B, or even an A, when it came to the actual preaching, but managing the congregation brought his average down significantly. There had been that Bible study session that went astray, a funeral, a catfight, and Rebecca's return to Easton, Maryland.

He had to admit that there had been some high times too. Finding a comfortable balance between church and work, and having an opportunity to minister God's Word were blessings. The church anniversary, in particular, where he encouraged Rebecca to minister in dance alongside him, stood out as a milestone. He had felt as if he had hit a rhythm that would only get better, until his family hit a huge bump in the road—his dad's secret indiscretion from the past and its eventual impact on the family dynamic.

Just then his dad, William Henry Donovan Sr., crossed his field of vision, ending Will's introspection. Will stood as his dad draped his overcoat on the back of his chair.

"Gentlemen." Pastor Donovan nodded to the others. "Son." He shook Will's hand. Their handshake, though formal for a father and son, was warmer than the mere murmurs from the others.

It was comforting for Will to see his dad behind his desk again. It had been determined that watch night was the night. He would be resuming his role as senior pastor, on top of his duties as school chancellor, after a topsy-turvy sabbatical. His father's eyes and expression seemed to be communicating something that Will could not read.

Deacon Contee, his father's right-hand man, and by all accounts, Will's right-hand man while his father was on break, stood. He cleared his throat ceremoniously, and it became clear to Will who was running this particular meeting. Will knew that Deacon Contee didn't mince words, so he knew he would not be left in the dark much longer about the details of this mystery meeting.

"In light of recent . . . discoveries, it has been decided that Pastor Donovan should retire as both pastor and chancellor of the school at Grace Apostle, effective immediately." Deacon Contee's eyes were unapologetic; his demeanor suggested he was ready for a rebuttal.

Will looked at his dad. They were both temporarily frozen in place. Recent discoveries equaled one thing: his dad's long-term affair with Madame Ava Lucas. His dad hadn't made an all-out confession, like famed televangelist Jimmie Swaggart's tearful televised admission to the like in the late eighties. His father had simply walked Gail, his daughter and the product of that affair, down the aisle recently at her modest wedding, held at the church. Although an early retirement was the same sanction Will had suggested, out of anger, be imposed on his dad when he first found out that his dad had cheated on his mother and the late first lady of the church, this dethroning felt more like a beheading.

"Hey, wait, I am missing something, like when this decision was made and by whom," Will remarked. "Doesn't the person retiring usually deem when he is no longer able or no longer desires to hold the position? I mean, c'mon. My dad has been a dedicated pastor, colleague, and friend to this church community for nearly fifty years."

"The pastor kept an extramarital affair a secret from this board and the entire church body. He deceived us all," replied John Lyons, the former chairman of the deacon board, which was held in emeritus standing now.

Will tempered his words for this patriarchal figure, whose history with the church dated back to his dad's early days as pastor. "The pastor is your friend. Isn't he?"

For an older man, Deacon Lyons was quick with his reply. "So was First Lady Donovan a good friend to Ethel and me. All the women of this church would see his infidelity, his secret, as an act of treason even after all this time."

Will dug his heels into the floor where he sat. When his mom died a little more than fifteen years ago, he had felt very much like the ground had given way from under him. He had struggled for a long time to regain his sure footing. Finding out about his dad's affair had shaken his foundation again and had left him with the same feeling of uncertainty and vulnerability.

"No one can claim ownership over this—the shock, the hurt, the grief. It didn't hit anyone the way it hit me," Will asserted, a little too passionately for the case he was supposed to be making.

"The fact is your father stood up there in the pulpit and preached against adultery and promiscuity when he was doing that kind of thing all this time. I think he ought to stay out of the pulpit," Deacon Contee said, chiming in.

Will was taken aback when he heard what was really an echo of his own words. He had heard of war room sessions with church elders that ended with a recommendation and a final say on the pastor's penance. Men were fallible. There would always be sin. Was there no one present who was willing to give his dad a second chance besides him?

Charlie Marks, the head of the six-member trustee unit, spoke. "This is a church, for heaven's sake. There is a certain standard for its leaders. I mean, my marriage is not perfect, but I've never gone outside it. Never will."

Deacon Contee continued making the board's case, painting a picture that Will wasn't sure as interim pastor was objective or his own projection. According to Deacon Contee, whispers of Pastor Donovan's indiscretion would surely turn into sparsely attended services, cries of concern throughout the congregation, all-out outrage, and calls for his removal. This was the only way for him to bow out gracefully. They would allow him to announce his retirement and accept an honorable discharge.

Will was thinking aloud. "This is a church, like Trustee Marks just pointed out. Forgiveness and restoration should not only be taught but also applied—"

"Forgiveness begins with the truth, Will," Deacon Contee said, cutting him off. "An admission, an apology."

Everyone looked to Pastor Donovan, who had stood silently throughout this whole crucifixion. Will didn't know who his dad's publicist was, but obviously he had advised his client to plead the Fifth. His dad was expressionless, and it angered Will. *Jesus,* Will murmured in his heart. He was working through his own process of forgiving the man, but his dad wasn't making it easy by being elusive about the details that could possibly exonerate him or at least convince this board to be lenient with him. He wanted more than anything to know the depth and breadth of his dad's affair with Madame Ava. When did it start and end? How did he reconcile his transgressions with God and his calling? Why wasn't his father trying to make a heartfelt plea for his integrity, for his ministry?

Will was done talking. Obviously, there wasn't anything worth fighting for anymore. He thought of Rebecca yet again. He didn't know what was worse, his dad giving up so easily on a ministry he had been in charge of all his adult life or Rebecca giving up on them before they had begun. Sure, folks would talk about him and Rebecca hooking up. Loving Lucas women apparently was a part of his hardwiring. Will knew one thing. He was tired of agonizing over things he and his father could have changed or done differently. His dad had strayed, and he couldn't have made Rebecca stay. If and when she came to miss the water out here in Easton, he'd tell her she had her own well willed to her by her mother, not to mention his love spring that she had left behind.

Will realized the conversation was circling around him while he entertained those thoughts. His dad's voice brought him back to the conversation.

"The ministry, I understand. But why the school?" Pastor Donovan asked. "I may not have founded this church—or, in your eyes, upheld its ideals to the best of my ability—but I can say that I did lay the foundation for this school."

"Who saved it come audit time?" Deacon Contee was fast to say.

Pastor Donovan pursed his lips. "You called a friend of a friend, who tightened up our books. Anyone could have done that, Contee."

"You didn't, Pastor." A flash of anger came from Deacon Contee's eyes. "You know full well what we went through to get the accreditation and the state vouchers that help to fund the school. We can't risk any of that. If the state even got a whiff of a scandal, it would be over like that."

"The only way they would get a whiff is if someone is airing dirty laundry." Pastor Donovan plopped down and looked around, as if he was already resigned to the fact that it would be the last time he would sit there as pastor. "Huh, we all know how easily that can happen, don't we, Contee?"

"You ran off our biggest contributor in Madame Ava Lucas when you played Casanova in her household," Deacon Contee said. "No wonder that woman went to her grave despising this place."

In an instant, Will's dad was up out of his seat again. Will felt the need to step in between the two opposing sides to avoid a scuffle.

"Don't you dare spout my circumstances like you care about another living soul except yourself in this matter. You don't know the burdens I bore because of this, and you certainly wouldn't comprehend the grace I've been shown." Pastor Donovan stopped only to wipe the spittle from his lips. "A righteous man repents to his God. I recommend you start."

Will was seeing a side of his dad and Deacon Contee that he had never seen before. How long had he and his father been feuding like the Hatfields and the McCoys? His dad had created a monster, as Deacon Contee had apparently become really comfortable filling in as chancellor. Will was sure that Deacon Contee was ready to do that job permanently.

"Gentlemen, let's keep things decent and in order," Deacon Lyons remarked, his voice doing more to temper emotions than Will's physical barrier when he stood between the feuding men. He propped both of his arms on the arms of the chair to raise himself upright with authority. "Who will take over?"'"

"Let's not forget, I've groomed my son. He's faithfully fulfilled his basic training and served here. My reputation shouldn't ruin his chances," Pastor Donovan was quick to add.

"Will may fill in as interim pastor, but we will look for anyone else who would like to be a permanent replacement, to be fair." Deacon Contee looked around at his cohorts for support. Then, turning his attention to Will, he continued, "At that time, if you, in good faith, want to continue to serve in the capacity of pastor, you must apply like the rest."

Will was reeling from the fact that the all-out feud had shifted suddenly to this all too-casual conversation about his future in the ministry, and he was unable to respond before his dad interjected, "Who do you have in mind to run the school? Will a board decide that? A vote? Who?"

Deacon Contee paused in mock reluctance. "I guess I am the only one who has experience. We're in the middle of a session. It would be too disruptive to bring in someone new and teach them the day-to-day operations now."

"Of course," Pastor Donovan said, turning suddenly and grabbing his coat. "I guess everything has been decided. Good day, gentlemen."

Will made haste to follow his dad out the door and catch him as he entered the outer office. For a man of seventy-five, Pastor Donovan was extremely quick. Will made sure to close the office door behind them before grabbing his dad's arm, which was stiff now with indifference. "Wait, Dad. I know this is . . . ridiculous, but let's let them say their piece."

"There is nothing more I need to hear. Contee has been undermining me for a while now, but just like he said in there, we never had time to train anyone else. You were always working. I could barely get you here on Sundays to preach. I think they made themselves clear. I'm out after fifty years, and you've barely got your foot in the door right now. After all this family has sacrificed for this place, huh? You can sit and listen to their stipulations if you want to. Grace Apostle apparently is no longer my affair."

Wrong answer, Will thought. His father couldn't have chosen a poorer set of words, and Will couldn't resist the jab. "Tell me this wasn't just an affair or about the one you shared with Madame Ava, that your ministry and the sacrifice you talked about in there, and all that I've tried to emulate through the years was about Christ, right?"

Pastor Donovan lifted his arms and let them fall in exasperation. They slapped loudly against his sides. He turned to leave as hastily as before.

Will felt a tug of allegiance to his dad, despite all they had been through. Walking away from Grace Apostle did not compute to him. This was his dad's church. What were they going to do at Grace Apostle without him? "Dad, you're the very fabric of this church. I know that, and they know that. You're still very much in this. I still consider you my pastor and mentor. What do you want me to do?"

Pastor Donovan turned. With glassy eyes, he approached Will, coming to within an inch of his only son, as if he was going to hug him. He spoke at a low volume so that only Will could hear, even if the door to the inner office were open. "Give 'em hell. Remind them it is a very real place. Study. Preach your heart out. I mean, come out swinging, Will, because they already have. If you ever dreamed about being a pastor, it's your time. This is your time, son."

Chapter 2

Rebecca Lucas needed to move. She wondered if she should pull out of her apartment's lease now, since some of her bags were still packed from an extended stay in her hometown of Easton. It was Thursday night—the official beginning of the weekend to the neighbors in her apartment building. Without a doubt, cash would be pooled together, a keg or two would be shared, and something would come crashing down, including a few partiers who had trouble navigating the stairwell. Rebecca remembered depending on her youthful complexion nearly ten years ago, pretending to be starting graduate school, when she leased the second-floor, rent-controlled unit, used for off-campus housing at Salisbury University. She had been in two similar units before, when she actually was in college: one in the community called College Park and the other in a subdivision called Merrifield. Her propensity to pay three months at a time and to stay out of trouble protected her middle-aged hideout. When she'd asked the landlord if the local university was a party school, trying to gauge the habits of the other renters, he'd told her that any school was a party school when the alcohol was flowing.

The alcohol was certainly flowing tonight. The ear acid of heavy metal came seeping through the ceiling from the floor above as Rebecca set cartons of Chinese carryout in front of her for a late dinner. She went for the fortune cookie first, as she contemplated calling the police and issuing a "disturbing the peace" complaint. It was only 9:30 p.m., so the three guys above her were starting earlier than usually with their inconsiderate antics that affected the entire building. Maybe she felt more bothered because she was getting older and less tolerant. She needed time to get some food in her, pop an aspirin, and find a boulder to sleep under. She cracked the cookie at the fold to extract the fortune, as if to find a solution to her dilemma. What the fortune said caused her hand to be suspended in the air and her mind to be plagued by recent events: *There is a difference between running scared and running free.*

Running was what she felt she had done when she returned to Salisbury a week ago from Easton: running from rumors, running from reality, and most of all, running from Will. Rebecca hadn't expected to get so close to her best friend, Will Donovan, in the four and a half weeks she had been at home to bury her mother. Having him near had her seriously contemplating staying. They had always been so close that they were practically brother and sister. Then their feelings for one another started to grow. On the verge of an ill-conceived love affair, the two of them found they shared a mutual sister, which set Rebecca's exodus from her family home in motion. That was too close for comfort for her.

Rebecca and Will's relationship had eerie similarities to their parents' relationship, her mom and his dad's adulterous affair, which went on for decades. Although neither she nor Will were married, Will was in a relationship when their feelings began to bud. Their parents' secret had imploded like an air bag that couldn't be stuffed back in. Rebecca and Will had survived the impact, but she had run before they could assess the damage to the future of their relationship. She had vowed to stop playing with him, to create the space that would keep them from toying with the idea of taking their friendship to another level. She was alone at Christmas.

Now Rebecca was going back to work after a mixture of her bereavement, sick, and personal leave had been exhausted. She would be trapped in the nine-to-five grind again. The thought made her toss the fortune and the cookie aside and wolf down the lo mein noodles from the carton. Nearly five weeks had passed since she stepped foot into Sanz, Mitchum, Clarke, and Associates. She picked Friday to get reacclimated to her work environment. It was exactly one week before many of the attorneys would claim their own time off for New Year's. As far as her caseload and trial prep went as a paralegal, she wanted to hit the ground running, set things in order for the New Year.

The next day Rebecca clung to her sixteen-ounce Colombian roast as life support to get her through the day. She practically had to reintroduce herself to the firm's fifth-floor administrative assistant, Celeste, after she called out to the slightly older woman to hold the elevator on the ground floor. No greeting and no apology came from her colleague when they came face-to-face after Rebecca sacrificed her umbrella handle to prompt the door to open again.

"Thank you," Rebecca said sarcastically before the elevator car became crowded with associates, who were just as rude, pushing them farther back with their wet umbrellas, their lawyer-speak, and their arrogance.

Their building had ten floors; the top five were occupied by the largest law firm on the Eastern Shore of Maryland. When the elevator reached the fifth floor, an older man in an all-weather coat pushed the CLOSE button so quickly that Rebecca and Celeste couldn't move forward and get off the elevator in time. The man acting as the lift operator then spoke loudly into his cell phone, letting the person on the other end of the line know his estimated time of arrival in the suite of offices on a higher floor. Having missed their floor, an indication of how insignificant they were on the firm's totem pole, Rebecca and Celeste shared a perturbed look.

They rode to the top, stopping on practically every other floor, and then rode back down to the very bottom before they could move to the front and take control of the roving beast that was their elevator.

"I see nothing has changed around here," Rebecca said once she was off the elevator and heading with her traveling companion to the administrative suite of cubicles and waiting rooms.

"Not a thing. I am glad one of us knows somebody that has enough pull to get a substantial vacation before vacation week." Celeste smirked.

Apparently, Celeste hadn't gotten the notice as to why she had been out, Rebecca thought. A "How are you doing?" would have been in order. Rebecca decided her business wasn't worth telling. They weren't friends. They had the same strained relationship Rebecca seemed to have with all women, one based on assumptions, envy, and petty arguments. She was thought to be worthless throughout high school because she didn't hang in a clique of girls that had boyfriends, gossiped, or had a fashion obsession. Then she was considered a wanton threat because the boyfriends of those same girls got wind of the fact that she had contoured her body and wasn't afraid to use it.

"I'm glad you're back," Celeste said, walking ahead to her command post, apparently in a hurry to grab something. Celeste grabbed a pile of papers and file folders with one arm. She turned at the precise time and practically shoved the stack into Rebecca's midsection. "Now you can pull your own weight."

Rebecca stepped back, not so much from the impact, but from the splash of her coffee. She fought to maintain her grip on the coffee cup. They were in a staring match, and it would continue, as far as Rebecca was concerned, until Celeste realized her hands were occupied. Still holding the pile of papers and folders, Celeste sighed heavily and begrudgingly followed Rebecca, whose gait was purposely slow. Celeste's shoes squeaked due to the slickness of the floor from the spilled coffee and the cheap polyurethane material her shoes were made from. Before even attempting to retrieve what Celeste had for her, Rebecca sat her coffee down and draped her fur-trimmed sweater on the hook to the right of her desk once she was inside her cubicle. They exchanged smug looks and the load of papers before Celeste turned to leave.

What was her problem? Rebecca thought. No amount of coercion or sweet talk could make Celeste fill in for a paralegal. On numerous occasions, she had let attorneys and their lackeys alike know she was an administrative assistant. She worked with Windows software, not Workshare, and she absolutely wasn't running back and forth across the street to the court-house. Bethany or any of the other three paralegals in the building might be called upon to assist in her stead, but definitely not Celeste.

Rebecca's desk was neat, and the pile of depositions and files that she now held would give her a time line of what had gone on in her absence. She walked to the break room before taking on the task of going through the pile and devising a to-do list from it. She needed to refresh her cup of coffee and, in doing so, checked off her first assignment. It was her duty to start a pot of generic roast for clients and guests who would check in on their floor. A sad cutout of a Christmas tree, tacked up on the huge memo board and cluttered with generic cards from random staffers, was the only reminder of the holiday that had just past. Rebecca concentrated on setting the coffee machine to brew so she could forget how she had spent Christmas day sulking and sorting through mail of her own.

She backtracked now to her desk to grab her calendar to confer with Celeste. Like a chess player did a chessboard, she studied her calendar and kept it up to date at all times. She had to know where all the major players were. Jacobs, God help him, was no doubt in court. That left Minor and Burke, whom she was uncertain about.

Burke. The thought of him gave her shivers. She used to think the way he looked at her was sexy, but now it brought a curl to her lip. Would he be in today or out wooing some client? Maybe he had started his vacation. Would he be looking for her to help him entertain his potential client list, like he had implied before she left? Hopefully, he had found someone else to harass.

Maybe she could get a reprieve today. Yeah, who came in between Christmas and New Year's, anyway? she told herself. Then she thought of all the attorneys in the elevator this morning. She bent back the corner on her agenda book, just thinking about it. It was crazy to keep dwelling on Burke's proposition to befriend his client, Walter Calhoun that had happened just one time and would more than likely not happen again. Her plan was to attack the pile on her desk while attacking her anxiety. She did a one-eighty back to her desk, but like a revolving door, she spun around again with a favor in mind to ask Cruella De Vil at the front desk.

Rebecca stopped at Celeste's desk and inhaled deeply as she waited to be acknowledged. "Celeste, since it's my first day back, I'm really, really, really trying to play low key today. It's like I'm not here. I wasn't even going to report until Monday, anyway. Until I can weed my way through this pile and get things in order, I'm no good to anyone, anyway. I'd appreciate it if you wouldn't tell Burke that I'm back here. I'm not saying to lie, but just don't make an announcement."

"Oh, no way, sista. Then he'll be loading me up with things to do, or he'll have me searching for Bethany, who, between the two of you, hasn't worked a weekend's worth of time this month." She leaned in, and although Rebecca found that odd, she leaned in as well to catch the apparent scoop Celeste was dishing. "You know, she's nearly four months pregnant."

Rebecca blinked several times as she digested the news, and wondered for a moment how much of her own business Celeste shared in this same manner with friends and foes alike. "Please, Celeste. I don't ask you for much."

"So you're hiding from Burke?" Celeste gave her top molars a satisfied suck.

"Not hiding. I'm just a little disoriented. See," she said, holding out her agenda book. "I don't know where anyone is in any of their cases. Jacobs . . ."

"Is due in court at nine," Celeste said, finishing Rebecca's sentence for her.

Rebecca shrugged and shook her head at the same time. "They do that to him on purpose."

"He does it to himself. He's served more court time than a repeat offender, but he's on a winning streak now. If he was smart, he'd hook up with seven and eight, like Minor is doing, working on a corporate bid. It should be interesting to see who between Burke and Minor wins an office upstairs first," Celeste said, referring to the status of senior attorneys, who were housed on the seventh and eighth floors.

Rebecca had underestimated Celeste's knowledge of office politics. Rebecca didn't want to play them, but it was good to know the house rules.

"He'll be in here, all right, without me saying a word," Celeste said.

Rebecca gave her a quizzical look. "Who?"

"Burke. That's who you're worried about, aren't you?" Celeste snapped.

Rebecca leaned in as Celeste had done to get her to pipe down. "What makes you so certain?"

This time Celeste backed away, as if Rebecca had some sort of disease. "One thing Mr. Kenny Burke can do well is sniff out fresh meat and money. In your case, meat he hasn't fully picked over yet."

Rebecca watched Celeste suck her teeth again, as if to dislodge remnants from her breakfast, before turning on her swivel chair. Rebecca was thoroughly disgusted. What did that mean? And what did she know?

Chapter 3

Rebecca could not ignore another call from her sister. Whether it was really early in the morning or really late at night, it was as if the phone took on an insistent ring when Gail was on the other end of the line. Rebecca always knew it was her even before checking the caller ID display. Gail never let the phone ring more than three times before hanging up. Then to add another layer of irritant, she would dial up again.

Rebecca was in the gym alone on the ground floor of the firm's office building, sweating it out on the elliptical machine before starting her shift on her second day back. She contemplated making Gail sweat it out as well with another unanswered phone call. She snatched her smart phone from the convenience tray at the last minute while adjusting her steps and the incline button to a pace that would allow her to hold a conversation.

"Yes?" Rebecca said.

"It's about time you answered a call. Is that how you answer the phone at your big-time corporate job? I was just about to drive to Salisbury to flat out embarrass you, ignoring me like you have," Gail replied in a threatening manner.

"No, I don't answer the work extension for personal calls, so, no, I don't answer like that. I knew it was you, and before you even make the trip, don't act like you haven't been so far into the clouds of marital bliss that you, yourself, are just connecting with Earth."

Gail giggled at the last part of Rebecca's statement. "What's that? Hold the line, Rebi."

Rebecca listened as Gail relayed all that Rebecca had just said to her husband of less than three weeks. This was followed by more giggling. Rebecca rolled her eyes. Would every call become a three-way now that Gail was married? These cutesy shared conversations gave her all the more reason to avoid her sister.

"Gail," Rebecca called in a regular tone of voice, trying to get her sister's attention. When that failed, she raising her voice slightly and tried again. "Gail. Do you want me to give you a call back while you talk to your husband?"

"Don't you dare, Rebi." All glee was gone from her voice. "I wanted to check up on you. I was wondering why you spent holidays alone when you don't have to. When are you coming home? We miss you. "

"I'm so sure I'm all the two of you talked about on your honeymoon."

Rebecca thought about home, 5920 Zion Hill Road, where she grew up, as opposed to 1515 Prairieville Lane, Apartment 2C, where she hid out. Her mother had willed the house in Easton to her sister before Rebecca even knew Gail was her sister. They both had been raised to believe they were cousins. Rebecca had released any and all emotional claim to the property when Gail and Milo married, giving her blessing, in a sense, for the newlywed couple to build their home there.

There was a slight hesitation. "We need you here on watch night. . . . The family does. It will be the pastor's last night," Gail said.

"What? Pastor Donovan?" was Rebecca's immediate response to the news.

"He's retiring. He told the congregation that it was a sudden decision." Gail's words hung out there.

Retiring or being forced out, Rebecca thought.

"You know me and the pastor talk once or twice a week. I've asked him about his decision. He says it's time, but I know he's just protecting me," Gail revealed.

Rebecca had noticed how Gail kept referring to her father as "the pastor," as if she didn't know how else to refer to him. Her newly discovered parents had to feel like a mismatched pair to her, the pastor and the Madame. It was hard for any of them to fathom, but there was no denying now that Madame Ava and Pastor Donovan had shared more than the same space at the same time. They had the paternity test results to prove it.

"I guess this is the price we pay for the fairy tale. Things are not the same, Rebi," Gail said sullenly.

Gail didn't clarify her last statement or offer up any other information. Once again, Rebecca could hear her brother-in-law in the background, no doubt consoling Gail. Rebecca wasn't going to play mental games with Gail or herself by pretending she wasn't interested in hearing about another special somebody in their "family." Putting distance between herself and Will didn't erase him from the map, or from the real estate he took up in her heart and head.

Rebecca asked, "Where does Will stand in all this?"

Freakin' out, I bet.

"You could ask him yourself. You know?" Gail replied.

There was silence on the line. Then, with a heavy sigh, Gail relented and began telling her about the hunt for the next Grace Apostle pastor. To be fair, she said,

Will would have to complete a candidate application and go through the same vetting process as anyone else applying for the job. In the meantime, he would preach, serving as pastor in the interim.

"So, you see, we could use your support here," Gail said.

We?

Rebecca felt she had to mend her bleeding heart before she could lend her heartfelt support, let alone face Will. And that wouldn't happen anytime soon. Despite Gail's smugness, Rebecca felt her sister was quite content with her role as the go-between. She hoped that she didn't have being a matchmaker in mind as well. It wasn't in the cards for her and Will, especially now that he was making a bid for pastor. What she couldn't understand was why he had to jump through the hoops of being a candidate. He was already the assistant pastor. He should be a shoo-in. One thing she did know was that she would have marred his reputation for sure if their relationship had continued along a romantic path as he had hoped. Things were best the way they had ended up.

"Should I tell Will you asked about him?" Gail inquired.

"If you must," Rebecca said, deciding to be just as snide. To show she was perfectly comfortable discussing him, she asked, "Do you talk to him much?"

"Of course I do. You know, it's funny he never asks about you," Gail said to Rebecca, then almost immediately had to answer for her insensitivity to their third party. "What?"

Rebecca rested her right hand on her chest, as if to perform a compression on herself after the blow to her ego, while Gail spoke to her husband. She had made her choice to leave, most likely losing her best friend in the process. It sounded as if he was really done with her.

"As I was saying, he doesn't ask, but he wants to so badly. I can tell. He loves your cuckoo behind. Forget the madness we kicked up. My mom and my dad equals my mess. It has nothing to do with you and him. Take it from me, Rebi. Don't fight love in the form God wants to provide it," Gail said.

Rebecca found it hard to breathe. She slowed to a stop on the elliptical, although she knew it would do little to help her recover her normal respiration. Rebecca just remembered another reason she wasn't fast to dial her old number. "You can't believe the ramifications of *our* mother's affair are only germane to you? What I can't get you all to understand is that maybe it isn't God's will for me and Will to be together."

"Did your 'here today, gone tomorrow' hyperactive tail talk to Him before running off? Have you ever considered that maybe *Will* is just that? God's perfect *will* to calm you down?" Gail asked, emphasizing the word *will*. "Honestly, I don't know what I am going to do with the two of you."

"Leave us where we are, one in Salisbury, one in Easton," Rebecca said, her breathing shallow between each word. Just listening to Gail spout on was giving her a mental workout. "I've got to go, sis. Time to hit the clock."

"All right, but give what I said some thought, and if you hear a knock on the door, don't be surprised to see me on the other side of the peephole," Gail said.

Thoughts of her conversation with Gail lingered in Rebecca's mind as she ended the call and collected her stuff. Rebecca felt that she had had enough reality shoved in her face in the past month to ever believe her story could have a fairy-tale ending. She grabbed her towel, which was draped across the handrail, and almost screamed when she saw the reflection of a man staring at her in the gym's mirror. He was suited for a day of work, as opposed to a workout. It was Kenny Burke—a classic wolf in sheep's clothing.

Chapter 4

"No wonder you are in such good shape," Kenny said. "Looking good, real good, angel."

"I haven't been gone that long for you to have forgotten my name." Rebecca exhaled loudly, getting over her initial fear but trying to sidestep his path all the same.

She had to admit Kenny Burke was magnificent to look at as well. He had a stare that could pierce stone, and was a Laz Alonso look-alike, with thick dark lashes that would make a woman envious—which was not to say he was at all effeminate. He had strong masculine features set against a backdrop of pure honeycomb. Of course, it would have been hard not to notice another black face when she was immersed in a sea of majority white coworkers on a daily basis, but someone so fine had been a daily fix of testosterone when she first started working at the firm. The fact that he was a black attorney, something she had aspired to be at one time, made him all the more attractive.

Kenny was an equal opportunity philanderer, though. She had considered herself lucky when they shared a lunch date. And a few weeks before her extended break, he had followed her into a supply room for what she was sure would have been a sexy interlude if it weren't for Celeste butting in. Now she considered him the mistake that had never really happened.

He casually shifted, his hands in the pockets of his slacks, blocking the only aisle between the elliptical and the treadmills. "I'm sorry to hear about your mother. You should have told me. I would have sent flowers."

"Really?" Rebecca smirked, remembering how he lit into her at a recent status report meeting of all fifth-floor associates and their aides. Apparently, she made him look bad by not being able to speak to the status of any of his cases. As if he had anything going besides schmoozing, Rebecca remembered thinking. She wondered if there wasn't more to it than that. He wasn't stupid. She knew he could sense that she was avoiding him, if Celeste hadn't told him straight out. "You went a little far with your boilerplate comments. I do a little more than just customize forms all day. It was like you were trying to make a case for my incompetence. What a great way to start back to work."

This time Kenny gave the money shot, with all thirty-two perfectly capped porcelain white teeth gleaming. He replied, "I can't have the office feeling like I am showing you favoritism by letting you off easy because we're both black or have hopes of being great *friends*. I'll admit I'm a butt hole. I know I'm the one in the office people love to hate. It's a strategy, angel. Actually, I'm really as cuddly as a bear. You should remember that."

She was trying to erase that familiarity and replace it with professionalism. He was a bear, all right, Rebecca thought, but she had never had to cross him before. She was coming to realize his bite matched his bark.

Kenny stroked his goatee with his right hand. "I'm a resources man. I like to surround myself with good people. The firm is definitely not using you to the best of your ability."

Rebecca pondered the implications of his words. She could pretend, but she knew full well how he intended to use her. She remembered something he once said. *Walter Calhoun is ready to drop the handling of his business commitments, not to mention his money bags, over to us. I've come to find out that all he requires to loosen his grip completely is a bit of your time.* He hadn't brought it up since she returned to work, and she hadn't asked. Now her peace had been compromised. No more morning workouts for her. She couldn't risk him tracking her down like this, not when she was alone.

"What do you want, Kenny?" Rebecca asked. "I told you the other day that the Mixon settlement has been a bear to close. I have to track down documentation, now that I'm back. Plus, I'm scheduling for Minor and Jacobs . . . interviews and possibly an arbitration. If you're starting something new, you might have to grab Bethany."

"I don't want Bethany," he said, mumbling something to the effect that Bethany was of no use to him in her present state. Then, with a brisk lick of his lips, he said, "I want you."

It was the ambiguity that made her want to scream. She could never read his sincerity. Did he want her or want a favor? She could handle the former more so than the latter. He was charismatic, she thought, if only he could be tamed. Now she wondered with each bat of his eyelashes if he could be the necessary salve for her heartache. Hadn't that been her remedy in the past? Get over one guy by replacing him with another?

Rebecca knew she had to take control of her thoughts. She felt differently now. Plus, she didn't feel like she wanted to get over her heartache as her thoughts drifted to Will. He was proof she had made a decent choice in her life, even if they couldn't be together. She reminded herself that she had retired the checkered flag she used to signal her interest to men. She needed to be alone and gainfully employed. Apparently, Kenny looked at her and saw the old Rebecca from six weeks ago, the one who literally tried to wiggle her behind into his good graces.

"I don't belong to you," Rebecca retorted. "What about my obligations to Minor and Jacobs?"

Kenny shooed off the mention of his colleagues as if they were a nonissue, and a flash of his Invicta watch almost blinded her. "I need you on my team. You'll see. It has its benefits. I'll look out for you. You think Minor or Jacobs would do the same?"

"About that—" Rebecca began.

His hand went up to halt her. He placed his finger to his lips, as if to signal that the walls suddenly had ears. "I want to make sure we are on the same page too. I'm out for the rest of the day. We'll talk about this at a more appropriate time later." He checked his watch, turned, and headed for the men's locker room door. As he walked away, he tossed a comment over his shoulder at full volume. "A strategy session. Brew River Restaurant on West Main. Eight p.m."

Brew River Restaurant was on the Wicomico River, which made the temperature ten degrees colder than the typical winter day. Not since leaving Easton had she thought about her suggestive attire. She was glad she had had a chance to replace the slim-fitting skirt and white blouse she had worn to work with a one-piece pantsuit toned down a bit by a blazer. The pier side ramp trapped her right heel as she walked. She had to shake the heel of her two-and-a-half-inch pumps free, and then she hastened inside. Burke was sitting in view of the entrance, at a bar side table. He didn't see her arrive, nor did he appear to be looking for her.

The setup was not what she had expected. A cozy candlelit table seemed more clandestine and more like Burke's style. Why had he chosen the bar, where puffs of smoke and bits of conversation were shared secondhand? He didn't acknowledge her greeting. He cursed as she took her seat, and pushed aside an appetizer platter. She noticed a ticket and a chart of some kind laminated on the tabletop, where he was tracking his odds in keno, a lottery-style game. She should have known he was a betting man. He threw a hand in the air for luck and cursed again as the monitor displayed the results of the game, while Rebecca looked on.

A waitress with a huge golden mane appeared out of nowhere, grabbing empty glasses off the table beside them. Kenny tossed what looked like a twenty-dollar bill on her tray, signaled that he wanted to continue to play by rotating his hand, and said, "Let 'em ride. I'm playing all night. You still have my numbers, right?"

"I got you. Bring your tickets right out, sweetie," the waitress replied.

Rebecca got that Burke was rude, but ignoring her and ordering without her was extremely offensive. She reminded herself that this was not a date.

He popped what looked like a fried jalapeño bite in his mouth before turning his attention to her. A slow smile crossed his face. "Take your sweater off. Stay awhile."

Although she was uncomfortable and just a bit chilly, she did as he had instructed. The gentleman in him emerged as he grabbed the collar of her fur-trimmed sweater to aid her and hung it on a nearby hook. His gaze penetrated her spine and caused her to shiver.

"Have some?" Burked gestured toward his platter.

Rebecca politely shook her head.

"Tell me something. How long has Minor been working on that bid?" Burke said, starting in.

"I'm not sure exactly," Rebecca replied, having a hard time figuring out where he was going with that remark and what she should do with her hands at the same time. She settled them on her purse, which was still in her lap. "It couldn't be that long. I came back, and he was working upstairs."

"They say the groundwork has already been laid. They can't offer me a spot." He looked at her for confirmation.

Rebecca shrugged her shoulders. "Sorry. I have nothing to do with the boys upstairs. To my knowledge, he hasn't been promoted, if that's what you're concerned about. He's just helping out."

Burke drew an imaginary line in the air from her eyes to his with his fingers, as if to signify they were on the same wavelength. "Are we going to do this?" He finally spoke as if she had already fallen into bed with him on a proposition.

Rebecca looked around for the waitress before responding, "What exactly?"

"Are we going to accept our lot in life at Sanz, Mitchum, and Crybabies?" He drew his face up in a ball, as if mocking the name wasn't enough to show his indignation. "Or are we going to make history, make partner before forty, add a little ginger to their spice rack?"

His ultimate goal was out in the open, and it was all beginning to make sense to Rebecca. "Well, it seems as if *you're* on the right path." He was supposed to be so brilliant, having graduated in the top 5 percent of his class. What was stopping him from applying himself?

Burke popped another pepper in his mouth and proceeded to speak with his mouth full. "Don't think for a moment there is a glass ceiling for you and me. It's really made of cinder blocks, with giant-size Road Runner anvils sitting on top of each one. You've got to be He-Man to bust through. Your boys, Jacobs and Minor, know it. They inherited the Acme Company, which manufactures the roadblocks."

Really? Rebecca couldn't believe they were having a conversation peppered with Looney Tunes references. Who was this little boy trapped inside this gorgeous man's body?

"That's why they work you to death, angel. It's to keep you from helping a brother succeed," he continued.

Rebecca wanted to tell him he was all wrong. No one was more of a team player than Anthony Jacobs. She loved that working for Jacobs was labor intense. He was also passionate about his job, like Burke, but in a different way. No task and no staffer were beneath Jacobs. It was a little disappointing that a perceived bootstrapper like Burke would come up with plots about "the Man."

"But I have a plan. And no one, no one is going to derail me." He slammed the table several times, leaving Rebecca to wonder how many drinks he had had before she arrived. Then like a man who channeled multiple personalities, he changed from Mr. Extreme to Mr. Easygoing. "Let's order."

When Burke signaled the waitress, she appeared immediately. The waitress uncurled a long receipt in front of him, and he stopped to review his numbers. She placed a menu in front of Rebecca with a smile and turned to Burke, either to be dismissed or to do his bidding. Before Rebecca could crack open the menu, Burke was ordering. It took her a minute before she realized he had ordered Maryland crab cakes for her and the fresh catch of the day for himself. Then he tapped his keno ticket on the empty place setting and ordered the seafood Alfredo and the slow-cooked prime rib, enough food to feed at least two more people, before dismissing the waitress.

"What is going on, Kenny? Are you expecting someone else?" Rebecca asked, standing with her purse in hand. Although she felt more like the carnage they had ordered and were about to consume, she realized she sounded like a jilted girlfriend who had just found out her boyfriend had someone else. All she kept thinking about was Walter Calhoun.

Burke reached for her arm and brought her back down to her seat. "Calm down, angel. It's just me. It's just us," he said in his best reassuring tone. He held on to her arm and slid closer to her, as if she was a flight risk. "I have a huge appetite, if you know what I mean. Now, just sit still. You're about to make me miss my numbers."

The pressure of his grip was pacifying. He reached into his jacket pocket with his free hand and pulled out a tin of chocolate peppermints, the exact kind they shared the rare times they went to court together. He knew she liked them. He was scanning the monitor and then his ticket while she tried to hide the delight in her eyes. He had even remembered she loved crab cakes, but apparently, he had forgotten that she was old enough to order them for herself. He was close enough to her now for her to detect that he wearing the cologne that smelled like the ocean. She had told him on numerous occasions that she liked it. This was a setup if ever there was one. He had thought of everything.

Oh Lord, she thought. What made her think she could match his wits or outsmart him?

"Awww," he called out when his winnings didn't match his investment at the end of another round of keno, but he could barely be heard over the clamor of the bar. He inched past coworker into co-conspirator range and whispered, "Five million dollars."

Rebecca looked into those eyes that pierced right through her, wondering if they could detect her questions before she asked them. She squirmed. She breathed in only when she had to. She refused to speak, refused to be baited by such a ridiculous figure. She needed a GPS to even figure out what position she had gotten herself in. Where was the waitress? She needed a drink.

Burke cut to the chase. "You're gonna finish law school, right? Walter Calhoun is our skyrocket past the ground level. He's got five million dollars' worth of assets, projects, and properties all over the entire peninsula he's looking to negotiate in the next five years."

Rebecca recoiled at the mention of the man's name, and Burke tightened his grip on her arm. She knew she couldn't leave if she wanted to, at least not without a bruise or a brawl. She watched his eyes darken and circle the bar, and hers followed his lead. "Is he in town? Here? Is that why you ordered so much food? Tell me what's going on."

"What's going on is that you are going to go out with him," Burke said.

Rebecca shook her head, because her voice was on strike again.

"Make nice to him, angel, like you do with me. Boost his overly inflated ego."

Rebecca closed her eyes, as if to activate her internal voice recorder. She had a feeling she had to remember this conversation verbatim. She had to tell him this would not fly with her.

"No," she belted out right as the waitress appeared with their food. Rebecca hadn't heard her approaching. She couldn't smell the aromas wafting from the platters. She had definitely lost her appetite. Burke looked unmoved. He smiled at the waitress as she placed the prime rib before the empty chair at the table. Had she said anything at all?

"Any luck?" their waitress asked, content to engage only Burke in conversation. His closeness to Rebecca made the waitress at least glance in her direction. She wondered if she could signal her distress to the waitress.

"None whatsoever," Burke said lamentably, impaling Rebecca with his eyes. "I need a good luck charm."

Burke had reached his limit of small talk and turned to both his grilled mahimahi and the pasta dish, which apparently was for him. Rebecca looked down at her crab cakes and then at the prime rib, which had a marvelous scent.

Burke dropped his fork with a clang and dramatically rubbed the length of his face with his hands once the waitress walked away and was out of earshot. "Listen to me, darn it. The only reason the old geezer talked to me was that I was standing next to you, although I had been going through my expense account with tee times and tequila. He now thinks I work at Dairy Queen somewhere and can hook him up with the swirl. So, as much as we both know you wanted me to tap your resources, I fell back. I didn't want any conflict of interest. Get me?"

Rebecca watched him stab at his pasta and take out his disdain on his linguini. She grabbed her own fork, figuring she should eat a bit of her food to have something in her stomach, even if she felt she might bring it up later. She had brought this on herself with her relentless flirting. She had wanted to be drafted onto his team, but not at this price.

Lord, help me, please. She tried scooting her chair over, and he grabbed her seat from behind and slid it back toward him.

"The way I figured, it couldn't hurt to bring you along in this deal. I am putting you on to something big. Don't be a fool. I'm talking a few business dinners, like the one we are having now. That's all it may have to be. Seal the darn deal, angel." His tone was even and calm, despite the fact that he was gritting his teeth.

Rebecca digested his words. He might as well have called her Anna Mae as Ike Turner would have said to a young Tina Turner. This was his hard sell. There was no way she wanted to be with someone so jaded, and there was no way she could continue to work peaceably at the same firm, under his direct supervision. He had spoken the language of harassment fluently, and she was knowledgeable enough to be conversational in it. There were certain things she had to convey as well.

"I'm not comfortable with that at all, Kenny. I'm just not." She managed to say it before the waitress came to check on them again.

"Everything all right?" the waitress asked.

Kenny realized then that he had been so engrossed in convincing her that he had neglected to check his numbers. He cursed, cast his fork to the side, and began to rip his tickets up. "I guess my luck has run out. Do me a favor and wrap up this meal for me, angel, and bring the bill."

Their waitress retreated with the prime rib, as if she was happy to be given something to do that was as far away from their table as possible.

Burke looked at Rebecca as if she was every bit a disappointment to him as he was to her. Although she was sure she was trembling, she stared back. He leaned in. This time his breath misted the inside of her ear. "You know I'm uncomfortable too, so uncomfortable that I've volunteered to help revise the no-fraternization policy we've both been violating by being here because of awkward times like this."

Rebecca pulled away from him and stood up so quickly, he lost his balance. "Then there is nothing to prevent me from passing on to HR everything you just asked me, told me, and suggested to me as well."

He smirked, looking up at her. "You could do that if that's the way you want to start out your New Year. As a matter of fact, I already assumed that was your next move. You must have forgotten who I am. I'm the butt hole, remember? I've already wrangled in a quarter million on retainer. They listen to me. You're just the crybaby assistant trying to crash through the glass ceiling by compromising yourself with the firm's most prized associate."

Rebecca snatched her sweater so fast that it brought the coat rack and the attached umbrella stand to the floor before ripping a giant hole in the sweater, at the nape, beneath the manufacturer's tag. The racket caused by her departure was apparently drowned out by the sound of a bar patron who had found the luck that had been eluding Kenny Burke all night.

Chapter 5

Will read a facsimile entitled "Pastor" that had been left in the tray of the copy machine at church, realizing that it was an advertisement for the very position he hoped to hold at Grace.

Conduct religious worship svcs & perform other spiritual functions, i.e., wkly Sunday svcs; coordinate funerals/wedding svcs associated w/ beliefs & practices of Christian faith; train leaders of the church community; and counsel members based on spiritual concerns. Req. master's degree in Divinity. Forty hr/wk @ prevailing wage. Job in Easton, Maryland. Grace Apostle Methodist Church. Send résumé w/cover ltr. Attn. Deacon Joseph Contee for interview.

It was hard for Will to think of his next steps until he thoroughly contemplated the missteps of his predecessor. He had thought he had time to ease into his position. Will thought about his dad's legacy as pastor, which Pastor Donovan himself had spoken so eloquently about over a week ago, at his father's farewell service. He had handed Will the mantle of his office, his own leather-bound Bible, as a reflection of his hope that his role as pastor would pass on to Will as well. One affair, which he had left out of his speech, had cost him his ministry, and the lesson was, "Don't mess up."

To the applause of all who wished his dad well, and to the executive board's chagrin, Will had accepted the gift and role as pastor all in one gesture. It was like passing the baton. This early morning fax was Deacon Contee's response. He was casting the net far and wide, according to the header on the fax's cover sheet, not only for his dad's replacement but for Will's as well, before he even got started.

Can Contee act as the employer, accepting résumés and interviewing on behalf of the congregation? He is just a deacon, Will thought. He remembered that Contee seemed to be the one with authority at the executive board meeting as well. All of that would change when he took over, Will decided. He didn't know if he was accepting the challenge of actually applying for the pastor position in spite of Contee's cockiness or to spite him.

Forty hours weekly? That meant he had to drastically reduce his hours at the Perdue plant, if not totally give up his job, a fact that Will had anticipated and to which he had given nonstop thought. He'd met with the GM of the soybean plant , Jessie Joseph, the same man who had brought him on board eight years prior and had constantly tried to increase Will's work capacity and promote him to a managerial or a supervisory position. Will had never accepted the role of pushing papers and standing over people, partly because his schedule at the church wouldn't allow for the extra hours, but also because he loved to get his hands dirty. He loved fielding the lot and doing quality control experiments with each crop sample. Jesse had joked about how Will would be prolonging Jessie's own retirement when he left them with a managerial void. The meeting had ended with an awkward gesture of admiration.

All Will had left to do was put his resignation in writing and send it to the corporate office in Salisbury. As he put his letter in the fax machine facedown, he hoped that he had thanked Jessie enough for his mentorship.

Before dialing the numbers and pressing SEND, Will thought about the fax he had taken out of the machine and had set aside with its confirmation. What if he gave up his job and his seniority status at the plant, only to be the next one ousted at Grace Apostle when they found a better, more suitable replacement? He wished the entire congregation were just as confident about his leadership capabilities as Jesse was. He remembered the faction of the membership that gave him a chilly reception at his father's farewell.

Will shook those thoughts off. His father had taught him that no man had ever taken on something great without a little fear, which he then battled with a lot of faith. This was a test of his faith, for he couldn't have one foot out of the boat and the other in it. He had to walk on water.

Will felt a twinge of anger creeping its way up his torso and seeping into his chest. He jabbed the ten digits that would connect this fax machine to the one at the corporate office thirty miles away. He admitted to himself that he was in no disposition to take over the role of pastor. Lately, he had meditated about his own misery. His prayers had been laced with insinuations and ultimatums, like, *Lord, if I do this, you've got to keep Contee out of my way.* Or, *a little help here, Lord! I can't possibly do this by myself.* His religion had become resentment, and he ran the risk of being burned out before he even got started.

The more he looked around, the more his chest heaved. Since his dad had always served double duty, he had one main office at the church and a kind of alcove area, or window to the world, downstairs in the school. Contee had completely taken over both. The chancellor had a bigger space than the preacher at this point.

Will smacked the SEND button, which awoke the fax machine. It responded with a muted dial tone, then a loud whirr, and it quickly cranked his letter midway through, then stopped. Will's eyes widened as he tried to see if there was an error message on the control panel. He realized at that moment that he had left his glasses somewhere, so he slapped the side of the machine, as if to bring the text explaining the problem or the remedy into view. He tried to dislodge the paper manually, but when it didn't budge, he stopped, not wanting to rip it. He was all set to manhandle the fax machine when he heard a group of people approaching.

His hands were raised and fisted like those of a madman when Contee burst through the door with a formally dressed man, a woman, and two children off the pages of an ad for Ralph Lauren kids' clothes. He brought his hands down slowly. At that point he decided to leave the stupid machine and the resignation letter for Contee to deal with. If Contee managed to dislodge the letter, then he'd be properly informed of Will's plan to devote his time and energy to winning his father's spot. Before he could vacate the room for what Will felt was another closed door meeting he knew nothing about, Contee spoke, his voice unusually cheery.

"Will, I'm glad you're here. This is—" Contee began.

"Minister Danny Glass," Will said, interrupting the deacon, as he came face-to-face with the man and recognition took over. "My family and I have watched your father's ministry on TV for years. It's a pleasure to greet you again. I don't know if you remember, but your dad did a day of revival here. Oh, it had to be seven or eight years ago now."

It was a hot ticket that had brought a near capacity crowd into Grace Apostle that night, so much so that the young adults were separated into another room with the then practicing practitioner Danny Glass Jr. Will had sat in on Minister Glass's session and had found him to be a better orator than theologian. He and Danny were both PKs, preacher's kids, but Danny's dad had a ministry housed in a newly built facility in Snow Hill, Maryland, and was televised throughout the tristate peninsula of Delmarva on Sunday mornings, then rebroadcast late in the evening.

Danny extended his hand. "Yep, I sure do. In fact, I was with him then. I was telling my wife on the drive in." They shook hands while he introduced his family. "This is my wife, Marie, and my children, Megan and Tyler."

Only then did Will notice the bulge in Mrs. Glass's stomach. She was a pleasant-looking woman whose eyes danced in response to her name being mentioned, but her mouth seemed to be wired shut. The kids waved shyly as the little boy tried to lose himself completely behind the profile of his mother. He had expected the family of Danny Glass to be camera ready, not camera shy.

"Don't you preach too?" Danny asked.

Will wondered if Danny was trying to be sarcastic or if he really didn't know, but he wanted to set the record straight either way. "Called, studied, licensed, and ordained."

Deacon Contee inserted himself between Will and his guests. "Both of you are candidates for pastor here at Grace Apostle."

"Oh, really?" Will said to keep his mouth from gaping open. Danny appeared equally shocked. Will extended his hand again for Danny to shake after stroking his ear nervously. It provided something for him to hold, as he felt weak all of a sudden.

The two of them shook hands this time as if they were contenders in a championship bout, hearty and strong. Pleasant smiles shrunk to awkward smirks. Contee looked on as if he were Don King. Will sized up Minister Glass as if he might have to take him on physically. Will had a good three inches on him. He wished he had listened to his father and had come to church "Kingdom minded" by at least wearing contender's clothes, like a button-up shirt, instead of his long-sleeved crew neck and khakis.

Deacon Contee began filling them both in on the vetting process there in the middle of the office. They were told that each of them would preach on four to six consecutive Sundays, would teach Bible study, and would have free rein in the office to meet with and counsel members about their spiritual concerns. They watched as Deacon Contee backed up against the desk and flipped through the desk calendar. Will noticed Danny's eyes travel around the rest of the room and watched him curl his lip at the haphazard way things were filed and stored. Deacon Contee finally shared that it was the board's hope to have a church-wide vote and a new pastor installed by Palm Sunday.

"Does that sound okay to the two of you?" Contee asked, posing the question more to Danny.

Danny shrugged at the idea, and Will did too, figuring he could voice his complaints later, when he had Contee alone.

Will had other things on his mind. Where was the Glass family going to reside? Were they moving to town? More importantly, why on earth wasn't Danny Glass Jr. continuing to work under the tutelage of Danny Glass Sr. in Snow Hill? Danny should understand legacy because he was one himself. This was his turf, Will thought, and he felt Danny should have the decency to withdraw his application. Will considered for a moment his own rocky relationship with his dad. He wondered if Danny was like him and preferred to say, "Look, what I've done, Dad," and show off something that was his own, as opposed to asking his dad what he should do with what his dad had built.

Before Will could phrase a question, he became plagued with a greater concern. How many more Danny Glasses did Contee plan to parade before the already partisan congregation? "I saw a fax of the job announcement for this position, and we apparently already have two candidates. What's the cutoff?"

Contee waved off the question. "I'll send a retraction in the morning."

All of a sudden it became more important than ever to Will to get his resignation letter out of the grips of the fax machine. As much as Deacon Contee wanted to pretend he was neutral, Will could tell that he had his man in Danny Glass. *Heck, I'd vote for him too, with his perfect wife and two-point-five kids.*

"Actually, Will, you'll have a slight advantage by serving as interim pastor because Danny won't be able to relocate until February, when he'll start his probationary period. So either we can split up your weeks or perhaps we'll invite a guest minister," Deacon Contee announced. "You should ask your father if he has any friends in the ministry you all can call."

Why? So their sons can also become candidates for pastor? Will said to himself.

Ironically, Will was the one feeling disadvantaged as he looked around, with nothing much left to say. This was not the perfect handoff between father and son. What had once felt like a changing of the guard between him and his dad now felt more like a contested inheritance of the family home. Everyone knew the home's value, but the paint was peeling. Maybe Danny Glass felt like he could help restore Grace Apostle to its former glory. Will felt that his facade was flaking before everyone. Just then, Mrs. Glass escorted Megan and Tyler to the bathroom with a series of hand signals. At that moment, Will realized what he was missing. No one could add polish like a woman. No one else could turn a bachelor pad into a home, a church into a family ministry.

"Hey, Will, we're about to grab a bite to eat before Minister Glass and his family head out. Care to join us?" Contee asked, to Will's surprise.

"No thank you," Will said, approaching the fax machine again. "I need to spruce up around here a bit if we're going to have *guests*."

Chapter 6

She would not be expecting him; that he knew for sure. Impulse was steering the car off Route 50 West to Queen Anne's Highway. Her family owned a home that was just past the post office and bordered Wye Oak State Park. The houses were no less than twenty-five hundred square feet around here, and hers was unique, with a monogram of the family name hanging over the two-car garage.

Will hadn't considered the backlash he might receive until he approached her driveway. The last time he saw his ex-girlfriend, Veronica Deeds, she was naked and he was ending their eight-year relationship before he took a moral dive. He had never regretted the breakup, but sitting outside her house now, he wished he had orchestrated it better. He hoped to be able to communicate that to her, among other things.

An older version of Veronica answered the door. Will thanked God for favor that he didn't have to face her father immediately. Will didn't know exactly what Veronica had told her folks when she moved back home with them, but by the look on her mother's face, it wasn't favorable. There was a tortuous pause after Will greeted the woman who would have been his in-law, and then he asked to speak to her only daughter. He wasn't invited inside, into their cozy sunken living room, like before or even offered a spot in the entryway. He was treated like the neighborhood tough who was lucky they didn't call 911 for trespassing.

The next face he saw was the one of the person he had met all those years back in the college career center. Indignation was spelled out across her forehead. Will took a few steps backward to the base of the front steps, remembering from their last encounter that she had a mean right hook. She descended the steps half way before stopping. Now that he had her here, he didn't know what he had come all this way to say.

"Don't tell me you were just in the neighborhood," Veronica said.

Will smirked. "No, I came to see you. How've you been?"

"*Exceptional,*" Veronica replied.

Her choice of the word that they had used to describe their relationship was almost lost on Will as he took in the campfire hue to her skin tone. He was still attracted to her, check. She was so pretty, almost obnoxiously so, with her freshly arched eyebrows, her perfect French manicure, and her razor-sharp haircut, which was as blunt as her last answer. She wore a thin oversize sweater over her slender body, which let him know she didn't plan to stay outside in the cold for long.

He began to speak, but she beat him to the airwaves. "You're about a month too late for an apology."

She was letting him know he had little more than room to grovel, but he refused to get on his knees just yet. It was like she assumed he had come crawling back to her. Was that why he had come?

"My dad retired," Will offered.

"I know."

Will was shocked to learn that she had kept up with events in Easton since her departure. She was at least civil, but it wasn't safe to assume just yet that she was amicable. That was his next check mark—whether she had moved on completely. Then he remembered her meddling girlfriend Nina, who was infamous for spreading information, erroneous or not. "That's right—"

"Nina," they both said at the same time.

"Well, I'm going to take over for my father, or at least I'm going to apply. As much as I don't want to, I'm resigning from the plant, so I won't smell like wet sod anymore." He smiled, trying to force one out of her as well. She wasn't budging from her stance, though. "Grace Apostle is where my heart is right now, you know . . . where it's supposed to be."

Veronica crossed her arms across her chest. Will could not tell if she was losing patience or body heat. "Nina also told me your little friend left town shortly after I did."

Will yanked his earlobe and dared to look her in her eyes. "Rebi and I were never together, not at all, especially when the two of us were together."

Veronica cast her eyes in her neighbor's lot before bringing them back to him. "So, let me get this straight. Are you telling me you've figured out where your heart is supposed to be in all areas, or is it in Salisbury?"

In so many ways, he thought. His mind drifted to the Perdue plant briefly, then meandered to Rebecca, creating too long of a pause in his present conversation.

"You better be glad I don't have the key to my dad's gun cabinet. I don't have time for this," she huffed, turning to leave. But then she snatched herself back around just as quickly, adding, "I told you that you would end up vying for your dad's position, and here on my doorstep, sooner than you thought. When I used to bring up your dad's retirement and how we should prepare to take over, there was always resistance and resentment. For a supposedly smart man, you leave yourself ill equipped every time because you don't plan. I don't know what you want from me, Will, but you need to get to the point of why you are here real quick."

Her comments reinforced what he already knew. To her credit, she had been the architect of their relationship, and he was in dire need of some blueprints. Was it worth the effort to try and rekindle what they had had, knowing he would be locked into the plans she would put in place this time? Would she share *his* vision? They couldn't be ripping off corners, or partial or whole sheets of the Bible, trying to get on the same page about submission. For some reason, at that moment, he thought of Mrs. Glass.

"So?" Veronica queried.

"Would you let me please . . ." Will managed to say. She had killed his game, not that he had had much to begin with. "I did want to apologize to you, actually."

Veronica shifted but gave him an expression that let him know to make it good. His blanket statement wouldn't cover what she perceived was the wrong he had done her. He had to spell out how he could make it right. Words eluded him for a moment.

"I'm sorry about the way things ended, and that we both didn't try hard enough to remain friends or at least keep in touch. Sorry about not being completely honest," he told her.

Veronica sighed heavily. "Is that it? You're in need of a friend?" She paused. "You could have saved your petty apology and a tank of gas after all you put me through. I'm back here with my parents, for God's sake, at thirty-one, starting all over. I suggest you get it together, get it from the baker, the florist, and the jeweler—at least two carats—before coming back, and then I'll consider keeping in touch. Good-bye, Will."

Will watched her turn to go back up her front steps, wondering if he should go after her. Instead, he turned as well. His time was up. He realized he had gone knocking on the wrong door. She was right; he wasn't well organized or very brave. He knew a bout with Veronica was safer than being rejected again in Salisbury. That, his heart couldn't take. It was fruitless to try and reinvent the wrong relationship.

"I heard your dad has a daughter," Veronica said with a curled lip, almost snickering, from her pedestal at the top of the landing. "Rebecca's cousin, if I'm correct. So what does that make the two of you, second cousins?"

Try estranged, which is exactly where I should have left this relationship, Will said to himself. She didn't know the half of it, but that didn't stop her and her best girlfriend from spreading news about his father like it was whole. Will didn't even stop. Rebecca was part of the reason he was here in the first place. In an effort to sneak out of town, she had tried to appeal to him to give his relationship with Veronica another try. Although his anger had him feeling reptilian, he walked, and did not crawl back toward his car.

Chapter 7

Rebecca found the most remote corner in an empty conference room to temporarily crouch in. She was so tired, yet it was just midday. She was tired of ducking and dodging Burke and assignments that pertained to his caseload. In the week since the meeting with him at Brew River Restaurant, she had been invisible. His eyes glossed over her when they both were in the same room. She had thought that all had been forgotten, or at least she had hoped. After a few cleansing breathes, she tried out her lips to see if she could be a whistle-blower. After what had just happened, it was apparent to her that it was time to go to HR.

The associates and their aides didn't punch a clock. They were in and out all the time. If an employee wasn't at court or if their presence wasn't required at a meeting or at the attorneys' catered lunch, then the basic operations of the firm generally shut down between 12:30 and 2:00 p.m., allowing the employees the freedom to run errands, go on lunch dates, or have trysts.

The latest incident with Burke had happened while Rebecca was taking a break in the staff lounge, holding up the short line, dredging the wells of her purse to come up with change for the vending machine. A lone hand had reached over her shoulder, grazing her collarbone, with a dollar to lend, which the slot of the machine gladly accepted.

The fresh tide of his ocean scent preceded his act of generosity. "Make your choice," he said.

Rebecca recoiled, taking a step back at the sound of his voice and at the realization that his statement was a double entendre. "Gosh, Burke, you scared me."

"Make your choice," he said again.

"I already have," Rebecca said, keeping her purse cupped in her hands between them.

He stood in mock surprise and looked around at Keller and Branham, who were both waiting for their chance at the snack machine, as if to solicit their reactions. "I don't know why you're scared or angry, or whatever this attitude is that you have toward me. I should have trusted my instincts and just walked the other way when it came to you." He put on his theater voice. "We tried this thing between us, and it didn't work. We can't keep sidestepping each other, and I don't think I can take another verbal battle with you. It is unprofessional and is starting to interfere with our performance. Let it go, Rebecca, please."

Rebecca watched as he locked eyes with Keller, a sandy-haired associate, before whacking the machine, which immediately dispensed a bag of SunChips, her favorite. This time she was left stunned as he walked away. She looked at Branham and Keller, whose eyes suddenly dropped to the floor. She grabbed her chips in a hurry and scampered off in the opposite direction in search of the hiding space she now occupied in the empty conference room.

As she rose from the floor, Rebecca yanked on her oversize purse, as it was crushing the remaining SunChips beneath it. Then she kneeled over and grabbed the bag of SunChips. She had to pull herself together before going to Human Resources. She contemplated whether her disheveled appearance might lend validity to the claim she was about to make. Where did she begin? How much should she tell them? Burke obviously believed that their relationship was more involved than it actually was. She thought of the chair massages she had initiated, among other things, all of which she considered harmless flirting. Had he beaten her to HR and told them all about that stuff, or had he just been bluffing the other night? Rebecca smirked, trying to convince herself not to be concerned. After all, his whole career was a bluff.

So why won't he leave me alone?

Once again she fished around in her purse. She had asked Jacobs if she could basically tag along with him to court. Bethany had prepared his case, but due to her pregnancy, she preferred to stay stationary. She searched for her cell phone to check the time and to call Jacobs and see if he had already left for an afternoon at the county courthouse.

He picked up on the second ring and answered with his adorable Southern drawl.

"Jacobs, where are you?" Rebecca asked.

"Across the street," Jacobs said, which meant he had made the short walk from the firm to courthouse. "I literally just got here. I couldn't find you. Where are you? What's wrong?"

"Burke," she whispered as she walked toward the closed door of the conference room and rested her back on it, as if the cavalry were outside.

"Don't say another word. He's pushing the envelope, isn't he? I hear it in your voice," Jacobs said. "My God, is this man crazy? He can't do that to you."

Rebecca took solace in his concern and was relieved that she hadn't had to go into great detail. She didn't know exactly what Burke was doing, but she didn't want to get Jacobs further involved. One moment she was just another colorless peon like everyone else in Burke's world. Then, this morning, he had used a broad stroke to paint her as a jilted lover. Things were not so clear-cut, but she feared they were on their way to becoming totally out of control.

As if hearing her thoughts, Jacobs continued, "Take it to Human Resources. Today, Rebi. Think deposition when you talk to them. Tell them everything." He paused for a moment before adding, "I mean, I'm early, so do you need me to come back?"

"For what?" Rebecca asked, trying to fathom what Jacobs could do for her besides hold her hand.

"To make a strong case to have Burke canned," he said.

She was silent on the other end of the line for a moment. "No," she finally said. She had to tell it, and she had to tell it all, and she preferred that no one besides the person she spoke with in HR hear the sordid details. Jacobs had helped her figure out Burke's angle, though. He was trying to get her canned. Case closed.

Chapter 8

Rebecca knew she was dead in the water when she found out the chief EEO specialist and the head of HR was a woman. Insecurities about her past relationships with women were reinforced when Phyllis Humphries gave her a once-over worthy of an MRI while being introduced by her receptionist.

What is it? Rebecca wondered. She considered that her skirt might be too short or that her blouse, which kept riding up, might be a tad sheer in Ms. Humphries's opinion. Rebecca wasn't going to give the woman the satisfaction of seeing her tug at her clothes in an attempt to perfect herself.

Making matters worse, Rebecca stumbled on a loose wooden plank at the seam of the door as she made her way into Ms. Humphries's office. Ms. Humphries stood from where she was seated in a feeble attempt to come to her aid if need be. She was an extremely full-chested woman who had made the horrible mistake of wearing an A-line dress that tented out and made her look larger than she was. She directed Rebecca to the chair across from her. When they both were seated on the opposite sides of the desk, Rebecca began to tell her that she wanted to make a harassment claim against a coworker.

"Name?" Ms. Humphries said blandly, apparently in the middle of a major project, because she continued to write notes and shuffle papers in and out of the colored file folders that were on her desk.

"Rebecca Lucas," she offered.

"No, Ms. Lucas. The name of the person harassing you," Ms. Humphries demanded. She pulled a form from a pile in her in-box, propped it on the stack of folders, and began to write. Only then did she look up.

Burke's name got caught in Rebecca's throat, and it took her a while to pronounce the one-syllable name. "Burke. Kenny Burke."

"I see," Ms. Humphries said.

Rebecca looked into Ms. Humphries's eyes, which were pools of the purest shade of blue, in an attempt to discern exactly what she did see. Did she know Kenny Burke? Had she talked to him?

"Is he your direct supervisor?"

"Yes, I'm an aide to one of three attorneys. He's one."

"I see. Do you feel your job is being threatened?"

Rebecca didn't know how to respond to that, so she tilted her head and pursed her lips in thought.

"Is this harassment one of a sexual nature?"

"Yes. I mean, no . . . not exactly," Rebecca replied, correcting herself, getting her words as tangled as her hand was in her purse straps.

Ms. Humphries was a machine gun firing off questions, and a marksman surveying how each one landed. "No or not exactly?"

"Not entirely," Rebecca answered.

Ms. Humphries huffed, "Semantics is important when you're filing a claim. It's best to be mindful of what you report. So, is it safe to say the two of you were in a relationship?"

Rebecca was once again at a loss for words. Once again it was a matter of interpretation. A relationship with Burke had been her goal until his stipulations made that goal unattractive and unattainable. She was trying to figure out how to put that into words, how to paint herself in the best possible light.

Ms. Humphries dropped her pen on the desk and waited for Rebecca to unshield her eyes before saying very pointedly, "Our no-fraternization policy is very clear and is in place for a reason. We have no desire to know or police your personal business, Ms. Lucas. Quite the contrary. No one cares if you and Mr. Burke elope and have a bunch of kids. Relationships are messy, especially ones with mismatched expectations. All we ask is that you keep it out of our hallways and supply closets."

Rebecca felt as if her heart had skipped a beat. Ms. Humphries knew something. "Have you ever had a circumstance where there was a counterclaim, like a case of one person's word against another's?"

Ms. Humphries blew a puff of air and stared at her for a short while. Her initial disdain seemed to have lifted, and it looked as if she might go into rescue mode. "More often than I care to mention. Mr. Burke has been coming to us about you for a while now."

Rebecca couldn't believe what she was hearing. She had just gotten back from a month's stay in Easton. Before that she had thought she and Burke were cool. Had I been harassing him? she wondered.

"Can we start over? I think I've been too conservative with my answers in an effort to protect him . . . protect myself. I think you need to hear the complete truth."

Ms. Humphries peered at Rebecca as if to say sarcastically, "You think?"

Rebecca in turn pushed PLAY on her internal voice recorder until she heard nothing but Burke's voice, his coaxing, his insinuating, and even his threatening comments from the night at Brew River Restaurant. She told it all, ending with the words "Then he said he was coming here."

"And he said all this over dinner, or was this a business meeting?"

Rebecca remained quiet as she thought of Burke's words. *A strategy session.* "I can't tell you what it was exactly. He asked me to meet him, and maybe I am an idiot, but I did. You can believe it or not, but I feel like a pawn in some sick game of his, and I don't want to play."

"It's not my job to believe or not to believe. It is my job to find a resolution so the work of Sanz, Mitchum, and Clarke can continue, Ms. Lucas," Ms. Humphries said, finding a fresh file folder to place Rebecca's claim into.

"So, what are the next steps?" Rebecca asked anxiously, pointing at what felt like the contents of her soul scribbled on the carbon legal form that she had just signed. "Where do we go from here?"

Ms. Humphries was quick with her response. "Well, a notice is sent upstairs. I follow up within forty-eight hours or wait a week and a half for the partners' answer. More than likely they'll place it back in my hands or encourage some kind of mediation. If everything doesn't end happily ever after, like you so eloquently said before, it will come down to your word versus his or to whoever is more valuable to the firm." She laughed out loud, as if this scripted soliloquy had a maddening effect on her psyche. "Scratch that last comment. In any event, Ms. Lucas, you have your own recourse after that. Good luck."

Rebecca felt relieved, but she knew the matter had not been resolved. Somehow every good feeling she had had about getting Burke's crimes out in the open just went out the window. Words like *recourse* and *good luck* rang in her ears. She stared a moment at her file and wondered what would become of it. Then

Rebecca stood, holding her copy of the claim, and proceeded to the door.

Ms. Humphries called out a final warning. "Watch yourself, Ms. Lucas."

Rebecca looked down to find herself past the door frame and realized Ms. Humphries wasn't talking about the loose floorboard.

Chapter 9

Will wanted a new lease on his life. He kept telling himself that change was good, but he was doing little to psych himself into believing it. He was having a hard time transitioning from a general laborer to a laborer exclusively in the vineyard of the Lord. Not only was he supposed to open his church house and pulpit to his competition, but corporate's response to finally receiving his resignation down at the Perdue plant was for Will to train his replacement. So he drove in twice a week. The coworker who was next in line seniority-wise was in no way ready to step up, and Will was in no way ready to step down from his role and his only hold on Salisbury.

He at least had an excuse to travel the familiar arteries in and around town when he was done. Set on autopilot, he allowed himself to do a drive-by that would place him in Rebecca's footpath. As far as Will knew, she lived across Route 13, off Nanticoke Road, which extended through the city to the highway. *We could have made it work*, he thought as he drove the forty-five miles practically in his sleep. Maybe it was he who had made too big of a deal about her leaving and the distance between them. Then he realized it was more about the line she drew when leaving and the emotional space she created when trying to sneak out of town.

He slowed the car to a crawl, imagining her life from this vantage point: the park in her subdivision, the crosswalk at the light, and the coffee shop down the street. He used the driver's side controls to crack the window open slightly as if to breathe her air again.

Will suddenly picked up speed to catch the green light in an attempt to elevate his mood, which had also fallen. Pride would not let him call her. He often imagined what he would do if he actually ran into her, and he knew it would be predicated on the circumstances. He left his wondering behind as he made a left at the university, taking the scenic route. He marveled at the expansion of the college and almost lost his bearings when he came upon a church adjacent to the rear end of the campus.

Dogwood Community Church was always an interesting stop on his tour. The landscaping was always evolving. There was everything from exotic plants and bushes to perennials of every shade and variety, which bloomed every spring and summer. It was obvious that they put a lot of work into the sides of the brick-faced edifice. Recently, though, Will had noticed changes for the worse at the hands of the same man who was out front now, in the dead of winter, seemingly feeding the once vibrant patch of earth something from a bucket. He was a white man with a white priest's collar visible under a fleece L. L. Bean pullover. Will pulled over under the belief that someone should have to answer for their sins.

"Hey," Will called from the curb once he was out of the car. "What kind of church is this?"

The man turned, bucket still in hand. "Oh, uh, it's nondenominational." He paused and looked up at the building, as if seeing it for the first time. "We're not your traditional church. We save souls and edify people, but we do not necessarily follow an organized religion per se." He put the bucket down and approached the car slowly when he realized Will was lingering. "I'm Monty Cutler, by the way. I guess you could say I'm the, uh, pastor and prophet of the house. And you are?"

"Will, Will Donovan, landscaper and lover of life," Will said, more concerned with pointing out the patch of ground the man was tending than displaying his preaching credentials. "May I ask what it is you are doing?"

"I have no idea." Pastor Cutler looked again at his building, as if in a quandary. "Trying to reintroduce life, I guess you could say."

"I stopped because I would notice this place often in my travels. I remember the exotic plants and an impressive flower garden right there," Will said, meeting Pastor Cutler where he stood, then venturing farther onto the property while pointing. "Recently, I've seen you during the heat of the summer or the bareness of the winter, you name it. It's like you purposely gutted this place. No offense, Pastor Cutler, but you destroyed most of what was here."

Pastor Cutler put up his hands in surrender after a deep sigh. "I did. I'll admit it. I don't know how to explain it, really. That was a time when I thought it was over, you know? I thought I was done with this place. I had actually put it up for sale, until my epiphany over a year ago. See, this is my wife's garden. I know I'm probably still in the doghouse for this one."

"Well, I'm sure she is a forgiving woman," Will assured him, knowing now that destroying the garden was a symbolic gesture of something greater.

"You're right. She is also a lover of life," Pastor Cutler said with a somber pause. "That makes you, my friend, a confirmation. I'd give anything to restore this patch to its former glory."

Will could see the hopelessness and doubt in Pastor Cutler's eyes. He had had the same look in his own eyes recently, a sign that he knew deep down that things could never be as good as before.

"Let me help you," Will said.

Pastor Cutler cracked a wry smile.

"But you do realize its winter, right?" Will asked.

"I was so desperate, I consulted with this guy, who sold me this," Pastor Cutler said, once again lifting the bucket. "He told me to mulch heavily and said something about a window covering helping when it's cold."

"He was probably talking about a cold frame to keep as much heat in as possible, which can work if it's a mild winter or if this were a south-facing field and had direct sunlight. It would also have helped if you had had the forethought to plant a few winter seeds before the first frost." Will sifted through Cutler's bucket with his bare hands. "This is mostly tree bark. Where's the peat moss? Do me a favor. Stop buying this, and stop listening to whoever is advising you."

Pastor Cutler stuck one hand in the air, as if taking an oath. His eyes shone brightly with the hope of a new beginning. "I promise. Besides you lost me at the cold frame. So, Will, lover of life, do you think we can get it back by spring? It might be minimal, but I'll find a way to pay you."

Still in his heavy work pants and boots, Will knelt on the ground to examine the beds. He sniffed, not trusting that in his desperation Cutler had not used chemicals to choke out what his wife had birthed. "I'm not going to lie. This will definitely be a major project. Some of the plants that are left here would be due to bloom again if you had not dug up or damaged the roots. We need to remove anything that's dead or dying."

Will jumped to his feet, dusting his pants at the knees. He was thinking that it was not a bad idea to start fresh, after all. He didn't know where he was going to get the time, but he had to devote energy to this project, if not for Cutler than for himself. It could be his outlet or his backup plan, depending on whether he was voted in or out at Grace Apostle. The heavy work would come in March and April, but at least he could prep the soil now.

"What about that bush? Can it go?" Will asked.

Cutler was on his heels immediately. "It stays. Leave this to me. These are Sandy's roses."

"Have they ever bloomed?" Will asked incredulously as he looked to the twine that still bound the fresh transplants among the more mature bushes. He didn't remember seeing roses on his previous drive-bys.

"It was her dream. Just tell me what to do with them. I'll dig and dung it. I know it might be crazy, but there will be roses this year," Cutler said, looking to Will to further affirm his belief.

Dig and dung. Will smiled. Besides being horticulture 101, this expression was from the parable of the barren fig tree in the Bible. If only Pastor Cutler understood how well Will knew the "last chance for atonement" message from that parable. He was living it.

Staying true to the parable, Will added, "I guess we can grant these roses a pardon for another year. God is merciful."

"Amen," Cutler agreed, studying Will curiously.

"But roses can be tricky," Will added, wondering if the pastor was hanging his hat on more than roses. "What happens if they don't bloom for you all like in times past?"

"They have to. The Cutlers are believers." He wagged a finger at Will. "I trust you know about a lot more than plants then you've been letting on. It starts with a big word called faith, huh? You were sent this way."

Will thought about what Pastor Cutler had said. Could God have sent him, and if so, was he here for Cutler or the other way around?

Pastor Cutler grabbed his bucket and a pair of outdoor gardening gloves, which he had abandoned earlier. "If you have the time, I'd like to show you the storage closet where Sandy stored her supplies. I don't know what we're going to need, but it may be back there. Oh, and maybe some of the kids can help out too."

Will checked his watch. *I'll meet the family and roll out,* he thought. Although he wanted more than anything to get his hands dirty with the prep work here, he heard the voice of his dad urging him to come out swinging, and he knew he had to begin his prep work back home if he was going to get his own church.

Chapter 10

Pastor Cutler's church looked gutted on the inside. Will now considered Dogwood Community Church a distraction and believed that its leader, whom he was now following through the front lobby, was more seriously touched than he had previously thought. There was a tarp in the vestibule area, and there was a rough outline on a cloud-filled wall, the beginnings of a mural.

Will cleared his throat. "How many kids do you have?"

"Anywhere from ten to fifteen at a time," Pastor Cutler said over his shoulder.

"Huh?"

They came upon a small bank of computers in the same hallway before Will could wrap his head around what Pastor Cutler was saying. A few young adult males sat in front of the monitors, too engrossed in various social networking sites to look up. Will, being curious, was peeking his head into what would be a sanctuary in a normal church when Pastor Cutler stopped to urge the gentlemen to join them in what he called the forum. A few groans and complaints accompanied the young men's labored movements. They looked at Will with wariness and mistrust, as if he were the one who had brought an end to their leisure activities. These were Cutler's kids, and the sanctuary was their forum.

The forum was devoid of pews, and in their place was now a rough circle outlined by a hodgepodge of chairs. A few other young people in random college apparel occupied some of the chairs; their book bags and gear sat on other chairs. Aside from one guy and one girl who were carrying on a conversation, the others were socializing on mobile devices or otherwise hanging out.

Will shifted his focus to Cutler, giving him a wry smile of his own, before they entered the forum themselves. "What kind of church did you say this was again?"

"Nondenominational and nontraditional, to say the least," Cutler replied, raising one hand in its defense. "In times past we held weekly services like any other church . . . until my time away. At that time, I assigned all my members to a friend of mine who has a church in Fruitland. Like I told you, I nearly closed my doors for good, until I started coming back here to pray, check on the place, or pay the bills. Students from the college, Christians, they would swing by 'cause we're in close proximity to seek advice, some from the campus choir who used to sing selections on Sunday or perform concerts here or others that just needed solace from campus life. They missed the tradition of going to church, I guess. I started opening the doors a year ago for them. It's a new direction for me—a new life for this church."

Will was both put off and intrigued by his ideas. Murals and computer access in the vestibule? Could a church that was centered around college kids be kept sacred enough to also be Christ-centered? It was so far from Grace Apostle and the ministry he aspired to lead. He assumed this type of spiritual crisis center was Cutler's answer to his own midlife crisis.

Cutler gave Will a hearty pat on the back before propelling him forward. "You should definitely come by some Sunday. We fortify ourselves right here in the forum. Don't we, guys?" Pastor Cutler nodded his head and looked to a set of his kids whose heads were in motion as well. "Danny over there is a gifted musician, and several, like I said, are in the Gospel choir. It's the most genuine and free expression of praise I have ever witnessed."

Will refused to comment with at least eight pairs of eyes trained on him. He wondered whether, in all their *praise,* the Word was also being taught, but who was he to judge?

Cutler introduced Will and the project of restoring their campus garden to his less than enthused congregation. Although Will tried to stress that there wasn't much to be done during this season of the year, Pastor Cutler egged them all on, asking them to at least work at tending the soil, pruning, and planning the garden.

A particularly friendly kid and the only young woman in the group was the first to speak up. "Hey, so what you're saying, Mr. Will, is when we come here, we should expect to get dirty, 'cause you're going to put us to work using rakes and shovels and stuff?"

"We've got the perfect tool for you, Trixie," the young man beside her responded quickly. He baited everyone by delaying the punch line for a second. "A ho."

That apparent inside joke garnered a response from nearly everyone in the room. The young man narrowly escaped a slug from the young woman, whose eyes registered the wound inflicted by his inappropriate comment. Pastor Cutler started to intervene, but they were all distracted by a new arrival, who seemed to just appear out of nowhere. A preppy young man wearing a button-up shirt, an argyle sweater, and a bow tie stood in the spotlight at the doorway. The length of his manicured Mohawk was highlighted ash blond down the center. He managed to get his hand out of his skinny jeans, which were cuffed at the ankles, to wave hello.

The same young man who had made the lowbrow comment said, "Ethan?"

Hearing the type of chatter that arose when gossip started to fly, Pastor Cutler left Will's side to greet the young man. "Welcome. I'm Pastor Cutler."

"Ethan." His arm seemed to levitate at his side, and then he pointed across the circle at a fellow student. "Marcus lives in my dorm. He told me I could come by and, you know, hang out with you all."

A sound that could be classified only as a catcall came from somewhere as Ethan's and Marcus's names were tossed around the circle. One kid who was sitting beside Marcus actually got up and changed seats, extending his hand to the now vacant seat for their new guest to take. Still another student began hastily preparing his stuff to leave, as if his bunker had been invaded. Marcus, a similarly skinny kid but whose appearance was more traditional than his friend's, looked as if he wouldn't be able to pick Ethan out in a line up, leaving Ethan looking genuinely confused.

"Ethan looks like he might work best with a ho too," said another young man, who was doing a bad job of whispering.

"Shut up, Keith. Always cosigning. Get an original thought of your own," shouted Trixie, obviously still sensitive about the earlier reference to the same garden tool.

"Hey, Ethan, we're about to plant something. You might want to take your loafers off before they get dirty," someone shouted.

Will just took in the scene, thinking to himself that he had witnessed firsthand the same kind of bickering and backbiting at Grace Apostle when he was pastoral assistant there. He was there to assist Pastor Cutler, but it wasn't his job to referee this time.

"What is this? Maybe we're showing off 'cause we have company. Is that it?" Pastor Cutler queried. "I just bragged about you all to Mr. Will. This is a huge embarrassment."

The cocky kid who had started the whole thing bopped over beside Pastor Cutler and draped his arm around him in a conspiratorial fashion. "No, Pastor Cutler, you don't understand. Word on the street is ole Ethan is a, you know—"

"A loved one," Pastor Cutler said, cutting him off. His slate-blue eyes, which seemed to have permanent tears in the corners, somehow turned darker. "Let me tell you something. Everyone is loved in the eyesight of God. Everyone is a loved one. Now, you can be as close as conjoined twins or as distant as cousins twice removed, but kin is kin. We share the same bloodline and inheritance, and we will treat each other with—"

"With respect. That's right, Pastor Cutler," Trixie yelled in the ear of the young man next to her.

"At least he has the decency to pull his pants up," a less vocal kid noted in Ethan's defense.

"I'm out. Next thing you know, he'll be trying to sit next to us in the dining hall," proclaimed the tall boy who had begun gathering his stuff earlier, lingering to see if anyone was going to take the same stance and leave with him.

Ethan thrust one hand away from him in an exaggerated manner. "I'm so sure that will never happen, Ricky."

Ricky stopped and flailed his arm for emphasis. "Hold up. Don't say my name like I'm one of those dudes you get down with."

"I believe it's best that you go if you can't stand being open to all people due to your reputation," Pastor Cutler admonished sternly, pointing the way.

Will noticed that Pastor Cutler's face had flushed to a near cranberry color. His simple yet serious words were enough to temporarily squelch the controversy that was brewing with the others. He waited until his dissenter, true to his word, left the forum and exited the building to save face.

Pastor Cutler faced his kids. "We're all different. I've been at this a long time, and I haven't always been on the right side of history as far as the community is concerned. When this area was divided by our stance on racial equality, Sandy would say to me, 'Monty, when at war, you don't turn your back on another soldier enlisted or drafted into His service. This is a church. We acknowledge those who acknowledge Christ. Got it?"

Pastor Cutler looked around and waited until all the heads, even Ethan's, nodded in acknowledgment of his statement. "Now, I am assigning you, Bruce, the responsibility to pick out a scripture from the Bible that reinforces my point for the next forum."

His arm still hooked around his leader, Bruce eyed Pastor Cutler. "And what's your point again?"

"We're all loved ones," Trixie explained. "Like your fifty million stepbrothers and sisters."

"Yeah, like your cousins and dem," someone squawked in attempt to keep the mood light. The comment was followed by some much-needed laughter.

"Or your auntie who sends brownies in your care packages," Ethan said, chiming in. "I'm just sayin', they are scrumptious. Y'all must taste them."

All eyes were back on Ethan, and even Bruce's eyes shone with newfound respect. Maybe it was the promise of brownies, but others dropped their standoffish attitude as well.

"Does everyone else get an assignment?" Bruce asked, looking from Pastor Cutler to Will.

"Naw, you'll be fine," Pastor Cutler assured him. "You are going to help me lead the discussion and, hopefully, help me lead by example as well."

"Seriously, Pastor C, I got it. Everyone should be treated the same," Bruce pleaded as everyone became bored with his dilemma and resumed socializing, as if they had been dismissed from class. "I have two tests in the next two weeks I have to study for. I don't know if I have time to go fishing for a scripture."

Will was chomping at the bit. He felt compelled to become involved somehow in the lesson, so he leaned over to whisper in Bruce's ear a scripture that immediately came to mind.

"Acts ten, somewhere around the thirty-fourth or thirty-fifth verse," Bruce repeated aloud verbatim after Will fed the reference to him.

"Hey, no cheating," Pastor Cutler said, wagging his finger, amused. "Consider yourself blessed, Bruce. That was a freebie. Read it and remember it for the next time we gather." This time Pastor Cutler moved in conspiratorially. "'Cause guess what? I bet Ethan came here needing to hear this word. Go see when everyone else plans on getting back together."

Will watched Bruce bop off, wondering whether he would digest that ministry morsel. Will checked his watch quickly, then looked up to find Pastor Cutler wagging his finger yet again, this time directly at him.

"Lover of life, Will Donovan, and apparently, lover of the Lord. I know now I wasn't mistaken about you. Try the spirit by the spirit. I bet you know a little something about that also. I'm afraid we didn't get that far in our groundwork today, though. Sandy would say I'd get sidetracked on a one-way street. I don't want to tie you up. I'm sorry to have wasted so much time on this."

"No problem. That was necessary," Will said, shaking the man's hand. "I like your approach."

Both men started a leisurely walk toward the door.

"Do we have you coming back soon?" Pastor Cutler asked.

"I suppose I've been drafted, so I'll be back next week this time. In the meantime, I think I'll help myself to a helping of what went on today and I'll create a sermon out of it to bless my congregation with as well." Will winked.

Chapter 11

Rebecca was working under the misconception that the firm would protect her, that Ms. Humphries, representing the firm's HR department, was Olivia Pope, the famous fixer from the TV show *Scandal,* and that everything pertaining to Burke and his caseload would be handled. A formal mediation between her and Burke was apparently not a time-sensitive issue as long as the firm's interests were being served. Rebecca had done her own arranging, evading, and fielding of solutions around their inner office to limit her interactions with Burke.

They had a commitment to task policy at the firm, which meant that if an associate or an aide touched a case, it was his or her responsibility to bring the pieces together that were necessary to complete it. Others could sign on, but no one could abandon a case. That was why Rebecca had a pinch hold on the Calhoun case file, which she held at arm's length. *How did this get on my desk?* she wondered.

Rebecca knew how. Her fellow first-floor paralegal, Bethany, was on temporary bed rest. With no official word from HR, no one else on the floor was supposed to know about Rebecca's and Burke's countercomplaints and therefore know to keep this file out of her in-box. She almost sniffed the air. It reeked of Kenny Burke. He must have signed her onto the Calhoun case six weeks prior, when he first came to her with his proposal for her to entertain the wealthy tycoon. She was liable.

Rebecca leafed through the contents of the file to confirm her fears. An impromptu meeting about the future of Calhoun's holdings to be held at 2:00 p.m. left her with a voluminous amount of reports on building codes, zoning, and other regulations to research and prepare.

Being an aide to three attorneys was like being in a relationship with three very different men. You had to cater to their individual needs. She and Jacobs had a true partnership. He saw her as an equal; they planned the future of a case together, often checking in with one another for any updates up to the last minute. Minor liked it sterile. He lived by the creed "Why have two meetings when things can be summed up in one?" He usually asked for things with ample time to spare, and he got precisely what he ordered. Burke, on the other hand, was the boyfriend who would disappear for days and who would leave you feeling uncertain, but when he came around, he hogged all your time. He required extra paperwork, pep talks, and pretense.

She swallowed hard and sank into the swivel chair below her. *Breathe and think,* she told herself. If she handed off or otherwise ignored the case, she'd be negligent. If she started the preliminary work but didn't finish it, she'd look incompetent. After the third rotation on the chair merry-go-round, she stood on unsteady legs and stomped off to Human Resources, only to find out that Ms. Humphries was out for the day. Her no-nonsense receptionist was fast to point out that no other EEO specialist could speak to a complaint Ms. Humphries had initiated. It was Murphy's Law, and not the loose floorboard, that literally had Rebecca tripping this time.

Rebecca felt she had no recourse. She glanced up at the ceiling once she was back in her cubicle, as if to ask the Lord, "What now?" She powered on her desktop computer, having resolved to burrow herself in her office for the next several hours, doing the necessary research. After all, it was an in-house meeting, not off-site. Maybe this would be strictly business. Maybe Burke or Calhoun had not engineered it to be something more. She'd set to work on preparing for the meeting and whisper a prayer that she wasn't being set up in the process.

When Rebecca felt she had prepared a decent enough summation, she was proactive this time and went looking for Burke, instead of the other way around. She would apprise him of the status of the report in the hallway if need be, just to avoid an actual meeting, like they did sometimes when he wound up in court and was unprepared. They had twenty minutes to hash it out.

She dipped into each meeting space and cubicle on their floor in search of Burke, but to no avail. She began to worry that no meeting had actually been planned and that this was just a hoax to get her further involved. That concern led her to the front desk, where Celeste had access to the corporate calendar and the meeting schedule.

Rebecca tried her best to temper her frustration. "Celeste, I have a presentation for the Calhoun case with Burke at two o'clock, but it wasn't marked with a meeting space. When did we stop marking the location?"

"I'm sure it is in one of those billion and one e-mails flushed down from above. Dive in or take your problem to someone else," Celeste replied, leaning back in her chair like a queen on a throne.

Rebecca's words clawed their way through her clenched teeth. "Can you look up the room?"

With arms crossed on her desk, at the base of her computer, Celeste casually looked at the screen. Rebecca noticed how the annoying receptionist always appeared to be chewing something, even when she wasn't eating, like a cow chomping on cud. The phone rang, and Celeste happily halted her pursuit of Rebecca's information to filter the call.

"If there is a delay in this documentation, I'm going to make sure I mention your name," Rebecca said, raising her voice to be heard over what sounded like a personal call.

Celeste rolled her eyes and pursed her lips as she studied the screen again. "Well, I'll be doggone. Burke has made his way to the top."

"What are you talking about?"

"His meeting is in the partners' suite, tenth floor," Celeste said, still staring at the screen while shaking her head. "He clawed his way there, and I can only guess how you hitched a ride yourself."

Rebecca knew she should walk off with the information she needed, but she felt she had been slapped in the face yet again. She waited until a client who had walked up with an inquiry was assisted and returned to his spot in the lobby waiting area before giving Celeste a piece of her mind. Rebecca leaned in. "You are about as unprofessional as they come. I could care less about a tenth floor meeting. I didn't ask for any of this. This wasn't my goal, my desire. I am tired of you or anybody else insinuating that I am here on anything but merit. I come early and stay late, trying to fulfill my obligations to this firm, so don't think for a minute I hitched a ride on anything."

Rebecca felt an arm bearing down on her shoulder and heard the voice that was currently haunting her dreams.

"Whoa, whoa, whoa, ladies. Must I referee?" Burke looked around, no doubt for witnesses who were enjoying the scene as much as he was. "Ms. Lucas, you're needed upstairs. I think you are finished here. You're coming with me."

Rebecca jerked away from his grasp as she made final eye contact with a stunned Celeste. Then Rebecca and Burke made their way to the bank of elevators around the corner. Even after they got in the elevator, Burke was beaming, and she was still boiling from the altercation with Celeste. She reflected on how she had let her emotions get the best of her as she looked at the person she should have directed her anger toward. He hit the buttons for the next three floors, as if he was unsure where they were going.

"Get it together, angel. We don't have time for your angry black woman routine today. I told you I was putting you on to something big. Today is the day to show and prove."

"And no means no. Whatever you're planning or scheming, make sure to count me out. Here," she said, thrusting the file in his chest once the elevator doors opened to an empty lobby on the seventh floor. "It's the zoning restrictions your boy is going to run into when he tries to build on the bay side."

Burke chuckled while pressing the OPEN button on the elevator panel, delaying their ascent to the eighth floor. He cast his eye up and down the corridor on the seventh floor to make sure no one was coming before replying, "You think I need that? When a client has a boatload of cash, you can best believe I've studied his interests. I shared that tidbit with him when we were yachting *bay* side. That old fool had us on the water in the wintertime. Do you think I'd trust an aide, especially one as disloyal as you? You've got to be out of your mind. You're just the chocolate mint in the centerpiece candy dish, but thanks for signing on. I knew you were a smart girl."

"I didn't sign on. I was coerced, and that is exactly what I'm going to tell Ms. Humphries when she gets back. So if you'll excuse me, I'm done," Rebecca said, attempting to leave the elevator, but Burke blocked her way as two gentlemen entered.

"Up or down?" one of the guys asked.

To Rebecca's surprise, she and Burke both replied, "Down."

Although there were two other people in the elevator car now, Rebecca felt she couldn't breathe after the doors closed, trapping her in with Burke. He settled in for the ride down with one hand in his pocket and the other holding the file. His smoldering eyes were on her and about as threatening as a drawn gun. As bad luck would have it, both newcomers got off on the sixth floor, leaving them alone again. Rebecca didn't attempt to move, and Burke jabbed the tenth-floor button with his thumb to take them back up once they departed.

"I am going to explain this once," Burke said, coming dangerously close to her as she hugged the far wall. "The firm, HR, and Ms. Humphries are prepared to let our case simmer and dry out on the *black burner*. We mean very little in the overall scheme of things, and our rift means even less. It's a black-on-black crime, like you and Ms. Firecracker back at the front desk. It's on their *black burner,* angel. We might as well be rival gangs in South Central somewhere. They are waiting on us to take one another out or make a truce."

Burke looked at Rebecca, as if waiting for her to respond. Her mind raced along with her heart. Could that be why she hadn't heard from HR about mediation or moving to another assignment?

His speech became faster and more intense as they neared their floor. His eyes, trained on her body, now made a slow trek back up to her face. "I can think of a hundred and one ways of keeping the peace with you *after* this is over."

Rebecca snarled and batted at his hand, which was hovering around her midsection. "You can stop the ad campaign. You stopped being the prize to me a while ago. Just leave me alone and we'll get along fine."

And it was true. She could vaguely remember the time when his smile, his scent, and his touch were a triple assault to her senses.

Burke stepped back while releasing a sinister smile, as if he hadn't heard a word she had said, "Yeah, okay, whatever you say. Look, Skip Clarke, the grandson of one of the partners, is waiting on us. He's signed on as well. I guess you can say he needs a home run after losing a half-a-million-dollar bid and soaking up *our* expense account while sulking in Vegas. His slap on the wrist is vetting junior attorneys, like me, while taking partial credit for our work. They must be passing out degrees at UMB. He's a regular Mrs. Doubtfire, baby-sitting me because he's blood, as if I haven't already proven myself. It's that glass ceiling."

Rebecca hoped he wasn't looking to her for sympathy. In some strange way, next to this Skip guy, she might be the only one Burke considered a friend, she thought.

Burke halted the elevator on the ninth floor as he launched into a speech that resembled his closing argument. "The strategy was to let Skip's banged-up track record keep all the buzzards in the firm off my kill. They slept on ole man Calhoun, and now I'm set to make a killin'. Skip will be waiting on us in Pop Pop's personal conference space, so don't screw this up for either of us. He spent all morning calling me Keith. Heck, I'll be Keith as long as they get my name right on the checks and the corner office upstairs. It's destiny, angel."

The elevator tour was over. Once the doors finally opened on the top floor, Rebecca was blinded by the light from the panoramic wall-to-wall windows. The opulent, wide open reception area, with its ornate furniture, marble flooring, and flat-screens displaying the latest Wall Street averages, was in stark contrast to their floor. Rebecca almost understood why Burke wanted in to this exclusive club so badly. In some strange way she wanted Burke to achieve his goal, or at the very least, she didn't want to be the one to hinder him. It would be another tragic case of crabs in a barrel.

A young gentleman, who looked uncomfortable with the fit of his Italian-cut suit, walked up, rounding out their motley crew. He adjusted his cuff links before extending his hand toward Rebecca.

"Skip Clarke, this is Rebecca Lucas, the one I told you about. She's got us prepared with all our paperwork," Burke declared. "Mr. Calhoun is *really* fond of her work."

Rebecca was hesitant to shake his hand, trying to decipher a code. Had any of them considered that she and Burke were branded? Had their complaints ever reached "the big boys upstairs," or was there actually a "black burner" mentality at the firm? She looked around, noting the air of confidence that nepotism and cronyism provided the occupants of this floor as they milled around. No one was hightailing it to court or stressing over mounds of case files. They at least had the luxury of breaking down behind closed doors when things got overwhelming, because their offices weren't cubicles. The disgust and disdain she felt over the office politics and her overall treatment at this firm didn't fit the decorum up here. *Self-preservation, Rebi. Maybe I too should play the game.*

"Nice to meet you," Rebecca finally responded.

"Cool, cool. The question is, do you have the most important documents?" Skip replied.

"If he is ready to sign, I've got the dotted line," Rebecca assured him, although her doubts were creeping back in. "It appears as if you all are set. Now, if you'll excuse me, gentlemen, I'll be getting back to my desk."

Both Burke and Clarke began to speak at the same time. Clarke had a particularly strained look on his face, as if he were reviewing memories of being on a ledge without a safety net.

"Now, I've told you, and . . . uh, Ms. Lucas, we wouldn't think of doing this without you," Burke said, hooking her right arm with his. "You've done the work, and now you should get the credit."

"Yeah," Skip said, cosigning, taking up the other side of her. "Lead the way, Ms. Lucas. I insist."

Chapter 12

Rebecca nursed her second glass of red wine while recalling the Calhoun meeting from earlier. Instead of being the candy in the dish, she had felt more like a lobster in a tank being presented to a bunch of diners who were interested only in devouring her. She had presented every report in the packet about every regulation and every zone that the wealthy tycoon planned to take over. Of course, Burke jumped in, using layman's term to explain any and every loophole.

Rebecca avoided eye contact with everyone in the room. Burke was in her head, and Calhoun was all over the rest of her with his stares and gaping mouth. He put her in mind of Alfred Hitchcock. He was definitely in the club with Donald Trump when it came to his wealth and the atrocious hair plugs scattered on the sides of his head and heaped on top of his head. As she drew nearer to him to have him initial the documents she had shared, she smelled his breath, which was rich with the scent of imported cheese, something they apparently served clients on the tenth floor. What she couldn't figure out was why they were still consulting with him. They were no closer to closing with this man than before. Calhoun, being the well-trained trapper that he was, had another snafu for all of them—another city on the Lower Eastern Shore, Hurlock.

"I thought we said you wouldn't be interested in townships that had an area of less than five miles.

What could possibly be built or expanded in Hurlock? You might as well snap up Vienna and Secretary while you're at it. I'm sure they are all in need of a new diner or a bait and tackle shop. C'mon, W.C. This is beneath brand building," Burke said, practically pleading for closure.

Calhoun pulled his bulky frame away from the table. "I said I wanted specs for anyplace that has a port or as much as a pier-side vacation home for my—"

The loud clap of Burke's arms dropping at his sides could be heard as both Burke and Skip rushed to finish Calhoun's sentence, saying in unison, "His yacht."

Then under his breath, so that Rebecca and quite possibly all those assembled could hear, Burke muttered, "His yacht needs a vacation home."

"They have this quaint little festival every year. Yes, Hurlock is the perfect place to rendezvous with someone," Calhoun said, unaffected by Burke's sarcasm. Then, turning all his attention to Rebecca, he added, "Have you ever been to Hurlock, Ms. Lucas?"

Rebecca's sister, Gail, who had been raised as her cousin, lived in the neighboring town of Vienna. Sure she had been to Hurlock, or at least she'd been through it, but she had no desire to share experiences of any kind with this man. "No, I haven't."

"Well, I guess my work isn't done here until I show it to you." He lifted himself from the chair, as if all had been settled. "How about we close this deal out on my yacht? You'll bring Ms. Lucas. We'll see if they let me dock in Hurlock. She and I will go over *all* the paperwork, iron out what needs to be straightened, and I'll give her a tour. We'll celebrate later that evening, and I'll sign on to Sanz, Mitchum, and Clarke. I'll have Lilly fax over the itinerary."

Rebecca tuned her radio to her favorite station to drown out the memory of everyone eagerly accepting Calhoun's invitation but her. When she graciously declined, she heard a male chorus singing, "I insist." The song that was now playing on the radio struck a chord with her. She had heard it before and knew it well enough to identify the artist as none other than Kirk Franklin. It was an inspirational song in the midst of the programmed love songs of the hour. Each refrain invited listeners to imagine themselves as God saw them. She tried her best to bring to mind her best likeness, but all she could imagine was what everyone else must see when they looked at her.

She made her way over to the decorative mirror mounted over her couch on the far wall. She peered into the mirror and saw her oval-shaped face and traces of blemishes on her skin, covered partially by her blunt-cut bangs and the longer pieces of hair framing her face. What did Calhoun, Burke, Celeste, and even Ms. Humphries see when they looked at her? A target? If not an easy mark, then they saw her as just easy. Easy as in weak when faced with her own urges and whims which was an accurate description of the woman she used to be.

The methodical tinkling of the piano keys through-out the song drew her into its musicality and message. It was introspection the songwriter was encouraging. She wanted to show she could be strong. She could imagine herself dancing to this song, a sway that would have her on her tippy toes at first, then flat on her feet like a seal, where she'd really grind into the floor before attempting a jeté.

Where was this coming from? No doubt from the creativity that had been unleashed during her trip back home, where she had rediscovered her love of dance, of choreography. She hadn't danced in the ten to fifteen years before that trip, and she hadn't danced since. How she longed for home right now, for the company of Gail, Milo, and of course, Will. She feared that she had completely destroyed the possibility of turning to Will again. He'd urge her to pray. Of that, she was sure. She felt as if she was in the middle of one soul-stirring prayer right now, as she listened to this song and imagined the possibilities of movement.

She had questions for God. How did she get here? Why did she come back to this? She wanted to blame her missteps on her mother, like she'd been prone to do in the past. Rebecca felt like yelling as the words of the song became intertwined with her conversation with God. When she heard the lyrics, "Over what your momma said and . . . ," she felt like screaming, "Healed from what my daddy did, . . ." She felt like leaping, and she did, but she was weighed down by sorrow. Her legs never reached their full extension, and she narrowly missed hitting the coffee table. She crumpled to the floor.

Just as she was about to get up, she heard the distinct thump of a broom handle on the floor below her from the apartment directly under hers. *Really? I'm disturbing you?* There, in the midst of unbelief and despair, she released torrid tears.

Her head and chest were in competition, pounding her frame. She had to stop the hurt somehow. She knew it would be suicidal to mix alcohol with pills of any kind, about as suicidal as her boarding that yacht with Calhoun. *It's time to give it all up.* She prayed a traditional prayer that spoke of how Jesus would help her. Hope's message, delivered through that song, began to revitalize her limbs, and she received an answer. She was tired of carrying this burden, so she handed it off to God. *Gone, gone, gone, all gone.*

No matter how they saw her, she no longer saw herself that way. Therefore, she couldn't continue to fall into their trap. The Calhoun case could either sink or swim without her. She would deal with the consequences, but there was no way she was getting on that yacht.

Chapter 13

Will's dad was the only one who could enter without knocking, introduce himself with a question, and start lecturing without a prerequisite.

"You know what keeps me up at night?" the elder Pastor Donovan asked as he entered the church office where had he worked for fifty years, carrying what appeared to be a bag lunch and a newspaper.

Will rose from his chair, pleasantly surprised and immediately conscious of the fact that he was in jeans and tennis shoes again. "Hey, Pop. So nice to see you. I know you can't wait to tell me. What have I done now?"

"Well, Will." His dad lowered himself into the chair on the opposite side of the desk. "Notice I said 'Will,' and not 'Pastor Donovan,' as I should, because I don't think you're acting like a pastor, a pastor in training, or even a minister, for that matter. It's not what you've done. It's what you haven't."

Will started to interject something, but his dad cautioned him with his index finger to let him finish his thought.

"Case in point. You're not holding appropriate office hours. Sister Albright called me personally to say she couldn't get an appointment with you all last week. I tried calling myself and couldn't reach you here, on several occasions. I ended up having two very awkward conversations with Contee. So I, Pastor Donovan Sr., ended up meeting with Sister Albright myself at the TCBY."

"There you go, Dad. Got yourself a date," Will said.

His pun skidded on dry earth. It wasn't even remotely funny to a man who had just buried the second love of his life, and it reminded Will of his residual anger toward his dad because of his affair. Will cleared his throat, which set off a delayed cough from his dad, as if both were trying to drown out the echo of Will's last statement.

"I've met with Sister Albright myself a week or so ago. I'm in transition. What can I say, Pop? I've been busy," Will added.

There was no way he was going to let his dad know he had been busy helping another ministry with a landscaping project. That wouldn't be completely accurate, because he had spent as much time inside Dogwood Community Church as he had outside. It had been like a ministry field trip. He had plans to head that way that afternoon.

"Recognizing the needs of your congregation is a part of a pastor's job. My first task when becoming pastor was studying the rolls. I learned the name of every member. No one wants to sit and listen to you every Sunday if they know you don't know them, and they can't get in contact with you throughout the week. I had a standing appointment with Sister Albright and several others. That is how I built up a Rolodex of resources to help the saints out when they were in a pinch. She's going through a transition right now as well. Losing a mate, retirement, empty-nest syndrome, and Social Security have a lot of *your* members, members of my generation, uncertain about the future."

Will held out his hand, as if ushering that thought right back to his father. "That seems like a perfect ministry for you to tackle, Dad. You can't stay bitter at your executive board for asking you to step down. Let

God convict them on their intentions. I need you here, on my team, advising me."

His father harrumphed. "That's right. We are all loved ones. What a memorable 'Kumbaya' moment. Seriously, son, that was a great message. No one said you couldn't preach. It's the behind-the-scenes ministry I'm worried about. Your modus operandi has been to delegate, get it off your plate."

Will knew when he was being indicted. He felt like he had when he was a little boy and had to face his dad because he was in trouble. He had to give him a satisfactory answer or the wrath was coming. "I'm doing my best."

"Are you? 'Cause I think you have a lot more to give— a lot more to prove." He moved forward in his chair and tossed the newspaper, which was no bigger than the television guide, across the desk for Will to see.

Will scanned the periodical and stopped at the banner. "The *Society Pages*. When did they revive this? Really, Dad, this is what you are reading now, in your retirement?"

The *Society Pages* was Easton's version of a scandal rag, much like the *Star* or the *Inquirer*. The writers had always been anonymous, and the paper had always been printed independently by the Pritchett Family Press, who were, ironically, members of Grace Apostle. The *Society Pages* had long been the locals' gauge of what was trending. Widely distributed, it gave every gossipmonger his or her fill of ammunition.

"Just read it. Page two," his dad said.

Will found the page. His eyes immediately settled on the article.

A Faux Farewell

A local pastor celebrated his golden anniversary by announcing his retirement. The announcement, which caught many off guard, led the Society Pages to ask whether this was a decision or a demotion, as it is rumored that the good reverend has not always been a good boy. No matter what, the void could have left the congregation scrambling to find a suitable replacement to preserve the church's traditions and lead the congregation with innovation and integrity into the future. However, there is a son—a legacy who was weaned on scriptures and the ways of the church. Crisis diverted or cover-up continued?

Michael Jordan did it, even Jay-Z. They both announced the end of an era with their retirement, only to return to the same arenas they had played in or performed in. Both were at the top of their respective fields—a king on the court and one on the concert hall stage. They hung up their hats, the hoopla died down, and the game went on. Instead of truly stepping away, the kings returned under the guise of elevating the game or educating the field of contenders for the throne. I ask again, is it a new game or more of the same?

A legend is only a legend when it stays in the past, and a legacy is limited to working in the shadows of the past. No new blood breeds, no new opportunity. As I see it, a retirement is a chance to open the field and find a leader who will be a game changer.

Victory eluded Michael when he returned, and Jay-Z had to watch several others occupy the top of the throne. In the case of this historic church, on any given Sunday it's any man's game. Recently, Pastor Jay-Z's son, Lay-Z, announced to the church that their system of electing a new leader involved a mini internship of viable candidates and a final vote. This should get exciting, and this Society Pages staff writer will be there every step of the way. It will be interest-

*ing to see how this congregation, left with the final say
of who its new leader will be, will respond when faced
with a new game or more of the same.*

Will reread the caricature painted of himself in
words. *Lay-Z*. It would almost be funny if it wasn't
so disparaging. He was far from lazy. Though the
moniker was not from his dad's own pen, it reflected
his dad's sentiments. Will had read a fair share of the
periodical's contents in the past. This new writer had
the specific tone and point of view of someone younger,
hipper. He or she also had an inside track to what was
going on in their church.

"This is defamatory. I can't believe . . ."

"A pastor stays on top of these things," his dad said
when words failed Will. "It doesn't name names, which
makes it speculative. Although very unreliable as news,
it is protected under First Amendment rights, as is
your generation's social media. I've checked with our
lawyer and the source itself. There was a stack in our
multipurpose room, near the community board and
what you called the free enterprise space. So much for
a spirit of Ujamaa."

Will stared at his dad in amazement. He truly never
stopped. There was a lot more to the job than what he
had bargained for, and there was a lot left to be learned.
He looked at his watch and figured he'd be late getting
to Pastor Cutler and the kids, if he showed up at all.

"I guess we know where their vote lies," Will said,
resigned.

"I never won the Pritchett clan over, either. Made me
wonder why they chose Grace Apostle as their place of
worship. You won't win them all, but you can't turn a
blind eye to this kind of rhetoric either," Pastor Donovan said matter-of-factly, unwrapping a sandwich in
wax paper before chomping down on what appeared

to be tuna fish. He pointed to the paper between bites. "You've got to speak against this from the pulpit this Sunday. You've got a couple of days to prepare something. Yeah, you need me here, all right—to play defense."

Will was thinking the exact opposite. Why give credence to it at all? He agreed with one part of the exposé. How could he set his ministry apart from his dad's if his dad was calling the plays? Will thought of his competition and what the article said about legacy. Maybe that was why Danny Glass was coming to Easton. It might work out better for both of them if they switched places and got a shot at authenticity.

Will's dad had moved on to eating a bag of chips without so much as an offer of the burnt ones to his son. "I take it Contee is downstairs."

Will questioned, "Do you think he contributed to this article?"

"It could be him. You've got to watch him, Will." His dad brought his voice down, as if Contee might have installed a bug in the room to record them. "You've got to find time in your busy schedule to go downstairs and learn the ropes. I can tell you how, and as much as I don't want to come within a mile of the man right now, I will, but you have to be present. He's becoming irreplaceable. Don't let him totally take over. The kids, the congregation, the entire community have got to feel like you're in charge."

Will felt the vise grip of stress in his torso, from his shoulders to his lower back. He had to find a way to bear more weight. "I noticed they didn't allude to Minister Glass as my competition in the article. You'd think they'd have a field day given the popularity of his family. I personally haven't mentioned him in church, because it isn't my place. What's the big secret behind this guy, Pop?"

Will's question caught his dad in mid-gulp as he drank his bottled iced tea. "It's a war, and he's their secret weapon."

"No, Dad. I mean, why is he even vying for a spot in Grace Apostle's pulpit?" Will asked, trying his best not to sound whiny. "Have you heard anything through the gospel grapevine? It just makes me think he's running from something in Snow Hill."

His father's eyes widened, and he tapped his own head with his index finger after capping his drink. "That's a good question—a question that can make or break your campaign. You've got eyes and ears and office hours. Use them."

Chapter 14

He wasn't a guest anymore. Will shared Pastor
Cutler's enthusiasm about the gardening project and
had to find something to tinker with in the garden at
Dogwood Community Church at least once a week in
anticipation of full vegetation in the spring. He was so
inspired by the Dogwood ministry that he preached on
the subject of sowing and reaping, titling his sermon
"Delayed Planting Equals a Delayed Harvest."

Pastor Cutler's kids were helping him erect a cold
frame to incubate the soil, and they were planting a
patch of cabbages that spelled out the word *hope* on
the front lawn. His dad's comments about being more
present at Grace Apostle, plus Will's growing concern
that he would have to hand over the pulpit and would
soon would be living off severance pay from his job,
seemed to dissipate when he was working with the soil.

It was a brisk day, and the few kids that were there
had long since trekked back to campus. He and Pastor
Cutler were walking the grounds so that Pastor Cutler
could take more pictures of the work in progress to
satisfy the criteria for another community grant that
would help to keep his doors open. To Will, his friend
seemed to back into blessings, and he wanted to share
in that anointing.

They stopped at what they both prayed would be
thriving rosebushes come summer. Will had had a few
kids bind them to guard against the sometimes brutal

effects of winter. Pastor Cutler lowered his camera lens and knelt before the rosebushes, touching the earth beneath him. Will didn't try to carry on a conversation at this point. He had learned by now when Pastor Cutler was with him, but not *with him*. Will hoped Pastor Cutler could leave whatever worry or bury whatever burden he was carrying around right in that very spot. After a time, Pastor Cutler rose with the most unexpected request.

"Tell me about her," he said out of the blue.

"Her?"

Pastor Cutler clarified what he meant while taking aim at the roses once again with his camera. "Mom, auntie, sweetie. *Her*. Everyone one has a special female in their life."

Will could have asked the same of him. Although he had heard a lot about Sandy, he had not actually seen her, except for a giant-size portrait of both of them, which had the perfect proportions for the church vestibule but was now locked in the storage closet. She had left him, Will reasoned, and Pastor Cutler's life bore the scars. Will imagined this was the inciting incident that had led to his period of sadness, a period that had prompted him to give up the notion of a traditional church.

"My mom died when I was seventeen, and I am single. So, no, there is no special lady to speak of." Will breathed in a big gulp of air, surprised at how hard it had been to voice that. His thoughts drifted, and he felt he needed to add a disclaimer. "I fell in love with a girl, though, my best friend from high school, actually. She came back to Easton to bury her mom recently. Ironically, she has a life here in Salisbury. I have a life in Easton. There is nothing to really talk about there, either."

"Aha! No wonder you're here so faithfully," Pastor Cutler said.

"I guess," Will said, turning his back on Pastor Cutler and his lens to tend to the unseen. His friend was supposed to be getting a few candid shots, but Will felt oddly like he was in some television exposé. "I am supposed to be getting over it."

Pastor Cutler smirked. "Getting over . . . I've heard that before. It's easier said than done, I tell you that. I won't fault you if her name comes up every once in a while."

"Rebecca."

Cutler smiled. "Pretty name."

Pretty girl, Will thought but was too shrewd to say it. The myth that if he didn't speak of her, she didn't exist had been busted. Pride was bullying him to back down from this conversation.

Pastor Cutler examined Will without the lens. "You really love her."

Will pinched his right earlobe and thought to himself, *Like no other.*

Pastor Cutler took Will's picture at that precise moment. Will swiped at the barrel of his lens, fearful of what it had captured. They both chuckled.

"Your natural headlights got brighter when you mentioned her name. Do you know that?" Pastor Cutler said, shrugging his shoulders. "What are you doing here, packing dry earth with us? Are you kiddin' me?"

With a friendship so new, it was hard sometimes for Will to know what Pastor Cutler was getting at. "What do you mean?"

Pastor Cutler's goofball smile was more from amazement than amusement. "I mean, why aren't you with her? May I ask that?"

Will shook his head unknowingly. "It's a long story. The deck was stacked against us as a couple. She felt . . . she felt as if she'd bring controversy into my life and into my bid for pastor based on the past."

He thought about a recent conversation he had had with Gail, who had been acting as a go-between. Gail desperately wanted him to understand Rebecca and the decision that had led to her curt departure.

Pastor Cutler, now wearing his camera around his neck like a medallion, posed with one hand on his hip and the other resting in the front pocket of his khakis, as if really trying to understand. "Do you feel that way? Are you conflicted when you are with her?"

"No," Will said, drifting toward the front door of the church. He was uncomfortable going any further and wondered how to stop the snowball of this conversation from rolling and amassing his longing and bitterness.

"Gosh, how long is your altar call on Sunday? One second?" Pastor Cutler called to him. "We're preachers, for heaven's sake, Will. We're into pleading for people's souls. You give up too easily. You're a charming gentleman and everything, but charm doesn't measure up to a stacked deck. Have you got any fight in you?"

Will looked back to find Pastor Cutler shaking his head.

"You can't *really* be in love, and if you are, then I don't understand the way you love."

"You don't understand," Will countered. He felt as if he wanted to fight, all right. "You don't know the whole story. She gave up on me. She left me." *She was weary,* he thought.

"She's in Salisbury, which is walking distance in the grand scheme of things, waiting to be convinced. So she left you? How many times was that? Sandy had to have turned me down a half a dozen times. She was the one I wanted and, as it turns out, the one God used to make my ministry make sense."

Will decided to keep his mouth shut. He didn't need this. Why was Pastor Cutler taking the events of his life so seriously, so personally?

"Let me ask you, could it have worked? Can it work now? Should it work?"

Will shrugged his shoulders, not willing to give his inquiry much thought. Their conversation had already released the image of Rebecca from that heavily guarded section of his mind. Now she was free to traipse through his thoughts and steal his concentration.

"Not everybody can be you and Sandy, man. As perfect as the two of you were, she's not here." Will observed, figuring he shouldn't be the only one forced to face regret.

His comment left Pastor Cutler beet red and riled up. He seemed to bite down on his response for a couple of seconds before finally saying, "Yes, but I was smart enough to know her worth. Convince yourself that Rebecca is worth the fight and then go convince her, but don't you . . . don't you dare stand in my presence and mourn someone who can be found. Now, if you'll excuse me, I think I'm done for the day."

Pastor Cutler passed Will and stalked to the front door. Once again, Will was asking God why he had been left out in the cold.

Chapter 15

Rebecca checked her text messages for the first time the entire weekend to see if Burke had somehow gotten her new cell phone number. Her paranoia was put on hold for a moment when she spotted a surprising message in her in-box.

> Was in your neck of the woods, wondering how you are doing.
> Will

It was a mobile hug. Rebecca stared at her phone to determine when it was actually sent. Could it be possible that Will had business in town at the precise time she needed support?

She had to face the fire in the form of Kenny Burke and Skip Clarke this week. But first, she hoped to begin with a visit to Ms. Humphries. Will's text was just the boost she needed to walk into the firm. She had waited until the last half hour in the business day on Thursday to fax over the necessary paperwork for Mr. Calhoun to close the deal, with her regrets that she would miss the yacht party on Saturday. She had called off work on Friday and had literally stayed in bed the entire weekend. She thanked God that she had never entertained Burke at her apartment, but she didn't put it past him to find out where she lived and come bursting through her door.

Despite all the drama of living on edge, she was smiling now. She thought of the text that had been sent on Friday and the man who had written it as she contemplated a reply while she dressed. She didn't want to read too much into his message. His text didn't speak of reuniting. It was just an inquiry into how she was doing. She figured she could tell him best face-to-face. You didn't discuss harassment and helplessness in a text. Plus, she wasn't sure she wanted to fulfill the role of damsel in distress.

Rebecca stepped into a pair of wide-leg pants and heels to complement her button-up blouse before typing her reply.

> If you're ever in town again, we should meet for coffee at this place close to my apartment. It's not Starbucks, but it's good brew.
> Rebi

She put the phone down to gather her things. Her stomach churned as she grabbed a yogurt from the refrigerator. She realized at this point that she was as nervous about Will's response as she was about the reactions of her coworkers. Essentially, she had left all parties hanging at some point in time. Four and a half weeks had passed since she had last seen Will in Easton. Maybe time had healed his wounds. She knew seeing him again would just about cover hers.

Rebecca walked into the office at exactly nine on the nose, with a prayer that she'd be too absorbed in a new project with another associate to be worried about Burke's every move. Celeste wasn't at her desk, but her extra-tall, extra-wide figure came into view as Rebecca approached the cubicle area. Celeste was carrying a mug of coffee and had a smug expression on her face. She spoke as she approached.

"The *it* girl has arrived. Must be nice to have every-one hunting for you. I'll be sure to send out a memo that you've made it back," Celeste said, halting in front of Rebecca. "Before you even ask me to recount who or what, remember, I don't work for you. I dumped every message on the virtual message board. Happy reading."

Rebecca was more intrigued by what was in Celeste's mug than what was in her personal in-box at this mo-ment. She had foolishly skipped her usual coffee stop, not knowing if she'd be sharing a cup later with Will. She pointed, feeling almost jittery without her caffeine boost. "Is that from the break room? Have we gotten more filters in?"

"It's instant from a box marked 'Do not touch,' along with the other necessities I have to supply for myself in this office." Celeste walked on.

Rebecca wanted to ask the ornery administrative assistant why she didn't just quit if she had so many complaints, but she knew that a confrontation would draw a crowd, like it had the last time. No coffee and no one to run interference for her made the firm a hostile work environment, indeed, Rebecca thought. She pulled out her phone to dial her only ally on the staff as she made her way to her desk.

"Where have you been hiding?" Rebecca said, voic-ing her desperation through her teeth.

"Where am I always, Rebecca? The same old story. Our clients are being ill advised upstairs, and then they dump any and every commercial litigation on me to argue what's actionable. I have to argue nuisance over negligence before the judge at ten a.m. Can you believe that?" Anthony Jacobs replied.

Her heart dropped at the prospect of not being able to hang out in the office with him for the day. He had a way of babying her and keeping her busy at the same time. Rebecca figured maybe she could join him across the street after prioritizing her messages in the order that she would address them.

"Speaking of negligence, I've been left here with Burke again."

"Yeah, but he can't come within ten feet of you, right? I heard you were working upstairs last week. I assumed it was with Minor. I had to use the temp to help me. She's supposed to meet me here."

"They hired a temp?" Rebecca questioned.

"Roselyn, Rosalyn, something like that," he said, his accent slaughtering her name. "And another girl started Friday."

Rebecca mused, "I was out a month, and they didn't hire help. As soon as Bethany was out a week on bed rest, they hired two new girls."

"They're temps, although one is supposed to have legal experience," Jacobs told her.

Something did not compute. Maybe they had got word that Bethany would not be returning after her baby was born. But why two temps? She looked around the corridor before walking past the doorless frame to her cubicle.

Fear gave rise to a hushed admission. "Burke's case was in my in-box on Thursday, and I signed on the case . . . which involves Walter Calhoun, the guy I told you about from Dover."

His sigh could be heard through the phone. "Heaven's, girl, what were you thinking? That case should never have made it to your desk. You have a right to deny a case—that case in particular. That guy is known to bully his way into properties. We sign with him today. I'll be representing him in court tomorrow. I'm worried about you."

"I'm worried about me too. " At that moment she spotted a floral arrangement on her desk. She approached it cautiously, powering on her computer before searching the flowers for a card. "To sealing a sweet deal and making a new friend," Rebecca said, reading aloud the unsigned card for Jacobs to hear. The flowers' wilted leaves led her to believe that the arrangement had been sent before she left everyone high and dry. "The man sent me flowers."

"Whoa, what? I know I might sound like a broken record, but I want you to camp out in HR today."

Rebecca stared into the unknown in front of her, recognizing that despite what Ms. Humphries had previously said, she had no other recourse. "It's no use. What if they don't do anything?"

"Sanz, Mitchum, and Clarke can either protect you or release you, but you can't continue to work under duress. You're not working today. If HR can't provide a resolution, such as mediation or something, put the matter in someone else's hands. You get counsel and you sue. I have to go. The temp is here. I'll check in on you later."

Rebecca knew what Jacobs was telling her was true. It took her back to her prayer the night she tried to imagine what others saw in her. She prayed that God would take the anxiety that came with this job away from her, because it was becoming too much to bear.

She logged off the company computer without accessing the message board. She had been instructed by wise counsel not to work, but rather to encamp. With her phone still in her hand, she grabbed her purse and headed to the HR suite. Ms. Humphries was literally coming out into the reception area when Rebecca rounded the corner. She looked taken aback when she saw Rebecca.

"Oh, Ms. Lucas, I was just about to have Jocelyn call down to you. I heard you paid me a visit last week. I was asked to keynote a conference in Buffalo, New York. I got up there and got sick as a dog—a combination of the climate and the altitude change, I reckon. Come inside my office."

The small talk felt oddly contrived to Rebecca, who followed the woman, not expecting to be seen so quickly. She took a wide step over the floorboard in the doorway and sat in the exact same seat she had sat in when she made the initial complaint.

The two women looked at one another as if waiting on a jump start. Ms. Humphries sighed before accessing a folder in her in-box. Then she pulled out a thick padded envelope and inched it toward Rebecca.

"I'm afraid the partners have sent notice for your dismissal," Ms. Humphries said, delivering the bad news.

Rebecca's mouth flung open as if it were hinged at the jaw. Ms. Humphries's words forced the temporary collapse of her windpipe. She needed clarification and quite possibly mouth-to-mouth. She coughed out, "What? Why?"

Ms. Humphries took the document from the unsealed envelope and read from it. "They cited abuse of leave and failure to effectively communicate between the firm and its clients."

"That's Burke and Walter Calhoun, the very men I told you were harassing me," Rebecca screeched.

"Calm down, Ms. Lucas."

"I can't calm down, Ms. Humphries. I've just been fired. I had hoped that by coming to you, all this would disappear. I've been alone here, steadily having to protect and defend myself. The firm did nothing."

Ms. Humphries held up her hand in her own defense. "I'm sorry you feel that way. I told you to be careful, to advocate for yourself. The claim was filed, but I told you it was going to take time to hear back from upstairs. I can't say that I understand their reasoning behind letting you go. I put in an inquiry right before you showed up. Maybe they haven't put two and two together that we have a complaint from you that they haven't addressed. You have to tell me all that has taken place since then, though."

Rebecca took a deep breath to pace herself as she gave an account of the past week. She knew her time off was not the grounds for her release. It had everything to do with sealing the deal with Calhoun and him nursing his wounds when she didn't show up for his little yacht party. Rebecca stared at Ms. Humphries, unsure if she had come to the same conclusion.

"I have an eleven thirty appointment to prepare for. Like I said, I'm waiting to hear a response from upstairs, so I can push for an immediate mediation between you and Mr. Burke and a reevaluation of your termination," Ms. Humphries said, standing.

Camp out in HR. Rebecca stood on unsteady legs. "If it is all the same to you, I'll be waiting in your lobby."

"Trust me, Ms. Lucas, I'll call you when I hear something. Go—"

"Where? To my desk? Home?" Rebecca hung on the hope that she'd get an answer about what to do next. Instead, Ms. Humphries merely handed her the envelope with a hopeless shake of her head.

Rebecca walked out to the inner lobby with a determination she didn't quite feel. She settled in one of the waiting-room chairs. She waited. She watched Ms. Humphries eleven thirty come and go. So many events from the day crowded her mind and kept her occupied, from her conversation with Jacobs this morning to the card on her flowers that sat on her desk and the excuses for letting her go that were cited in her termination papers. Why did she expect a fair shake in the end? She now saw Ms. Humphries's closed door for what it was. It was indeed over. She asked God to release her from that spot, release her from the need to control the uncontrollable. It was out of her hands.

Then the tears fell. Rebecca used the sleeve of her blouse to wipe her eyes. Ten years at the firm had shriveled up due to what Burke had termed *the black burner*. She consulted her phone to see just how much time she had wasted sitting there today. She noticed that Will had sent her a return text.

How's 2:30?

It was almost one o'clock, according to her phone. She contemplated how much time it would take to gather her things in a pathetic cardboard box and take her walk of shame. Although she could very well leave that for another day, she knew that when she walked away, she would never want to return.

She typed her reply.

I'll be scooping up my cup in the next forty-five minutes and leaving work early. Worse day ever. Rain check?

The thought of what Will might think carried her around the corner to the bank of elevators and down to the fifth floor. Rebecca felt herself looking over her shoulder at every turn. Given the way her luck had been going lately, she expected to run right into Burke. She didn't even want to talk to Jacobs at this point.

Her heart began to pound when she saw that Celeste's chair was empty. Maybe she could get out of there unnoticed, she thought.

The impact of leaving a coveted position under these circumstances hit Rebecca once she was inside her cubicle. She took in the dimensions of the space she had occupied all that time with the firm. *Rebecca was here, but now she's gone. . . .* The thought of the already hired temps occupying her space had her contemplating whether she had left her mark on the firm. She shook her head to clear her mind and began snatching personal items from her desktop and drawers. They filled a plastic shopping bag that she had on hand. When it came to the floral arrangement, for some reason she wanted to keep the card. The rest she placed in the trash can.

Rebecca put her sweater coat on, grabbed the shopping bag, and left her cubicle. She did not stop once as she headed out of the building. A real determination carried her up the main hallway and past Celeste, who had returned to her post.

"I guess I'll go get that coffee now," Rebecca said with a combination smirk and sniff as she hurried by. "Don't worry about taking my messages."

Chapter 16

She did it again, Will thought, powering down his cell phone. It was just like Rebecca to bail on him. He didn't need this.

"Oh, let's meet," Will said, mimicking Rebecca. "No, on second thought, let's not meet."

At least she gave him a heads-up this time. He could imagine himself waiting in the coffeehouse for her and her never showing up.

Unless. There was a possibility he could meet her, anyway, surprise her on the way in or out of the coffeehouse, if she was accurate with her timeline. The only thing that she seemed to be certain about was that she was stopping for coffee. *'Tis the season for a grand gesture,* he thought.

No, he told himself. *Be here now.* He agreed with his father: there had been too much coasting on his part, too much business as usual. He wasn't an interim pastor anymore, but rather a pastoral candidate. He needed to be present when at church, establishing his ministry. He was amazed at what he could get done in one day by studying the desktop databases and speaking extensively to Sister Tyler, the church's part-time receptionist, to make sense of the church's daily operations. He had even arranged a meeting with the church stakeholders, including the state voucher committee, in this, the last week of his probationary period. He wished he had more time.

The next forty-five minutes. He had planned to take his daily walk through the school, something he had been doing to become relevant there as well. He stood and grabbed his phone to check the time. It was 1:30. *It was way past the morning announcement and prayer,* he thought. He needed to key certain parts of the school schedule into his "Remind me" app so he could speak to groups of students, as his father often had, without being obtrusive. *Maybe another day,* he thought, easily convincing himself.

He tried to ignore Rebecca's text message, which seemed to be almost pulsating at the top of his in-box. She was having the worst day ever, and so she was leaving work early? Maybe she was sick. Maybe Route 50 wasn't congested this time of day. Where were those speed cameras posted along the highway? He was en route to the coffeehouse in spirit before his body and mind could catch up.

Deacon Contee was outside waiting for someone or something when Will reached his car. He waved to him as he folded himself into his car. Will paused when he noticed Danny Glass pull up a second later in a car that was too sleek for their sand and gravel parking lot. Will forgot it was moving week for the Glass family, though where they were moving, he still did not know. He reminded himself to have his eyes and ears open when this guy was around. He couldn't help thinking that he himself should be upstairs and busy doing something church related to show that he had squatters' rights at Grace Apostle.

This coffeehouse better serve a mean caramel frappé, Will thought as he cranked up his car and slowly backed out of the pastor's parking space. He put down his window to extend a courteous greeting as he drove up to the pair.

"Hey, man, nice to see you again," Danny said, extending his hand. "I was looking to catch up with you here, get a feel for what Grace Apostle is all about. You know, observe."

"I'm sure Deacon Contee can handle that. I'm off to check up on a member," Will said, not a believer in issuing rain checks of his own.

Will gave a curt wave and drifted a considerate distance through the parking lot before he accelerated. He didn't know what to make of Danny's request to hang out with him. They were competitors, not friends.

After pulling onto the main highway, he increased his speed. It was impossible for him to be present at church when his mind was on Rebecca. He was doing exactly what he had said he wouldn't do. He was chasing her. From Pastor Cutler's perspective, that was the way to show love. There wasn't a day when Pastor Cutler's words didn't haunt him. Will thought that before Rebecca had decided to leave, he had made his feelings about her clear to her and that he had conveyed to her that he wanted them to be together. But maybe he had not shown her.

This was not a leisurely drive down Route 50, like when he was going to work or going to help out at Dogwood Community Church. This felt like a joyride. It felt irresponsible, reckless, but freeing. He could admit to himself now that he wanted more than anything to see her. He wanted to balance the coolness he felt with the surge of emotions cresting and breaking inside his chest. He was curious to see if he could or would still feel like putty around her—both needy and needed.

Thinking these things seemed to cut the drive time in half, but Will didn't stop to think about what would happen if she wasn't there until he crossed into the city limits. His mind was a map, bringing him closer to his target. His heart, which now felt like it was beating behind his ears, seemed to drop when he didn't spot her car in the lot immediately.

Will stared aimlessly through his windshield at the almost full parking lot. A passenger van, having loaded a diverse group of senior citizens, pulled off, exposing a few compact car spaces. There was her Hyundai Sonata. She was, in fact, there.

He didn't give himself time to doubt his decision. He put his Camry in reverse and backed into a corner spot. He exited his vehicle and shortened the gap to the front door with wide strides. Upon careful inspection, he spotted Rebecca in the line, brushing wisps of loose hair into a makeshift knot at the top of her head as she waited. He studied the tilt of her neck and the impatient way she swayed from side to side. He'd know her anywhere.

He went into stealth mode. With a finger to his lip, he asked those behind her with just a glance to allow him to get in front of them so he could surprise her as they inched forward.

Will waited for her to put her bid in for a simple large cup of French roast coffee before interjecting over her shoulder, "Make that two. Make mine black."

He didn't expect the shriek or the way she attempted to hoist herself on the counter in what appeared to be sheer terror. They were face-to-face now, but Rebecca was still guarded.

There were tears. "Will?"

"Yeah, like the guy you've been texting all day. Remember me?" He tried to appeal not only to her, but to the patrons he had conspired with, who now viewed his surprise as suspect and an impediment to their own service.

"Oh my God, you said the word *black,* and I thought you were—"

"Someone else, obviously, who has made quite an impression on you." *Some other dude,* Will thought.

With a hand still clutching the excess material of her shirt, she said, "You've got to be a mirage. Tell me you're real, 'cause I don't take to foolin' myself these days."

Will coaxed her off the counter in front of the order line, and she hugged him heartily around his neck. He felt the aftershocks of her fright. "You're shaking. Go get us a seat. Go ahead. I got this."

Will paid their tab and added stirrers to the coffee carrier before rejoining her. He sat down hesitantly and watched her snatch up her cup once it was on the table. She palmed the cup with both hands and brought it to her nose and mouth like a true friend. The aroma seemed to have a calming effect at least. They sat there like that for a while.

This was not at all how he had envisioned their reunion. *Silence?* Will felt as if he had both said and done enough already by surprising her. He too grabbed his cup, and they stared at one another over their coffee lids. Her face looked as if it were lit by a LCD lamp. It was scrubbed clean, so he could see the subtle changes in her skin tone. She looked flushed, as if she had just come in on a cold and windy day. She didn't appear sick, just tired, like a person who had been pushed to her breaking point.

"How is it that you're here?" she finally asked, shaking her head at the ceiling, as if asking God rather than him.

"Is that a trick question? I'm here," Will said.

"It's just your uncanny timing," she said, putting her cup down. "Your wonderfully *horrible* timing."

When was a good time to turn a friendship into something more? He had thought about his timing on the day of Gail's wedding. That was the day he had planned to propose to Rebecca, and the day she had planned to leave him behind.

"What's going on, Rebi?"

There was a tremor in her lips. She temporarily shielded her eyes. She sniffed, batted back tears, and said, "I got fired today, or I should say, I was wrongfully discharged."

"Oh, wow," Will said in a low voice, sympathizing. Everything was beginning to make sense to him now. "When you say wrongfully, how do you go about righting that wrong?"

Rebecca looked over her shoulder, causing Will to do the same, before saying, "I'm not sure I want to. It's been, like, unbearable since I've been back, but I didn't want to go running, like I always do. Look, I can't . . . I don't want to get into this here. If you don't mind, why don't we get out of here? I mean, if you don't have anything else to do for a while, my apartment is literally two blocks up the street."

They were on the move, gathering up their individual cups and discarding all the rest. They walked past several patrons either coming in or claiming the limited number of seats, with Rebecca leading the way. For a small coffee shop, it was quite busy. Rebecca did an abrupt about-face a few feet from the door.

"Oh my God, it's him," she said, her head bowed into Will's chest now. "It's really him this time."

Through the panes of glass in the doorway, Will spotted a well-dressed brother with a confident demeanor, similar to that of Danny Glass, walking across the parking lot, headed in their direction. Will felt himself sprouting an instant attitude. You didn't shy away the way she was doing from a mere acquaintance. Given that her job had been unbearable, maybe this guy was the real reason she just had to return to Salisbury.

"There is only one way out, and I'm not ducking and hiding. If this is your man or a jilted lover, you'd better let me know now."

"He's a coworker. The one I mistook you for—"

The one that has her scared to death, Will thought, surmising the truth. With no time to hear the entire backstory, Will stepped in front of her and grabbed her free hand. Just then Rebecca's coworker burst through the door, as if he were the new sheriff in town and in search of a confrontation. He paused, stepped to the side of them, and peeled off his Ray-Ban shades once he spotted Rebecca in Will's company. The man was eating Rebecca up with his eyes, while Will hardly merited a second look.

"Ms. Lucas, fancy meeting you out and about," the guy proclaimed in a rich baritone voice.

"Whatever. I'm so sure this is the only coffee shop on your route," Rebecca snapped.

The man glanced in Will's direction, then looked quickly back at Rebecca. "Can I speak to you for a minute?"

Will wanted to punch this dude. He felt like an observer caught in the smog of tension. He could feel her hand tense up and become sweaty as he held it. They were a threesome of chest heaves. Since no one had introduced him yet, Will placed his cup down on an unoccupied table nearby and stuck out his hand.

"Will Donovan, Pastor Will Donovan. And you are?"

With a quizzical look, the man gave Will a solid handshake. "Kenny Burke, attorney."

"Well, if you'll excuse us, Mr. Burke. We were just leaving," Will said.

Will dropped Rebecca's hand only to open the door for her. He picked up his coffee and ushered her through the door, leaving Kenny Burke wanting to say more.

Chapter 17

"You lead a very eventful life," Will said once inside her apartment.

"Don't start," Rebecca said, peeling off her sweater coat and stepping out of her heels at the door. She hung her key ring on a hook to the right of the door. She glanced toward the doorway that led to the kitchen. "I have nothing really to offer you to eat. I'm sorry."

He held up his coffee, now barely lukewarm, as if toasting something. "I came all this way for the coffee. I'm good."

He wandered around her living room, admiring the arrangement, and she hovered over him as if she was a tour guide ready to interject an interesting fact. Her furniture was heavy and ornate for an apartment, so different from what he had expected her living quarters to look like. Will stopped to pick up a framed picture of Madame, Rebecca's mother, Gail, and Rebecca. It appeared to have been taken within the last ten years. He focused in on their mutual sister and then Madame—the woman with whom his dad had had the affair. For the first time he noted major similarities between them all.

"Have a seat, *Pastor*," Rebecca said.

"Hey, I was trying to let the guy know that I'm prone to laying hands on people," Will said, the photo still in his hand. "What would you have preferred I say?"

"I would prefer to forget about the whole thing," she snapped as she found a spot on the couch after checking the peephole in her door.

She'd prefer to forget it all. Will wondered if this entire visit would be a part of that memory lapse.

Rebecca sighed heavily. "Thank you."

He furrowed his brow in confusion. "Huh?"

"For your wonderfully horrible timing." She smirked. "Seriously, I'm indebted to you for getting me out of there."

He joined her in the sitting area, taking a seat on a hard straight-back chair. "Since I was thrown in the middle of whatever was going on back there, I think I deserve some details—at least about what happened today at your job and why this guy came looking for you."

She closed her eyes and tilted her head back. Although reclining on the couch, she didn't appear comfortable. "I was being harassed. I filed a claim with the firm, but obviously they believed him over me. He probably wanted to rub it in. He's a jerk like that."

"Kenny Burke?"

She nodded her head slowly.

Will repositioned himself so he could sit up straighter. "So this guy stays, and you've got to go. That doesn't add up. He gets away with stalking you on and off the job?"

She lifted her arms out to the sides, then let them fall dramatically. "He predicted it. My claim must have been pushed to what Kenny referred to as the *black burner,* and now I am probably going to be blacklisted in the immediate legal community."

"How can a lawyer in a law firm blatantly harass a fellow coworker? That's criminal. Lawyers are supposed to uphold the law," Will declared. "That's mighty stupid of him, and presumptuous at the same time."

"Presumptuous?"

"Just like you said, he thought either he'd get away with it or you'd go along with it," he practically shouted.

"I guess you assumed I'd do the latter. Great. Why don't you offend me also? Look, I'm not making this up. There are people who believe they are above reproach. It's the same way a preacher can preach from the pulpit every Sunday and blatantly . . ." Her last words trailed off.

They had hit a wall hard and fast. Will wished he could rewind the entire conversation, but he kept imagining a good-looking brother working with a good-looking sister and the type of harassment she was implying. Maybe he should have laid his hands on that guy.

"My bad. Anything is liable to come out of my mouth. Sorry," she said, recanting as her eyes issued fresh tears.

"No, you're right. Some preachers sin blatantly, and I didn't mean that I didn't believe what you were saying about this Kenny dude." Will thought about his recent study of the scriptures in the book of Romans, where Paul admonished the Jews for boasting about the law but breaking it all the same. It happened, and he and Rebecca knew it more than anything. They looked at one another pensively.

"What are you going to do?" he finally asked with a big huff. He felt like he should check the peephole now.

She shrugged before speaking. "It's so fresh. I wanted to lay low for a day or two. Give myself a chance to think."

Will's heart went out to her. He feared the circumstances had cast a shadow on this visit. He wanted to make headway in figuring out their own relationship, but she had more pressing things on her mind. It wouldn't be fair to press her.

There was a sudden blast of sound, and after his initial shock, Will realized it was music coming from upstairs. It took a minute for him to decide that the occupants had indeed chosen that volume and weren't planning on reducing it. He watched Rebecca bring her head between her knees. She arose with fresh tears.

"Not today," she shouted. "Did I not just say I needed time to think? To think, you inconsiderate jerks! Is that too much to ask?"

Was this a regular occurrence? he wondered. In all the confusion, Rebecca appeared as if she was arguing with God. He discerned that what she was going through was a spiritual process as well as an emotional one. She was fighting the process as she raged on at the actual person upstairs. He was eager to know how he would be a part of this process.

Before Will could tell her to calm down, she marched off to her kitchen and returned with a broom. Her face was balled up in anguish, and he wondered what she planned to do.

"Oh, we're going to come to an understanding tonight, 'cause I just lost my job and I can't afford to move," she raged.

Will watched in stunned silence as she began thrusting the broom upward into the epicenter of the commotion above, at the expense of her paint job, until the frustration and futility of her efforts began to tire her out.

This is insanity, Will thought. He could not watch any longer. He approached Rebecca and wrangled the broom from her hand. He laid it down on the floor and rubbed his own face with his hands before declaring over the noise, "Pack some stuff. You're coming with me."

"To Easton? I don't know. I don't want to impose. You know Gail and Milo just got married, and I don't want to tell them what's been going on," she replied, jumbling up her thoughts.

"You can stay with me. It'll give you a chance to decompress," he said.

Bewildered, she became a mannequin, acting as if she hadn't heard him or didn't comprehend his words. He hadn't completely processed what he had offered himself.

"Pack some stuff," he reiterated.

"Are you serious?"

"It's not much, but I promise you it's quieter than this."

Her lips formed an unsure smile. As he watched her saunter down the hallway to carry out his order, he couldn't help but think that this was not quite the grand gesture this pastoral candidate had planned on making.

Chapter 18

In a panic, Rebecca snatched her eyes open at quarter past eight. This was déjà vu. Sadly, she had awakened in an unknown bed before. She recalled that it was the worst feeling in the world, remembering a torrid night of events and a brain so numb it would allow it all to happen. It took her more than a moment to take in Will's earthy scent, which was lingering all around, but especially in his sheets. She sat up to take in the rest of the room, lit now by sunlight, and Will's collection of geek globes, and then she remembered the dismissal from her job, her apartment insanity, and the offer of respite.

She was in Will's T-shirt, in Will's bed, back in Easton. She felt both comforted and scared to death by that reality. In her haste she had neglected to pack her nightgowns. He had offered her a pick from his vast number of T-shirts and the use of his entire bedroom suite for the duration of her stay. She checked the bedside clock. She had slept for twelve hours. He was right; his house was tucked back off the road like her childhood home and was unusually quiet, which was apparently exactly what she needed.

Rebecca could hear signs of life now. It was Will in the hallway bathroom, which they would share. He was singing at full volume as if the pelting of the water in the shower was the perfect pitch. Reality set in. He had somewhere to go, and she didn't.

She dressed, anyway, to partake of whatever he had planned to eat for breakfast. Before she could get to the kitchen, she entered a huge sunroom with rows of folding tables seemingly huddled together in the corner, where the various herbs and other plants could get direct light. *This is his terrarium.* She wondered when he found the time to water all this vegetation, and figured the hardwood floor took the spills better than carpeting would. It smelled heavenly and earthy at the same time as she nosed around. She could detect both spicy and perfumed plants in the starter trays in front of the containers of huge potted plants.

"Is that you? Trading spaces? You're awake," Will called out.

She emerged from the sunroom, rolling her eyes at the thought of acquiring yet another nickname from him. "You're hilarious. You know that?" She took a glance around at the living room, which fed into that sunroom. "This place is huge. Did you build that extension, or did the house come like that?"

"Would you be more impressed if I did?" he asked earnestly.

Rebecca noticed he was dressed up, and it arrested her momentarily. She could see the imprint of a crisp white T-shirt under his starched white button-up shirt and striped tie. It was a good look for him.

When he realized she was not going to answer his question, he began to explain about the house. "I was in a town house and saw this place had a vacant sign about a year ago. I knew it was perfect for what I like to do, although at the time Veronica was set to redo this whole place. She hated it. I guess moving into a bigger place gave her ideas," he said with a smirk and a shake of his head.

She moved back toward the sunroom. Hearing that name had made her uneasy. "I wouldn't change a thing. Except maybe I'd add a wall of mirrors and a ballet bar in all this space right here. Seems like a tragic waste of space. Is that all the room your plants need?"

"I prefer to call them green friends, and, yes, they catch the sun rays better on that side of the house."

They shared a smile.

Will's expression turned serious as if he was shifting gears. "Speaking of Veronica, I went to see her."

"That's nice. Is your kitchen over here?" She pointed. This time she retreated from the conversation and the room.

"Wait, if I'm not mistaken, that was your suggestion when you left, wasn't it? That I should go see my ex-girlfriend—be with my ex-girlfriend?" He followed her into the modest kitchen and waited for her to turn and face him, his question a springboard.

She wondered if he expected her to remain shallow or to go deep with a response. She reluctantly turned around but decided to say nothing.

"She all but called me a sick inbred weirdo. She knows about my dad being Gail's father also, all the way in Wye Mills, but they haven't quite figured out that Madame is her mother. This whole thing is what got Dad kicked to the curb. Her little friend, our classmate Nina, and her family have reissued their pamphlet of lies, which is parading as a newspaper, with a lead story about their own ministry, telling the community they might as well say farewell to the old and usher in the new."

She hated being here at that moment and was ready to shed more tears. Did he bring her here to berate her about her choices, Madame's choices? Then she looked at him, caught up in his own soliloquy, and realized it wasn't about her. He was simply venting, wanting to be heard, or perhaps he needed a pep talk.

He appeared to snap out of his trance when she reached for a paper towel to discreetly dab her eyes.

"Any day now, I'll stop crying. I'm sure of it. Or I'll run out of tears. Better stay hydrated." Her comment gave her an excuse to search the refrigerator for something to drink.

"You didn't create this firestorm, Rebi. None of us did. Grace Apostle was bound to be torn apart. Hopefully, it is in God's plan to build it back up with me at the helm. It's gonna be hard. I need two thirds of the vote of the membership to maintain what my father built," he huffed. "Dad . . . he put so much into that place. You know, sometimes . . . sometimes I fear if I don't get this spot, and keep Dad connected to this ministry, he'll waste away. All this could be God's way of bringing him in for a landing, you know. He wants this so much for me. That's what's at stake."

She lingered open refrigerator, stunned by his admission. To think that she felt that she had all the stress. She felt instantly guilty. "Well, you know where to find me if it gets to be too much."

He sighed and smiled, as if he was relieved to get his burdens out in the open. "Yeah, same here."

There was an awkward moment as she contemplated whether it was appropriate to embrace him. She surely wanted to. His look showed he was facing the same quandary. A hug meant something different if you weren't together but were technically living together.

"I don't have to tell you to make yourself at home. Help yourself to anything," he said.

As it turned out, something caught her eye that might be the beverage she needed. On the counter was a four-bottle wine rack with one bottle facing bottom out.

He caught her staring longingly at the wine bottle. "Oh no, help yourself to anything but that." He extracted the bottle so Rebecca could see the faded label. He palmed the bottle with one hand. "This was my parents. They got it for their twentieth anniversary or something all the way from the vineyards of Naples. Dad said to save it to toast an extra-special occasion. I can't say that anything has ever fit that bill. This day and time are not it, either, boo."

She tried to shield her disappointment but shut the refrigerator door a little too hard. Coffee in the morning and a glass of wine or a hot toddy at night had become her norm. She knew she needed to lay off, especially with their current arrangement. She sought solace in his cabinet and was happy to find a can of corned beef hash.

"I'm afraid I don't have much stocked here, either," Will admitted. "What are we gonna do?"

"I'm cool," she replied, holding up her find. "And I saw bread and peanut butter in there. Anything else I need, I'll just run out and get. I mean, I did drive my own car."

His mouth stood open, as if he were relearning vocalization. "Ah, are you sure you want to be seen out and about?"

That let her know he certainly didn't want her to go out. The ground rules were out: no wine, no exits. She guessed that a party was totally out of the question. Before she could certify her fear that Will's house would become suffocating to her real quick, she realized his position. They were cohabitating. She didn't want to jeopardize all that he had riding on his election at Grace Apostle. She wouldn't be able to forgive herself if she blew it for him. As much as she rationalized it, it struck an eerily dissatisfying and familiar chord.

"You're right. I'm chillin'," she announced, appeasing him.

"I'll run past the store on the way in. Consider me your butler. Text me your requests. Now, wish me luck. I'm meeting with stakeholders at the state level so we can continue funding through the voucher program."

She was feeling very much like the opposite of a good luck charm. "You don't need my luck. You're blessed, right?"

He gave her the once-over, which made her feel as if her whole life had been read and registered by a bar scanner. "I'm down to follow where this leads me."

She was thinking that boundaries would serve him better than the hug he was waiting on now. Feeling conflicted , she settled her quandary by putting all her affection into a hearty pat on his chest.

Chapter 19

There was something to this suit and tie thing, Will thought. He felt he had wowed the committee, or at least he had assured them that under his leadership, Grace Apostle would remain committed to preserving its school as an educational alternative to the public schools in the area.

Before running into the supermarket, he checked his text messages to see if Rebecca had in fact sent a request for something. Instead, he found a text with a scriptural reference, her belated wish of luck. It was Ezekiel 47:14. "And ye shall inherit it, one as well as another: concerning the which I lifted up mine hand to give it unto your fathers: and this land shall fall unto you for inheritance."

Look at her, he thought. Somebody had cracked a Bible concordance. He smiled. He felt that text message called for a fabulous dinner, which he would prepare for her.

Later they talked about her inspiration over a steak dinner complete with baked potatoes and broccoli. They sat across from each other on bar stools at the kitchen island.

"Got your text. I was impressed. I didn't know you were a budding theologian. Ezekiel, huh?"

"Please. That verse and that whole book came to mind partly because it's where I stopped when I was supposed to be reading through the Bible when I returned home for Madame's funeral. I kind of gave up after that."

He couldn't get his broccoli spear down fast enough. "What? You stopped in the Old Testament? You do know you have the Gospels in a whole nother section to go."

"After you get through who begat who and the breakdown of the tribes of Israel and what they took poor Moses through? Don't get me started on King David. I had to stop. I might try again with audio."

Will couldn't contain his laughter. Rebecca bubbled over, and he got the impression that she hadn't thought of how ridiculously honest the whole thing sounded.

She was concentrating on cutting her meat and didn't look up when she spoke. "I know I shouldn't admit this to a minister, but I'm like, Lord, I know I am supposed to read this, but where am I in the lineage? Tell me when it gets to me, please."

"You must have skipped all of Psalms and Proverbs. You're in there, for sure. I got you," he said, resigned to the fact that he'd miss having dinner with her the following evening due to Bible study at the church. The least he could do was have Bible study with her now.

Will got up to get his favorite Bible. Once he was seated, he held it out in front of both of them, as if it were a mirror. "I see you, me . . . us all in here. Don't think of the books as a bunch of stories, but as mirror images of our experiences."

Rebecca looked up from her plate. "What do you see in there for me?"

Will's arms grew tired, and he lowered the Bible. "I see sinners' prayers, cautionary tales, redemption, and victory. This is all of us at the same time. Our life stories are all intertwined. I got you pegged as the woman with the alabaster box, the way you pour your heart out in an unexpected expression of praise when you dance. "

"How awesome is that," she remarked.

"Sometimes I wonder why I can't make the entire congregation see themselves as well."

"You'll never make a hundred percent of any population do or see anything."

Will had forgotten she was a realist and was thankful for her forthrightness. "Since you were searching the Scriptures, did it prompt you to do any soul-searching about your predicament?"

She shook her head. "I haven't gotten there."

"What do you feel?" Will said, figuring she had to have a gut reaction.

Their eyes connected, and he didn't like what he saw. It was the same thing he saw shortly after they found out about their parents' affair. She had found the off switch that changed her into an unthinking, unfeeling mannequin.

"I can't find the emotion. I just feel depleted," she admitted.

"What do you think is gonna fill you back up, Rebi?" He wanted so desperately to fill that space for her—to be putty.

She used her fork as a pointer, then brought that hand back to her mouth to catch any food from falling. "Why are you pressing me?"

"'Cause I can't stand seeing you like this," he said. *'Cause I'm anxious to get on to better times . . . our times.* "We go from steak dinners and smiles to complete depletion? I wanna see that courage I know you have."

"About what?"

"About Burke," Will said incredulously.

She shrugged and rolled her eyes at the same time. "What about him?"

This time he was the one who was pointing. "I'm talking about his ability to harass you on the job, then come looking for you. I'm talking about his ability to even be employed at the firm instead of you. His ability to rattle you, rob you of your joy. This guy ain't God, Rebi."

The fighter in her suddenly emerged. "I know that. He's far from it. I guess what you're really saying is that I need to figure this out fast and get to steppin'. You should have told me that I was on a time clock when you ripped me from my apartment. I'm not you. Revelations don't hit me so quickly."

"I'm not saying that at all. As a matter of fact, I'm not going to entertain the notion of you going back to the firm if you're not safe. So, if you want your old life back, we have to make sure this Burke guy is dealt with."

She looked at him as if he had just confessed to a heinous crime. "*Dealt with?* What are you saying?"

"What are you *not* saying?" *Why was she not crying foul?* he wondered.

She had her arms outstretched in a defensive gesture. "What makes you think I'm holding any information from you?"

"'Cause I think I know you," he told her. There was no more eating as he anticipated a response.

She was solemn, to say the least. She let out a sigh and on the tail end of it gave a sniff. "I put my trust in HR, in my job, in . . . I'm tired of putting my trust in people."

He stood to scrape his plate and take it to the sink. Once there he turned to look at her. "I hope that doesn't include me too, 'cause I'm here, obviously, to help you figure this out, and anything else you're ready to deal with."

"I hear you. Don't you have Bible study to prepare for?" Her eyes had glazed over. She used the napkin from her lap to wipe her mouth. "Now, let me do these dishes. It's the least I can do. Earn my keep."

Once again he had said too much too soon. He left her alone in the kitchen with her thoughts. He had to prepare his Bible study lesson for the next night. He wished he could take her with him.

Will lost his balance in the middle of the night, as he stumbled to the hall bathroom. He had been known to stub a toe or bump into the wall on similar excursions since he was only half awake. Remaining in a semi-sleep state made it easier for him to fall back to sleep after he handled his business.

The sight of Rebecca made him come to complete attention when he swung the bathroom door open. She was in the doorway of his room and was wearing his Perdue T-shirt and one of his button-ups as a robe. Her feet were planted in a pair of Ugg boots, and one bare knee protruded and was wagging back and forth, as if she had been waiting awhile.

He remembered that knee. He was sixteen, and in desperation his dad had dropped him off at the Madame's house in attempt to shield him from yet another rough night of nursing his mother, who was suffering greatly from the effects of cancer, in her final days. He remembered Madame clearing the entire top floor of the house for him, displacing Gail and Rebecca, who had to sleep with her downstairs. He didn't know if she was being extra accommodating or not by trusting him to stay put and not peek into or poke around in one of the girl's rooms. He was confused and vulnerable, and the last thing he wanted to do was be alone.

He remembered Gail gushing sympathy and Rebecca darting around her room to gather a few belongings. Rebecca wanted to share something with him, but Madame, who had never trusted that their relationship was purely platonic, had abruptly yanked her out of the room. When it was all said and done, Madame ushered him into his guest chambers and the girls stood obediently in the doorway, looking on, Rebecca wagging that knee. He didn't know how to take that knee then, didn't know why it was so intriguing. Was she trying to send a secret message? Was it a pity wag? Did she have to go to the bathroom? He felt guilty about his preoccupation.

Looking at Rebecca now, with her hair hanging at her shoulders, her body draped in his clothing, and that knee wagging, Will understood his fascination. He needed Madame or the man upstairs to keep him out of her room now.

He stepped out of the bathroom doorway, giving her the right of way. They changed places, taking up positions on the opposite sides of the doorway.

"Good night, Rebecca," he said with all the formality of a perfect gentleman, knowing his stare filled in the blanks of the things left unsaid.

"Good night, William." She pierced him with a return stare.

Only then did he realize he had greeted her in a T-shirt and boxer shorts. He didn't flex, but there was no need to hide now.

See you in the morning, Will thought. He knew a day of reckoning awaited them both.

Chapter 20

Rebecca was reading a text message backward. In part two of two, Jacobs had given her a name and a number, and in part one of two, he explained what he wanted her to do with that information. He wanted her to sue her former and his current employer. Being in-house counsel made him unable to represent her. Connie Doyle was an attorney at the law firm Princeton and Hope and was likely a classmate of Jacobs, as Rebecca remembered hearing her name before. As she scrolled up, she realized Jacobs had also given her an assignment: research wrongful discharges.

Will wanted her to go after Burke; Jacobs wanted her to go after the entire firm. What did she want? She wanted to suspend time right where she was. She looked around Will's cozy bedroom and knew that wouldn't be possible. A tented flip calendar reminded her it would be the first of February at the end of the week. The first of the month rent would be due on an apartment she had outgrown, and she didn't have a job. Time wasn't on her side. Decisions had to be made.

Had Ms. Humphries called? Could she at least get severance pay? *Not if I sue. That's for sure,* she thought. Those questions alone led her to find Will's laptop on his bookshelf and power it on. She almost cried when she found it was password protected. Just when she had set her mind to do something, she hit a roadblock.

Rebecca tried a few random codes—his house number, his birthday, his middle name—but nothing worked. There was a hint: my love. What did he love more than anything? *God.* She tried it, but the password had to be at least five letters. It wasn't *Jesus.* She was about to give up when she tried another word on a hunch, and it was successful.

Weary. That was one of his original nicknames for her.

She warned herself against imagining that this man loved her beyond measure, and there was nothing she could do to foul it up. She hadn't achieved love in all her thirty-one years. Why was this so hard to believe? Maybe it was for the same reason that she couldn't imagine herself taking on Burke or the firm and actually winning. *Weary.* She was falling into her old habits and thought processes.

The laptop became her constant companion and the Equal Employment Opportunity Commission Web site was her landing pad for much of the afternoon. Her mind was filled with thoughts of legal claims, untruthful allegations, and civil lawsuits.

Later in the afternoon, she stopped to take a break from her research, determined to return the favor and have dinner ready for Will when he returned. *What a wifely thing to do,* she thought. An image of him in his boxers the night before popped into her mind, and she wasn't fast to turn off the instant replay. She'd be lying if she said she didn't feel a spark from that encounter. She had to remind herself that there was a thin line between helping out a good friend by letting her stay at his place and playing house.

***

Will was in an obvious good mood when he got in. She served up spaghetti and salad. He spoke nonstop at the dinner table about a call he received at church. Apparently, a horticulture project he had always wanted to do with the upper grades at Grace Apostle, similar to the one he had started at Dogwood Community Church, a church in her area, would likely land them on the pages of Lower Eastern Shore Charter Schools spring catalog, according to the charter school committee chairperson. Rebecca tried her best to listen, despite what was on her mind.

"I imagine they have to keep me around now. Danny Glass was in the office to hear it and everything. I can't wait to get started," Will said.

"*The* Danny Glass?" Rebecca inquired.

"There you go. That's my competition, but let me stop you there. He's got enough fans, or should I say his dad has," Will told her.

She scrunched her face in confusion.

"Exactly," Will said, as if he could read her mind. "I don't know this guy's story. I'm reviewing the weekly bulletin before it goes to print today, and I find a half-page bio and a picture of him running in this Sunday's church bulletin as an introduction. I just hope Grace Apostle doesn't fall for the hype. It's cool, though. I'm done talking about that. What have you been up to today?"

"Nothing much. It took me all day to make this spaghetti bake. I'm no Martha Stewart," she reported. Everything else she chose to keep secret.

They quickly moved their after-dinner conversation to the living room at his request. There was a view any way you turned in this smartly decorated room. One side of the room held his flat-screen television, which was encased in the wall over an entertainment center. The other side displayed the reflection of the moon, which cast a celestial glow over his sunroom. It was so enchanting that Rebecca wondered why they didn't chat in the living room during the four previous evenings she had been there. They always seemed to retreat to their separate quarters. Tonight was somehow different.

When she took her seat opposite him, she had an overwhelming sense of melancholy, realizing, realistically, that she'd have to leave soon.

He leaned over and tapped her leg. "What are you thinking?"

She attempted a weak smile. "I'm thinking I didn't go out and conquer the world and face adversaries today like you did."

"It's been less than a week," he was quick to say. "I was unfair to press you the night before last. That's not what I brought you here for. You're supposed to rest, empty your mind. Your mind, though, not your spirit. Grace Apostle can have Glass tomorrow. I'm taking off. We'll go out."

Rebecca wanted to get lost in his eyes and anticipate her first day out with him back in her hometown. He seemed to be talking in a way that was opposite what she was thinking. She was thinking about statutes of limitations. Everything had a clock, even the amount of time you had in which to file a wrongful discharge claim. He was right to press her.

"How long can we honestly do this?" She tried to raise her arms in a sweeping gesture to illustrate their arrangement, but she possessed only enough energy to lift them a foot or so from her lap.

He inhaled and breathed out loudly before managing an unsure, "as long as you need."

Rebecca's needs seemed to grow each day. She was figuring now that she needed a hug from Will, and not that brotherly-sisterly type of embrace they managed to pull off while wanting more. He had once told her that with the opposite sex, he lived by the creed that he wouldn't take what hadn't been offered to him. She respected him for that. He was a true gentleman in that regard. She prayed she'd remain a lady during the duration of her stay.

He rose quickly and walked over to the entertainment center, retrieving one of the many remotes, as if he had read her thoughts and was getting away from her. He punched a series of buttons, and his sound system came to life.

"I know what you need, mopey," he said from the middle of the room. "Dance with me."

She watched him a moment to see if he was serious. He bopped to the beat of a familiar tune. When he realized his song selection and swaying weren't swaying her, he shuffled the songs.

"C'mon, Rebi. Don'tcha wanna dance? Do you wanna dance? Don'tcha wanna dance?" He asked, borrowing a line from Whitney Houston.

This was ridiculous. He was ridiculous, she thought, but he looked like he was having so much fun. He hit the buttons on the remote again, and she recognized the party anthem of their 1995 graduating class, Montell Jordan's "This Is How We Do It."

"I understand if you don't want to be shown up," he said, baiting her while doing his own version of the step and glide. "You were never much of a dancer."

She laughed while admitting he was more agile than she had suspected. He turned his back and continued to groove until the song seamlessly blended into Brownstone's "If You Love Me." Rebecca didn't know if she wanted to join him, but she definitely wanted this playlist. She sang along, and Will took that as an invitation to pull her off the couch. "Candy Rain," "Creep," and "New Jack Swing" kept them in the party spirit. They were in competition with each other. Just to be silly, they did their own versions of the Humpty Dance, the Tootsee Roll, and the Macarena with the snippets of songs he shuffled through.

He kept up and gave back vibrations that thrust them into a danger zone a couple of times. Quickly, they shifted back to an up-tempo hand dance. Rebecca was impressed with his partnering skills. She decided then that this was the way she wanted to be held and this was the person she wanted to be held by for the rest of her life.

He danced with his remote in his hand, a wireless connection between the man and his music. With the click of his finger, they were in a storm with a considerably slower tempo as the soulful voice of Johnny Gill was undergirded by crashes of thunder and rain. They dropped each other's hands as she backed away. He looked at her as if asking the question posed by the song's title and refrain, "Can You Stand the Rain?" She knew if she could wrap her head around an honest answer, it would explain to him why she had left him almost five weeks ago.

He came to her with his arms outstretched. Rebecca shook her head no immediately. Whether this was uncanny timing or a calculated move on his part, she was trying to be good, she thought to herself as she fanned herself with both hands.

Rebecca looked at him sheepishly, with an eyebrow raised, as she tried to rid her mind of thoughts of them intertwined like a pretzel. "You don't want none of this misery."

He frowned. "Don't tell me what I want. We're just dancing, right? Relax."

He pulled her close by grabbing handfuls of material from the sides of her tunic dress, in search of an appropriate hold. They resigned themselves to having that moment, standing close to each other but barely touching. The lines and definition in his chest and arms were more pronounced up close. Although he was clean shaven, his chin gave her forehead the most marvelous scratch. It was no holds barred now. Rebecca wrapped her arms around the small of his back and dropped her head on his shoulder determined to take a whiff.

This time he let the whole song play and the one that followed and the one after that. He had found a new playlist. Rebecca couldn't recall the titles or the artists, but their bodies found the rhythm and their lips found each other's. It was a luxurious exchange. He was the first to pull away.

"Let me get off you," he managed to say when he opened his eyes and steadied his breath. "You know what? You've got to go!"

Rebecca's eyes widened. "You've got to be kiddin' me. You're kicking me out?"

"Yeah, for real, Rebi. Can you go to your sister's house?"

She grabbed his arm in her confusion. "What? Why? We were just dancing, right?"

"No, I was doing just a little more than that. That kiss. Are you serious? I was straight up lusting. I'm not going to lie," he admitted with a sigh, a smirk, and a shake of his head.

"It's okay. It's whatever . . . We're grown," Rebecca said, thinking of whatever would get her back in his good graces and back in his arms.

"No, it matters. I better act like I know that there's a time to embrace and a time to refrain. Hence me getting off of you. I don't know. Us staying here together like this really muddies the water."

"No, it doesn't. There's plenty of space here. We've managed to stay out of each other's way."

"Who are we fooling? Last night I'm parading around in my boxers, and you in my T-shirt. Tonight we're kissing. Where does the train stop tomorrow?" he asked. "I'll tell ya. In a wreck at the corner of sin and shame. I don't want that for us. I mean, I want it, but not like this. I need to fall back, way back."

Rebecca had to admit she had been ready to take it there—the slow wine, the grind, then bedroom time. *Oh my gosh, I was ready to get it on with a preacher,* she thought. The mixture of anxiety and desire caused a burning in her chest. "It's nighttime. Gail doesn't even know I'm in town, and I'm supposed to show up out of the blue?"

He tugged at his earlobe as he thought. "You're right. And I promised you that you could stay here as long as you needed. You know what? I'll leave. I'll pack some stuff and go stay with my dad."

"C'mon, Will. I can't kick you out of your own house."

Rebecca considered the alternative, returning to Salisbury. *This is ridiculous and unnecessary.* One look at him barefoot and in relaxed jeans and a T-shirt, which housed those arms and the power they possessed, let her know he was absolutely right. One of them had to go.

"Let me go, please. It's the right thing to do," he said.

She found it hard to look at him now. "Will you at least come back and have dinner with me?"

"Definitely. We've got a date tomorrow, remember?"

Rebecca considered herself blessed as she walked to what was now her bedroom. While Will had had to watch her pack, she wasn't forced to watch him pack up and leave.

Chapter 21

"Hello?" Will's dad called from his back bedroom in the way one did when one heard an unexpected commotion and wanted to give trouble a chance to announce itself.

"It's me, Dad," Will said after entering the house with his own key. "Who else has a key to your house?"

He could hear the shuffle of his dad's slippers on the hardwood floor. Will hoped he didn't wake him. Since it was only nine thirty in the evening, it seemed his dad was going to bed earlier and earlier. Maybe he needed to be here to stop his dad's decline.

"Will? What's wrong?" Pastor Donovan asked, rounding the corner. He took the closest seat, at the head of the dining-room table, which was as far as Will had gotten. There was a bowl of fruit in the center of the table to encourage his dad to eat right. Since Will had upset his dad's rest, he decided to grab a banana.

"Nothing. I thought I'd stay with you. I need an intensive, residential pastor-in-training course. I haven't been using my most valuable resource to the fullest. Can you believe that after Sunday, the next voice that you will hear at Grace will be none other than Danny Glass Jr.'s. That's crazy. His dad has a virtual dynasty. Why is he in ours?"

His dad harrumphed, then peeled back the skin on the banana and then pinched off of it to take a bite. "First, banish the fear that Danny Glass has something that you don't have."

"I wouldn't necessarily call it fear," Will protested.

"You'll bring the Word this Sunday and weave in stories about growing up at Grace Apostle. Be gracious, almost sentimental in your approach, while thanking the congregation for helping to grow you up, for supporting you when your mom was sick and when you went off to school. You're a son of this ministry. It's okay to tell them you depend on their support in the end."

"Then what? It all seems so political."

"Bingo. It's about time you figured that out. The best thing you could have done was suggest I start a group of senior saints. I began calling them from my personal Rolodex. You may not be preaching after Sunday, but you can still court votes. Be present when Glass is doing his time. I intend to. Be helpful, even to him, but to a point," his dad advised, coaching him.

Will thought about being helpful and skeptical at the same time. It seemed so deceptive to him. They had interacted today, but Danny had been preoccupied with getting acclimated. The Glass family was not even staying in the 21601 zip code. They were renting in nearby Trappe. Will realized that while he feared the task of keeping up with Danny's fame, Danny had to catch up with his familiarity.

Will sat down at the table with his dad, ready to get into the real reason he was there. He felt like he had when he was younger and had to admit a truth that could potentially get him in trouble.

"Rebi is at my house," he admitted.

His father just stared at him with his hands crossed at the wrists, his discarded banana peel left on a napkin within his reach. "Why?"

Will cleared his throat. "She needed me. She's having major problems at her job, which may result in a lawsuit. I gave her a place to stay."

Pastor Donovan's eyes were wide and probing. "How noble and admirable of you, son. Is she having a problem with her apartment as well? C'mon, Will. I love Rebecca dearly, but there is always something going on with her. She's not short on drama. We need to stay focused, and you have a hard time doing that when she's around."

Will felt that was an unfair statement to make when his and Madame's affair had added to their drama tenfold. "I think what you meant to say was that we need to be praying for her. She's having a hard time, Pop."

"Why you, huh?" his dad shrugged. "I guess what I should be asking, if what Gail says is true, is, why her?"

"I love her, Dad. Probably always have."

"How long has she been here, and how long does she plan on staying?" Pastor Donovan rattled off the questions, as if refusing to hear what his son had just said.

"She's been here for a few days. She needs to clear her mind, and I don't want her to rush the decision she has to make."

Will saw questions behind his dad's eyes and an even more intense doubt. "You need to remain hands off, literally."

"I know that, Dad."

"I mean if church folks get a whiff of you and her, especially with you being their candidate, and even suspect you were fornicating—"

"I know the difference between love and lust. Rebecca rededicated herself to the Lord under my watch. She is the very seed of my first real harvest. It ran hot, and yes, maybe I am really here for a cold shower, but I cared enough to fight the flames and preserve both our temples." Will's voice was purposely loud, his tone decidedly accusatory.

His dad smirked. "Oh, you're a saint, son, and so much better than me. Is that what this is all about? Is that what you want me to admit? Let this not be a knee-jerk reaction."

"Reaction to what?"

"She's Ava's daughter!" he shouted. "Out of all the women in Easton, she just happens to be the woman my son falls in love with. How far do you think your relationship with her can go? Listen to me. The two of you are better off as friends, fam—"

"Don't you dare. Gail is my sister. It's perverse, and not at all the kind of relationship I desire to have with Rebi," Will said.

"That's exactly how the saints of God will view it."

How could his father not be happy about what had been years in the making? Perhaps his father didn't realize how long he and Rebecca had been friends, which showed Will how out of touch his dad had been when he was caught up in his own affair. Didn't he see how Rebecca complimented him?

Will stood abruptly, wanting to flip the whole table over. "I am not taking relationship advice from you. You had two women, and you're going to tell me I can't pursue the one I've chosen? The only relationship between her and me will be husband and wife."

Pastor Donovan put his hands up in surrender and remained quiet for a moment. He stood as well. "You can listen to me now or wait until marriage counseling, I guess, when I tell you the same things—things about taking your time, loving in and out of season, and in and out of the bedroom."

"I said we haven't slept together."

Will felt he was being very tolerant. He didn't know why his father couldn't leave well enough alone. His wound about his dad's affair with Rebecca's mom had only recently begun to close, but now he felt his stitches about to erupt.

"Look, Dad, I'm hoping this arrangement will work out between us. I'm here as your son, looking for shelter and pastoral training. That's it. You certainly don't get to tell me about marriage," Will stormed, punctuating his words by driving a finger into the table.

"I was you fifty years ago, on the brink of ministry, young, single, and lonely. You think I don't know the need to dig in, find someone who grounds you, so you can help ground everyone you minister to? Is Rebi gonna dig in with you? Is ministry what she wants? Answer that, if you know everything."

Will rejected his father's comparisons and muttered, "I know enough not to cheat on the one I love if and when I choose to marry."

Once again Pastor Donovan's hands went up. "Thy will be done."

That was his dad's way of saying, *"C'est la vie"* or *"Que sera sera."*

"I guess you can't curse and bless something at the same time," Will said snidely.

"Thy will be done. We say it to God, and He says it right back. He gives us free will to do and choose what we want for our lives, so who am I to say any different to a grown man? Hopefully, your decision won't bite you in the butt. Now, if you'll excuse me, I'm going back to bed. I trust you can see yourself to your old room."

Chapter 22

Her sacrificial lamb rang the doorbell at 1:00 p.m., as if he didn't possess a key or the deed to the property. He came bearing flowers, which made Rebecca thankful she had gone girly instead of casual on her hair and make-up. He did say it was a date, she reminded herself. His eyes did a dance of appreciation over her, which rekindled a bit of the heat she had felt last night. When he bent to kiss her on the forehead, the full steam came on. He was casually dressed in deep blue denim jeans and a V-neck pullover. They didn't linger in the house, but rather went quickly to his car, which was parked behind hers, now in the carport.

Although they had spoken on the phone that morning and briefly the night before, she was still trying to define the cosmic activity that had shifted their relationship.

"So, tell me, who was that playlist reserved for, Preacher?" Rebecca said once he was in the car.

"I'm sure you don't want to go there with me, Rebi," Will said smugly.

"I'm just trying to gauge how many people you've previously engaged in a dance off."

He turned the key in the ignition but did not shift gears to pull off. "Real talk, who are you reserving yourself for? Answer me that."

That question caught her so off guard, she had no choice but to tell the truth. "I'm . . . waiting. I guess.

I'm waiting for God or someone to tell me that I am not making Mama's mistakes."

"All right, all right, I can respect that," he said, then hesitated, looking in the rearview while backing up. He was reflective as Rebecca took in the scene along the back roads, which she had never paid attention to before.

Will cleared his throat after a while. "I can tell you that God is telling me that you're the one. I seek His face, you know. I just believe He's gonna keep bringing us back together in these extreme circumstances until we get our act together. As stubborn as I wanted to be when you left, I am always going to want this . . . this relationship to go further. I am always going to err on the side of us."

She wasn't fast when it came to putting into words what she was thinking. She wished God would show her how she was supposed to fit in Will's world, besides waking up in his bed every morning. Or was that all he wanted and needed? She lived on extremes. She'd choose Will in a heartbeat, but with the next beat of her heart she wouldn't be entirely sure that there wasn't someone else better suited for him.

Rebecca tilted her head when he turned to look at her at the stoplight. "That would explain the uncanny timing. I'm definitely on the path. You're just ahead of me, as always," she said.

The back roads gave way to open road. Before she knew it, they were on Route 50, headed east and leaving the city limits.

"Where are you taking me? Are we going to Salisbury?" Rebecca asked.

"Yeah, I want to show you this project I've been working on, and in the process, maybe I'll show you that Salisbury isn't scary. Relax. You're with me. Don't you trust me?"

She gave him a drawn-out "I guess."

"Do you love me?" Will asked, taking his eyes off the road to be a spectator of her initial reaction.

She snatched her eyes away from him. "Wow, okay. I wasn't expecting that."

"Do you know the answer?"

There was a weight of expectancy between them. "Yes."

"Yes what?"

How dare he try to make me voice what I haven't rightfully earned? she thought. She loved him, but she wondered what she could possibly contribute to him that would equal everything he had given her.

"You know the answer to that."

His smile was broad and mischievous. "Good. Okay, I'm just trying to establish the basis for this relationship, you know, write a charter for this courtship, give it a time and a date so that we can register that we're an item."

"Oh, so you're telling me we're in a relationship? That's what guys do now?"

"You're doggone right. You just said, I am ahead of you on the path. Catch up, sweetheart. I wasn't kissing myself last night." He smirked.

She took aim at his cockiness and landed a blow on his arm. It was so like him to want to be so official. *So why aren't we spending the day in Easton, telling everyone?* she wondered.

As if reading her mind, he said, "Like I said, I want to show you where I've been spending some of my days. Then I'm going to take my girl out to eat. You may even want to go to your apartment and check your messages. Maybe a representative from your firm has called and you'll feel inclined to call them back or drop by."

Once again she felt the weight of his expectancy. That reminded her that a representative had called and had recommended that another firm handle her case. It reminded her that he was lending her his love and support in exchange for her depletion, indecision, and failure to emote. Maybe she'd even the scales by telling him about Jacobs's text message over dinner. Maybe.

Chapter 23

Rebecca thought Will was taking her to Perdue Farms, where he used to work. Instead, he pulled into a church lot not too far from her alma mater, Salisbury University. Will was like a superstar once inside the church. Big kids like the ones that lived in her apartment building immediately recognized him and began approaching and talking at the same time.

"Where have you been, Pastor Will?" one of them said.

"Working outside isn't on my to-do list today," another said.

"I'm just visiting today. Like I told you guys, there is not much to do, other than let nature take its course."

Rebecca had a chance to look around while Will was consumed with inquiries. The place looked as if it needed more than cosmetic work outside; it could stand a full refurbishment. She pulled her sweater closer to her because the church was as drafty as a warehouse owing to its airy openness and the folks coming in and out like a revolving door.

Will and the group of young men floated along like a cloud. Will checked over his shoulder to make sure Rebecca was keeping pace with them. He winked at her.

"Hey, I like the new sign." Will pointed out a sign as they were passing by that read MINISTER 1:2 ANOTHER. It was in the middle of what looked like a mural under construction.

"Ethan," said a young man ahead of them who was walking backward as they proceeded slowly forward.

Will looked at him. "Ethan?"

"Ethan and Bruce-Bruce," said the young man, correcting himself. "Guess what part Bruce did?"

They all waited on the punch line and laughed when someone delivered it. "The colon."

Who were these kids? Rebecca wondered, and who gave them permission to walk around and write on the walls like they owned the place? Will had told her the church was more like a community center. She couldn't wait to meet the shepherd of this lively flock.

"Where is Pastor Cutler?" Will asked when they reached the door of the sanctuary.

"Sometimes he closes himself off in his own little world. It's been happening a lot lately. A couple of times we couldn't even get in here," one of the fellows revealed.

Rebecca saw the look of concern on Will's face, which slowly faded when he realized he was being watched. "Maybe you guys are getting too rowdy and obnoxious for him. You got to take care of your leader, all right?"

Just then someone darted across the open recreation area. She sideswiped Will and caught him in a hug, keeping his arms pinned at his sides. She was followed by others, who had also been hanging out in what was called the forum, but they covered a lot less ground than she did in a lot more time.

"Pastor Will," she squealed. "I'm so glad to see you."

"Hi," another young man said.

"Ms. Trixie, what's going on, sweetheart?" Will asked, and she beamed.

Someone has got themselves a secret crush, Rebecca thought.

"Hi," the other young man said again, and Rebecca noticed he had been talking to her all along.

"Who dis?" one of his friends finally asked, noticing Rebecca as well.

"Bruce, aren't you in college? Speak like it, man," Will said, trying to swat at the young man, whose pants were sagging, revealing coordinated gym shorts underneath, but Trixie still had a hold on him.

"Must be Pastor Will's woman," Bruce said in an off-putting way, though he meant to be inclusive.

"Are ministers supposed to date hot girls?" asked the kid who had first addressed Rebecca.

"That's right. Everybody say hello to Ms. Rebi," Will said, ignoring that last comment. "She went to undergraduate school right here at Salisbury University. She came with me to check y'all out, so don't embarrass me."

Rebecca waved and mouthed a hello. A few kids walked off after the introductions, using this as an opportunity to occupy the computers, which were now free. Trixie abruptly let Will's arms go after he introduced Rebecca. Rebecca and Will exchanged looks when they noticed the tears gathering in the young woman's eyes.

Will hunched Trixie and whispered, "What's wrong?"

When Trixie didn't answer, Bruce, who was still around, spoke up. "Well, let's see. Besides all her friends bassin' on her in the café and her secret love affair, this is her normal attitude."

They all looked at Bruce with a mixture of frowns and scowls due to his insensitivity. Even Rebecca was tired of his wise-guy routine and was glad when he lost interest and walked away in pursuit of someone else's business.

Will grabbed Trixie by the shoulder. "All this over a guy? C'mon, cheer up. It can't be that serious."

Trixie's eyes widened with surprise, then all at once became sorrowful again. Rebecca was just as surprised at Will's dismissive words, considering that they had just declared in the car that they were in a relationship. This time she and Trixie exchanged eye roll for eye roll. Will excused himself to find Pastor Cutler, leaving Rebecca alone with the forlorn young woman.

Rebecca shrugged awkwardly. "You mind if I hang out with you?"

Trixie looked at her warily as she drifted toward one of the only remaining pew benches that lined the sides of the room. She was wearing a tan sweater, which hung over leopard-print leggings, and boots with heels too high for someone walking around a college campus. Rebecca watched her bring her leg up onto the bench and into her chest to rest her head on. That movement reminded Rebecca a lot of herself, of her efforts sometimes to make herself small. Rebecca knew what it felt like to be an outsider looking in during her early school days. It was during those times that she needed a friend and needed to be left alone all at the same time.

Rebecca pulled out a hidden stash of Craisins and extended the package to Trixie, deciding that there couldn't be any restrictions on food in this otherwise uninhibited space. She was at a loss as to what to say to this young woman, although so-called friends and secret affairs could have been pulled from the pages of her own life. Rebecca looked away, allowing Trixie the space to wallow if she wanted to.

"How is it gonna be a secret affair if everyone knows about it? That obviously means it was something." Trixie took a handful of Craisins from the package, which Rebecca had placed between them. "Everyone is fast to share my story. Bruce and 'em are a trip. I'm not supposed to know that his girl, Samantha, might be pregnant, and besides the fact that she's white, he's got this scholarship that can't support her and that baby when her racist parents denounce her. Marcus's mom died last semester, and just like Pastor Cutler when he lost his wife, he's one step away from going postal. Oh, and Ethan is tired of being in the closet. We all got our reasons for being here."

Rebecca looked around at the sanctuary with new respect. She wondered if she had had the kinds of problems Trixie had just described when she was in college.

Rebecca tried to sound as if she could relate. "It's rough, right?"

"I guess you're gonna say you know all about rela-tionships." Trixie smirked.

Rebecca thought about that statement. Outside of one or two boyfriends, she really couldn't remember a relationship in her adult life. She thought of the few guys whom she had allowed to wreak havoc on her self-esteem, and still others whom she had allowed in her bedroom, although they had barred her from their heart. Will was a definite upgrade. She thanked God for him then and now. Just then she remembered the sign they had passed, the one that read MINISTER 1:2 ANOTHER, and figured she should practice this, even if the guys, including her present beau, hadn't.

"No, in fact, I know very little. But I do know a lot about liking the wrong guy or liking a coward who won't admit he is the right guy. I know about women and what we can do to one another because of jealousy. I know how easily friendships can fall apart over a guy."

That was enough to tell the young woman that she and Rebecca were in fact kindred spirits. Trixie began telling her story, which was worthy of its own reality show. She and a few young women from the same area had established a friendship during her freshman year at Salisbury University. Returning to school for the fall semester of their sophomore year, they decided to live together in a suite in the dormitory known as Chesapeake Hall. At a party early on in the semester the friends became captivated by the same transfer student, Smith Chaney, from the University of Maryland Eastern Shore. They all weighed in on how fine they thought he was and put mock dibs on being his girl.

Smith made his choice by midterm, when he began showing up everywhere Trixie seemed to be on campus. According to her, he was funny, articulate, and down to earth. He never came to see her at her dorm and called her at random times, with the excuse that he had to be discreet because he was scouting a particular fraternity that he wanted to pledge before graduation. At another house party, the couple stole a few intimate moments in a back room. They were ousted by another couple who were ready to take a turn in the secluded spot. After that, all her girls, and everyone else, for that matter, assumed that Trixie was, as she put it, "an undercover ho," willing to get down at a party and get one over on her girls. None of them were more vocal about it than her roommate, Keisha. As a result, the seven young women in her suite began treating Trixie like an outsider.

A stubborn trail of tears streamed down her face. "Nothing hurts worse than a slap on both sides of the face. My own girls are spreading rumors about me, talking about how he don't really like me. He's using me. Every time I leave, they assume it's to be with him, as if they wouldn't do the same. Then I got Smith texting me, telling me to meet him here and there. I don't have time for all this if I want to graduate on time. I'm confused."

"About him?" Rebecca had her theories about this guy's character. Why wouldn't he stand up for her if he really liked her?

"About everything," she said. "I'm on the dean's list, but I'm not supposed to know when someone is being genuine or not. I think I know a real kiss from a fake kiss."

"It's time to have a heart-to-heart with your friends, and if they don't come around, make new friends. I hope that this will blow over for you real soon," Rebecca advised. "When's spring break?"

"I want to go home now!" Trixie screeched. "SU is already short on housing, so I can't switch dorms. I know my parents won't understand me quitting or even asking to transfer over something like this."

Rebecca draped an arm around the young woman. "You can't quit. You have a right to be here as much as these catty girls and this dude you're involved with. You have a right to make mistakes and receive an education as much as they do. You have a right to like who you like, but make sure he likes you in the same way. A guy is not worth a hill of beans, in my opinion, if he only takes what he wants but can't give."

Rebecca felt quite motherly. *Lord, please don't let these kids be wilding out sexually.* She hunched Trixie. "You know how Bruce's girlfriend got pregnant, right?"

Trixie nodded her head.

"That is not what you need right now. It doesn't stop the hurt, it does not make a guy love or like you more, and it does little to build up your overall sense of self-worth," Rebecca said. She wished someone had told her that when she was Trixie's age.

"So, you are telling me that despite the way that both you and Pastor Will came smiling up in here, you all aren't . . . you know?"

Rebecca narrowed her eyes at Trixie, shocked that she had the gall to think she had a right to that information, but she wasn't ashamed of her answer this time. "I am smiling 'cause for the first time in my life I am certain I love someone without having to fall into bed with them first."

Trixie closed her eyes and bunched her face up. "Why can't all this just go away? Why do I have to be the brave one and deal with this?"

Rebecca heard her own voice through the young woman's questions. Then she heard an inner voice with the wisdom of God, and it made Rebecca tear up as well. She knew the answer was as much for herself as it was for Trixie. "Because you were built for this. You're strong. You can withstand this adversity with God's help. You're really at an advantage being in a place like this. Make sure you learn as much about faith while you're here. That's what you need more than anything. Soon all of you in here will be on the other side of your tests and trials, with a testimony and a degree."

The young woman sniffed loudly, as if to put her sorrow in reverse. "How do you know that?"

Been there done that, Rebecca thought. She contemplated whether to tell Trixie her tales of times past or to share more recent accounts, such as her return home to Easton to deal with her mother's death or her run-ins with Burke at the firm. She decided instead on what seemed like the proper summation of the day. "I've walked that path. I'm just ahead of you."

The kindred spirits shared a hug just as Will and an older Caucasian gentleman walked over to them. Pastor Cutler seemed to be nodding his head in agreement or approval as he approached. He extended his hand to Rebecca with a wide smile, as if he couldn't be happier to greet another living soul. Rebecca wondered at that moment what Will had shared about her.

"You must be Rebecca. I'm Pastor Monty Cutler."

Rebecca stood. "Nice to meet you. Trixie and I were bonding, maybe because we're the only females here. I'm glad she has a place to come and get away from campus life. I wish I had known about this place when I was in school."

"Well, I told Will I didn't want to take all of his time. I hear you plan to spend his day off together, but promise me you'll come back."

Rebecca looked back at Trixie, who was looking on. "Oh, I will. I want to check up on my sister here. I'd also love to see the place when you're done . . . you know, all this." Rebecca's eyes took a trip around the forum.

Pastor Cutler chuckled as he looked around the forum. "I believe Dogwood will always be evolving. God loves fixer-uppers. Our weakness is His strength . . . yada yada yada. I'm sorry. You didn't ask for a sermon. Sandy, my wife, used to say, 'Don't bore me with Bible quotations, but challenge me with practical application.' Good thing we don't need renovations for Christ to show up."

Rebecca felt his sentiments rang particularly true, because they were all works in progress, and God had definitely shown up there today.

Chapter 24

His mama called him baby boy. Deacon Lyons and some of the other senior saints who had an allegiance to his dad had referred to him as Little Willie, until he'd asked them politely to stop when he went off to college. His sister, Gail, or Bit as he called her, always respectfully called him Pastor Will. Recently, he'd even been called merely a placeholder for his dad and Lay-Z in his role as an interim pastor by those who were not so certain he could hold the top spot. He was going after the title of pastor, hoping he'd forever call Grace Apostle home. So he felt a rush of melancholy as he was bringing to a close his last sermon before taking a break.

He had preached on the power pack, which many commonly thought of as a mixture of herbal supplements, like ginseng, to get one's day going or one's energy up. His power pack included faith, hope, and love. In his sermon he identified these as very specific qualities of his parents and the saints whom they had shepherded along the way. It was like an anniversary sermon, meant to spark nostalgia, like his father had suggested. He couldn't wait for it to be over. He hated preaching under this new microscope his dad had him under.

He wanted Rebecca with him, but he, with input from his dad, had decided they should go out and visit friends and family first before showing up at church as a new couple. Their sister, Gail, still didn't know Rebecca was in town.

At the end of his sermon, Will decided to ditch his father's script. "I've found if you need that added punch, an added lift, a boost, you've got to add prayer to your power pack. Take it once, twice, three times a day, continuously, without ceasing. Let me warn you, though, that you may overdose on His grace and mercy. The Bible says the effectual fervent prayer of the righteous availeth much. That means it reaps great rewards."

Will remained silent as he waited for his words to hit those in the congregation the way it had just hit him. He was still learning to be a receptacle of the Holy Spirit without gushing over with emotion himself. He was known to tap his foot, tug at his ear, or break out in song. Had he prayed enough for this moment and the moments to come for Grace Apostle? he wondered.

"One saint came up to me last Sunday and asked, how often do you utter a prayer? I got to say, it was a great question. She wanted to know, do you replicate that prayer until you see the manifestation of the answer, or pray it once in faith, knowing it will be done according to His will? I'll tell ya, we've not been taking prayer as prescribed in the good book. Prayer is not where you devise a wish list for God and are left with a lot of unanswered questions. It's reciprocal. You've got to speak and listen."

He heard his father shout out in agreement from behind him in his pastor emeritus seat. Deacon Contee appeared to squirm and signal from his seat in the deacons' row. He had slipped Will a note earlier to pass the microphone off to him after the sermon so that he could give an announcement of some kind from the pastor selection committee. Will couldn't comprehend

the audacity of Deacon Contee trying to get him to
wrap it up. He knew Danny Glass was present. The
fact that Danny hadn't joined him on the pulpit for the
Word, but rather was waiting behind the scenes for a
dramatic presentation, left a bad taste in his mouth.

What both of them had yet to figure out was that
neither of them was in authority. The Lord was revealing something to Will, and he was going to be obedient
and round out this impromptu lesson on prayer.

"Before I take my seat and turn this pulpit over to
another capable practitioner, I'd like to ask for your
prayers. The Holy Spirit is kicking my tail up here. He's
telling me and you not to be self-serving. My father,
the selection committee, and I decided when my dad
retired that it would be great to have a new pastor
installed by Easter Sunday this year. It's the Lenten
season, y'all. We have your gleaners ready today to
collect coins for those less fortunate. I'm asking that
we enter into this season with prayer. Let's suspend the
vote until the resurrection and be in prayer, every man,
woman, boy, and girl. Nothing should interfere with
our spiritual preparation. You know I'd love more than
anything to be your pastor, but we should all pray that
His will be done. Can we do that as a church family?"

Why did I say that? Why on Earth did I give them
permission to consider someone else? Will asked
himself. He heard his dad coughing. Will imagined
his dad passed out behind him. There was clapping
of approval, which showed that nearly the majority
of congregants shared his sentiment on that point.
Will could stall no longer. He packed up his favorite
Bible and took his seat. He closed his eyes and took
cleansing breathes as Deacon Contee's committee of
one took station at the floor-level podium.

"The harvest is plentiful, but the laborers are few. Grace Apostle, we should consider ourselves blessed that we have not just one, but two, worthy candidates. I have the esteemed pleasure of introducing you to a phenomenal son of the Gospel, a husband, father, laborer, and preacher."

Will stopped listening. He had read all these finer points in the bulletin. He felt Deacon Contee sounded like a sports announcer or a commercial hype man. The crowd began to shed the end-of-the-service antsies and became reenergized.

Will let his imagination run wild as Deacon Contee spoke. *In this corner, weighing in at one hundred ninety pounds, hailing all the way from Snow Hill, Maryland, is none other than the son of a spiritual heavyweight, Minister Danny Glass Jr.*

Applause. The congregation was actually on its feet, as if Contee had introduced Christ. Will scrambled to his feet as well and saw the Glass family, all smiles and waving, enter from the back and proceed down the aisle. They were picture perfect. The entire family joined Deacon Contee at the podium, where Danny begun a planned monologue.

Will managed a smile when Danny at least acknowledged him as a pulpit associate and fellow laborer. They were contenders indeed, and Will considered again their matchup. He could give the congregation nothing but the Gospel truth, whereas Danny delivered the glitz. Will gave them something to go home and study; Danny gave them something to write home about, share on Facebook, or text to a friend. Will looked out over the faces of the congregants, who were enthralled with what this man had to say. He knew they had long forgotten his points on the power pack. These people wouldn't be praying with him.

Will felt his dad tap his leg, and Will realized he was still standing. When he found his seat, his dad leaned over and whispered, "Nothing, I mean nothing, should take place after the Word has gone forth but the benediction. This is still Grace Apostle, and I got a mind to tell 'em."

"I didn't know about this, nor do I condone it," Will whispered back.

I didn't know, Will repeated silently. Will felt as if he was in trouble. What did his dad expect him to do? Silence the microphone? Apparently, Danny Glass hadn't been taught Sunday morning decorum like he was. In the end, Will was so numb, he gave the new rising star the opportunity to pronounce the final blessings of the benediction over the congregation. These were no longer his people.

There was a photographer, and oddly enough, Danny Glass wanted Will in the picture too. Will felt like a puppet as he posed for them and others as people with camera phones took advantage of the photo op. His dad circulated among the after-service crowd, shaking hands, ever the politician. Will wondered what could he say at this point. *Vote for me? Pray for me?*

When the photo op was over, Contee led Danny Glass, Mrs. Glass, and their two restless children to the back of the pastor's lounge and his dad's old office. Will wanted no part of that, either.

Will was ready to go home to Rebecca, where he could lick his wounds in private. He mapped out a path to the door. But first he had to get past the surprise visitor waiting for him in the back row. He had heard of chickens coming home to roost. He wondered what his ex-girlfriend, Veronica, had come back to brood about.

Chapter 25

The first thing he asked her was how long she was staying.

The next thing he told her was that he was on a spiritual retreat at his dad's.

He didn't like Veronica's response. She was scouting for a place to live, so she was staying with Nina, who had been instructed to take it easy until she delivered her first child. It wasn't working for her being back at home in Wye Mills with her parents. She now wanted to keep all her options open. She made sure he still had her cell phone number, and strongly suggested, as only Veronica could, that he call so they could catch up. He couldn't put into words that he wouldn't, and that she shouldn't wait for his call.

He wanted her as far away from Rebecca as possible, before operation "Get the right girl to the altar" went up in flames, just like his hopes of a clear victory at Grace Apostle. He had to succeed in something.

All he wanted to do was sulk and mope after the service. He drove directly to his home. Rebecca was there to receive him. She cradled his head on a pillow in her lap and listened to him in a way that showed they had connected as much emotionally as they had physically when they were dancing the other night. Somehow, during some part of the evening, a movie and Chinese food got ordered and their old yearbooks got pulled out. It was a perfect ending to an otherwise crazy day.

***

Will woke up the next morning ready to fortify his faith and his relationship with Rebecca. That night spent in his childhood room at his dad's, and away from Rebecca, had felt like forty days in the wilderness. His dad had wanted to talk to him about church matters when Will got in way after 11:00 p.m. at night. Everything in Will's mind had been settled, or he had let it go earlier with Rebecca. His nervous system was sending an urgent signal that it was now or never. He thanked God for the time off to spend with her. He was determined the two of them would be in prayer about their future, if no one else would.

Will dressed and left his dad's house. He drove across town to his house, only to find that Rebecca wasn't there. She had taken the car cover off that he had given her to use in the carport and had gone. He tried to stomach the anger and the twist of fear, thinking she had moved on and was back in Salisbury. He was coming to the realization that he couldn't keep her caged. She had to want to be there with him. He sat outside for a long while, as if he didn't have a key to his own home.

He sensed her all round his place when he finally let himself in—from the kitchen, where recently washed dishes were still drying, to the living room, with its the stack of fashion and urban-inspired magazines. He saw her soft ballet slippers, which she loved to wear around the house, curled up in the middle of his sunroom floor, as if she had been trying out the hardwood, and quickly realized she had not gone. She was coming back.

That led him to check what he had hidden in his bedroom, now that he had access to it again. In the right-hand corner of his top drawer was a small blue box. He felt all at once that the ring inside it, which had not seen the light of day, had to grace Rebecca's finger before she really did decide to go back home. *Could it be today? Should it?*

Be in prayer. How often had he uttered a prayer about himself and Rebecca? It felt like a million times over. Was it a lack of faith that kept him repeating his plea? He could probably have gotten engaged to Veronica and darn near married her in a week's time. Would that be enough time for Rebecca? She had said she didn't want to make her mother's mistakes. He failed to see how that would be possible.

Will took the ring box with him to the couch and palmed it as he texted Rebecca with his right hand, asking her where she was. He smirked as he thought about how he was unable to get the bulging ring box out of his pocket the last time and how she nearly detected it. He stood and concealed the box on the highest shelf of his entertainment center, in a bowl of decorative mosaic spheres. Then her reply came in.

In a meeting. TTYL.

She returned forty-five minutes later, wearing a formfitting skirt and blouse and toting coffee in a familiar cup, letting Will know she had been to Salisbury. She looked as if she wanted to turn down the peck he wanted to offer her, but she leaned in, anyway, to where he was propped up on the couch.

"Wasn't I with you yesterday? How come I didn't know about this meeting?"

Rebecca set her cup down gingerly before sitting next to him, then immediately picked the cup back up. "I guess we both have our reasons."

"Reasons for what?"

"Keeping secrets," she said after taking a swig of her coffee. "You got a call today on your answering machine. It was Veronica, asking you to let her know how she can help with your bid for pastor, because from the looks of things yesterday, you need it. She offered to talk to her sisters on the women's auxiliary on your behalf. I guess I wasn't the only one you saw yesterday, but it's cool, though."

He stole a glance at the entertainment center directly in front of them, possibly checking on the ring, though it was hidden, or thinking of a playlist that would smooth over this dilemma.

"I was just as shocked as you. I told you I went to see her in Wye Mills, and nothing had changed. She's still the same self-centered Veronica. She showed up in church, and honestly, I don't know why she's here," he explained, pleading his case.

She rolled her eyes at him. "She showed up there because she can. Should I show up next week?"

There was a moment where his mouth was left wide open. She was up and pacing to the kitchen with her coffee. He snapped out of it enough to get up and follow her.

"Sure you can, Rebi," Will uttered. "I didn't think you wanted to just yet, 'cause, you know . . . Plus, I want to introduce you around as my, you know—"

"*Introduce?* Like Contee did with Danny Glass? Like the people don't know me already." Rebecca placed the entire cup, lid and all, in the microwave and set it for thirty seconds. "I know I haven't exactly been bursting to get to church, either. I get it, Will. Veronica is Princess Di and I am Camilla Parker Bowles at Grace Apostle. She's more palatable."

He attempted to laugh it off. "What? That's not it at all."

"Could this be exactly what our parents were trying to avoid? They obviously remained close, even though Madame left church altogether. They could have dated in the eyes of the church after your mother died, but they didn't, because of appearances. Forget what they meant to one another."

"Come here. I don't want to talk about Veronica. I definitely don't want to talk about our parents. Our relationship is different. As far as I'm concerned, we're the reclamation of their affair. What I want to talk about is you. Are you gonna tell me about this meeting?"

She kept her distance as she sized him up over the top of her cup, which was now up to her lips. She blew into the spout and took an earnest gulp before beginning. "Another associate at the firm, a buddy of mine, gave me the number of a lawyer at another firm. I had a consultation with her to discuss my case."

"Good. So did she help convince you it's worth the trouble to go after this guy?" Will said, taking a seat on an island stool.

"Let's just say, I received my inspiration the other day, but it's not going to be pretty. She told me to prepare to finally have an offer of mediation with Burke. We'll see what comes of that, but she thinks we have enough for a civil suit against the entire firm."

Will studied the look of apprehension on her face. He was pretty dazed himself. It sounded more complicated than he had originally thought.

"Well, I'm off, so I can go with you."

She joined him at the island slowly and very dramatically took a seat on the other stool. "What if I don't want you to?"

Will's eyebrows knit. "What do you mean? I don't know about restrictions in court, but if Burke is going to be anywhere near you, then I want to be there. Why would you even want to go it alone?"

Though she had just sat down, she was up again, reaching for his arm, but latching on to his hand. "My attorney says Bryan Russell, a veteran attorney whose sole job is to represent the firm against law suits, sent a snide comment when she requested the mediation with an outside agency. She says he loves judicial sparring, especially when he senses a threat that he believes is a frivolous lawsuit. He's buddies with the son of one of the partners and has been known to get the second-generation Sanz to show up just for the sport of it."

"What does that have to do with me coming out to support you?"

She wiped her face frantically. "I was in hot pursuit of Kenny about a year ago. There. Now you know."

He threw his hands up as he stood to wiggle out of her grasp. He was trying to make sense of what she had told him. He felt that raw spot in his gut when he thought about what he had known about Rebecca in the past, about the men. Looking at her and the way she moved sometimes stunned him into silence, as if she were undressing in front of him. He knew what effect she could have on a man, but he saw more, wanted more. He couldn't help but feel she had been in hot pursuit of everyone but him. What did that say about him? The possibility of them?

"I wanted Burke way before I came back to Easton and up until he showed his true colors."

He resisted the urge to cover his ears like a child. "What are you trying to tell me? There was no harassment?"

Had they slept together? he wondered.

Her throat was hoarse from the tears she tried to choke back. "Sure, there was harassment, but he's going to try and claim the same. You can't sit in, even if we go to court. I wouldn't be able to breathe, knowing your sitting in there, hearing the things they will be saying about me, promise me."

She looked as if she could barely breathe now, and his heart wanted to go out to her.

"I feel like you're trying to make a fool out of me all over again," Will said. "Why don't you go be with him then? Huh? He apparently wants you to sacrifice your job for him. He's an attorney; he can take care of you, shelter you, come to your aid.

"C'mon now." Rebecca clawed at his arms, which were folded tightly against his chest, preventing her from embracing him. "I don't want him."

"No?" he asked.

"No," she replied.

Finally, he relented, and she hugged him like the long-lost friend that he had always been to her. He just stood there, allowing himself to be hugged and thinking about the ring in its box becoming a permanent fixture of his decor.

Chapter 26

He was giving Rebecca a break from having to answer to him, and himself a break from having to answer to his father. He wanted to visit the kids at the school, visit a music or physical education class, to hear the uninhibited sounds of laughter and see the innocence of self-expression. It was the liberation he had experienced when he watched Rebecca dance that time in church that he sought.

As he approached the front entrance of the church, he saw a bundle of newspapers, the newest edition of the *Society Pages*. Will looked around, as if he might catch the culprit who put it there fleeing the scene. He thought his dad had said he'd taken care of that. The individual papers were still bound together, so he grabbed the lot of them and carried them not to the free enterprise wall and the mail slots, but rather upstairs, where he planned to inquire about future deliveries and properly dispose of them.

Will was taken aback when he saw Danny Glass alone in the spot he had just occupied a week ago. Of course, he knew it was time for Danny to grace more than the carpeted runway of the sanctuary aisle. It was his turn to put in office hours, but Will wasn't used to seeing him without his puppeteer, Deacon Contee.

"Hey," Danny said, shocked to see him, from his spot at the desk, where he had a newspaper spread out in front of him.

"I know you are surprised to see me so soon," Will explained. "I'll get out of your way. I'm going downstairs to observe a few classes."

"Shaking hands and kissin' babies, huh?" Danny said.

Darn right, Will thought. His dad refused to let Will do a Romney and forget close to half the population of the church.

"I can tell you're one of the hardest workers in the game," Danny observed.

Tell that to your friends at the Society Pages. He brought the bundle of papers over and placed them down near the desk where Danny sat to see if he had the audacity to read that filth in the office. He glanced over to find that he was reading the *Easton Star Democrat,* and that the paper was turned to the real estate section, where several listings were circled.

"So, I heard you found a house in Trappe. That's kinda far, isn't it?" Will asked, towering over him now.

"Not really. We're renting with an option to buy. I'm used to a commute. When I was growing up, everyone assumed we lived in Snow Hill because the church was there, but we didn't."

"You all put Snow Hill on the map, the whole Eastern Shore, really. So where does the anointed Pastor Danny Glass live? Ocean Pines, Libertytown? Don't tell me you all lived in West OC."

Danny smiled devilishly. "If I told ya, I'd have to kill you."

Will smirked, finding the scissors in the supply corral to cut loose one of the binding strips that was holding together the papers so he could extract one. Although Danny seemed cool, Will thought twice about perusing the paper in front of him, just in case the writers had another spoof on the church.

Danny disrupted his thoughts. "What is our role at the school? I mean, we dabbled in a lot of things at I Am the Way Ministries, but never education."

Will's goal was to become chancellor of the school, like his dad had been, or at least to relieve Contee of his duties as the interim chancellor, but he kept that to himself. "Contee hasn't shared any of this with you?"

Danny shook his head. "A big fat zero. You know I was the youth minister at one time at I Am the Way, but Deacon Contee seems to have it handled. Me and my siblings went to public school, but I guess a Christian-run school is much like an extended Young Christian Disciples Camp."

"Aw, man, not YCD. You're taking me back," Will said.

"You went too?" Danny asked.

"Did I? It was more like I was drafted every year."

"Me too. It was like *The Hunger Games*. Each church had to send two representatives, one girl, one boy, and when no one volunteered, Dad went into this spiel about sacrifice. There was no television, and everyone had to share that one phone. I hated those camps, man."

It made sense to Will that they would share this experience. They were around the same age, and both were preacher's kids. Will reminisced, but he didn't share Danny's loathing for the camps. He was fine once he got to the sleepaway camp. The classes were actually interesting.

"The best part was the basketball and the honeys," Danny noted.

"You ball?" Will asked, ignoring the reference to the female disciples.

Danny pushed back from the desk to stand, as if he were about to find a court and demonstrate a move. "All day."

"You know, I wanted to, but I was too much of a nerd. I never could seem to balance my studies and leisure time."

Danny adjusted his pants at the waist and kicked out the static cling in his slacks. "Man, please, and you want to be pastor? This game can consume you, like it does my dad. You better find that release button."

Danny's likability meter was rising. Will felt he had made a good point. What was his release? He did enjoy growing his plants and fooling around with a plot of land. A lot of his free time now, though, was devoted to spending time with Rebecca and hopefully winning her over.

Will bent to pull out the latest issue of the *Society Pages* from the bundle, which had to be a special edition, because it was scarcely four pages folded. Once again, they had made page two.

Discarded

Charities will usually accept discards, and churches are the biggest charity of them all. They throw out, recycle, and otherwise pass around their leaders. The Society Pages *was there when a local historic church announced the retirement of its pastor, and we continue to be there, front row, center, for all the drama that is bound to happen.*

One of my favorite card games to play with my family is Tunk. In that game you must match pairs, two of a kind, if you will, with cards in your hand or pluck a card. Those cards that are useless, you discard. We now know the two candidates in the running for the top spot of pastor at the church I mentioned earlier. At first they appear like two of a kind. Both can claim, "I'm a son of a preacher man," but the differences between the two couldn't be more evident. Move over, Lay-Z. There may be a new sheriff in town. One of them will be plucked up, and one will be discarded.

Who vets these candidates? Someone should card these preachers wanting to be pastors, inspect their credentials, and make sure they've come of age. If not, this church is bound to elect a card-carrying member of the entitled who is out for the title, and not for the growth and maturity of the church's members.

Will was tired of getting a paper cut each time he read this publication. A picture on the opposite corner caught his eye as he passed the article over to Danny. Will watched his mouth open, close, and open again as he read.

"Who are they talking about?" Danny asked.

"I think they are talking about the both of us. Check out that picture on the next page."

Placement was everything. The very picture he and Danny had posed for in church last Sunday wasn't paired with the article but had been placed under the paper's banner with other pictures of people in and around town. The picture was slightly off center, which led Will to wonder whether the image had been captured by the official photographer or someone in the crowd.

Will watched Danny pull the offensive page away from the rest of the newspaper, ball it up, and cast it toward the wastepaper basket before repeating the act with the rest of the issue. *Trash can hoops, my favorite,* Will thought and decided to do the same. It became street ball, putting up points, profiling, and presentation. They had the entire bundle to get rid of.

"Is Contee affiliated with this?" Danny asked, attempting a fadeaway jumper. "It was his idea to have the photographer in the first place. That's why I pulled you into the picture. I was trying to get you to get some of that shine."

Will was myth busting and didn't know what to believe. He felt Danny carried a pretty good shine all by himself. "It's someone in the church, if not him. We've got a family in the congregation who owns the press this mess is printed from."

"Wow. The saints of God get down like that here?" Danny asked in mock disbelief before attempting a hook shot.

"One of the members of this family is a girl I graduated high school with. Never been a fan," Will added.

"That's the one you were supposed to charm into confusion," Danny said without reservation. "You never married?"

Will felt ashamed by his answer. "Naw, but I'm working on that." Maybe it was the bravado that came along with shooting hoops, but Will felt the need to be just as cocky as Danny was. "I might be down the aisle before you're done with your four weeks."

"I hear ya. That's why you asked for an extension past the Resurrection, to get in the honeymoon. Wait, I think I might have met your fiancée in the office here Sunday," Danny said, frowning at the recollection.

"Couldn't be," Will said, trying to think of whom he might be referring to. He was tired of shooting and blocking shots.

"Tall, tan, looks like a model," Danny remarked, practically drooling.

A bell went off. "You must mean my ex, Veronica."

Danny stopped mid-shot and smiled. "Oh, okay. The ex still has backstage access, huh? I understand how that goes. Do you have enough people around you to run interference, though, just in case? You all don't have any armor bearers?"

Will didn't know what Danny was talking about, but he was sure they weren't talking about the same thing. "You didn't come with your own? I would think that some in that big ole ministry at I Am the Way would come with you to support your pursuit of a new ministry."

"What about we do that for each other?" Danny suggested.

The question still remained which one of the two would assume the role of pastor. Just when he thought that he might have a friend in the ministry and that it would be fun to go after the pastorship with someone grounded and down to earth, Will felt like he was being baited. He didn't want any part of the foolishness Danny was partaking in. Will now regretted everything he had shared with him.

Danny appeared to be pondering something. "Veronica, huh?"

Although their relationship was over, Will wanted Veronica's name out of this man's mouth. "What about your wife? How's she? When is she due?"

Back behind the desk, Danny stared into space for a minute before replying. "She's well. My second baby boy is due in less than three months. Look, I'm sorry if I offended you. I'm just getting to know people. Excuse me if I happen to notice a pretty face first."

Will ignored Danny's mumbling and began picking up balls of paper that had rebounded out of the now full can. He pressed them on top and into the others in the can. His head was swarming with ideas. It was time for him to go. He gathered up the remaining third of the papers that were left intact.

"I come from this. This is in my heart. The Gospel is in my heart," Will said, clarifying what he thought was an evident difference between them.

Danny stood as if ready to block a shot, although their game of trash can hoops had long since ended.

"I guess you're suggesting it's not in my heart as well. God's doing a new thing in my life. No offense, but however it comes, I need this."

Will felt there was nothing left to discuss. Neither one of them was backing down. As he walked toward the office door, he said over his shoulder, "So let the best man—the chosen man—win."

Will had taken the remaining copies of The *Society Pages* with him, and it gave him great satisfaction to place them in the Dumpster with the other trash from the church and the school that had been discarded.

Chapter 27

They were three legal minds. Jacobs had come across Courthouse Row to the law firm of Princeton and Hope for Rebecca's strategy session. If Rebecca couldn't have Will with her, Jacobs was the next best thing, although she thought it was a risky move for him and the future of his job. As it turned out, Jacobs and her attorney, Connie Doyle, were quite enamored of each other. She was blond and had the cheeks of a porcelain doll, which stayed rosy despite her efforts to look professionally conservative without makeup. It was fun watching the two of them. Jacobs had turned down a position at Princeton and Hope, thinking his interest in Connie would be a breach of the firm's no-fraternization policy. Rebecca wished she had been so wise.

Mediation was a few hours away, and they were still debating if it served their interests to go. The hardest part for Rebecca was knowing what she wanted her outcome to be going into the session. Did she want her job back, or did she want punitive damages or compensation for her time and suffering? Did she simply want to target Burke like he had targeted her, or did she want the big fish at the firm?

"Offering mediation is the firm's way of giving her a last-minute invitation to the dance. Either she can be happy and buy a dress and go or she can intentionally stand the jerks up, who didn't give her the consideration in the first place," Connie observed.

They were seated at opposite ends of the conference room. Rebecca was on the couch, and Jacobs and Connie were slightly elevated in swivel chairs, which they kept twisting intentionally so their knees would bump.

"I'm a litigator, not a mediator," Jacobs declared, "but if it scapegoats Burke, then it's well worth it. I can't tell you how much of a jerk this guy is. It is a moot point to do mediation, unless Burke is fired as well or—"

Connie finished his sentence. "Or she is reinstated."

"Burke being fired won't happen from mediation, will it?" Rebecca asked, chiming in. "They are looking for a mutually agreed upon solution. Who would agree to their own firing?"

"Don't worry about Burke. He has no say, because he's still employed by the firm," Connie replied. "We treat him like the face of the harassment in a portrait that is framed by the firm. They will have to speak to his actions and what they allowed to happen to you while you were still employed there."

"Well, I definitely don't want to be reinstated if Burke wasn't terminated," Rebecca said. Burke strapped to a chair with no say was almost laughable to Rebecca, until she thought of how he operated. What had he armed the firm's lawyers with? Would she be equally as willing to unload her tell-all arsenal?

"Ask Tony. It's always my intention to prepare a case in a way that will result in the best decision for my client by a judge. This is just a stair step to that end. Being a law firm, they have a clause that forces mediation before litigation. So after today we can tell them they can keep their stinkin' dance. We got a better offer."

They were like peas in a pod. Connie was trying to be funny, and *Tony* Jacobs was eating it up, but this was Rebecca's life. "Aren't you afraid to take on Bryan Russell?"

Connie shook her head. "I was born for this. This is what I went to law school for, outsmarting the big boys. The question is, do you want to dance?"

Her statement made Rebecca think of Trixie and Will at the same time. She wanted to dance—to go after Burke. He was the reason she had disappointed Will and was away from him right now. She wanted to dance, but she had a feeling it was bigger than Burke.

They settled on their terms, and those were the first thing on the table once they arrived at the mediator's office. It felt oddly like her mother's estate hearing, with parties crowded around a conference table, looking for their piece of the pie. There were two older Caucasian men, who, Rebecca imagined, were Bryan Russell and a representative of the firm, and then there was Burke, with a slick attorney whose hair was slicked back into a ponytail at the nape of his neck. She could smell both their colognes, which seemed to be clashing with one another, before she could see them. She and Connie were two women in a sea of men.

They had settled on reinstatement, but only if Kenny Burke was terminated, but they could live with Rebecca not being reinstated, provided the firm wanted to pay. In that case they asked for a compensation package consisting of her regular pay times five for pain and suffering, and an extension of her insurance and retirement benefits.

Mr. Russell automatically began to smirk. "Obviously, Ms. Doyle failed to point out to her client the severance pay contract in our employee handbook, which stipulates that severance will not be rewarded to employees who intend to sue the employer for wrongful dismissal."

They didn't intend on paying her anything.

"Let's take that off the table for right now," Connie said.

Mr. Brookstone, their mediator, was an extra-wide man with his own custom conference chair. "Yes, it seems we have a layer of claims that took place internally, where both parties filed a claim of sexual harassment against one another. It seems to be where this whole thing began. Neither was called into internal mediation at the firm. Since we have Mr. Burke and his lawyer, Mr. Williams, here, let's start with that. What were your complaints, disputes, if any, and how do you see them resolved within the context of the overall case?"

Mr. Williams cleared his throat before beginning. "My client has served the interests of Sanz, Mitchum, and Clarke and intends to continue his tenure there. Ms. Lucas's claim jeopardizes that. His status as junior associate became compromised when he met and became involved with Ms. Lucas, a junior legal aide. After the relationship went sour, their working relationship became nearly impossible."

"Correct me if I am wrong, but there was a no-fraternization policy in place, am I right?"

Rebecca hated these rhetorical questions. Brookstone had all the paperwork. She had hoped that they would not get into all of this. It was bad enough explaining her relationship with Burke to Connie, and then to Will. She was being stared at. Burke had a way of staring at a person without actually looking at them. She could feel the pull of his concentration through his blank stare.

Connie jumped in. "They both ignored it."

"Mr. Burke filed a harassment claim a month and half before her claim," Mr. Keith countered.

"He filed a claim when my client was on bereavement leave. And there is nothing on record that shows he pushed HR for mediation or a personnel reassignment, as Ms. Lucas has done several times."

Then came the free-for-all. They went there. As the lawyers engaged in judicial sparring, arguing about the definition of the term *relationship,* Brookstone sat like a bump on a log. Burke supposedly had receipts of dinners he and Rebecca had shared that were of both of a personal and a business nature, as well as names of witnesses to her defiant outbursts on the job. Rebecca felt as if she had been defiled. The only time Burke was asked to speak, he described the compromising positions and the state of undress he and Rebecca found themselves in while in the storage closet at the firm that one afternoon. They asked her one question directly, and it was about whether Burke's account was accurate, and she agreed that it was. The partners' representative and lawyers took it all in. She felt they all couldn't help but believe that she was a jilted lover, losing files and missing meetings in response to being dumped. It would have served them both right to be fired on the spot.

I was in a relationship with Kenny Burke? Rebecca asked herself silently. What made her think she could get this man on harassment when she had been a willing participant? He was supposed to be the face of harassment, but she was becoming the poster child. Why had she even filed a complaint against him? Then she thought of Walter Calhoun's and Burke's proposal. This wasn't just about her and Burke; it was a threesome. Had she or Connie even brought Calhoun up anywhere in the claim?

She pressed Connie about it during a break.

"It's best to keep that under wraps," Connie told her. "He's the new face of harassment and cover-ups, along with some other empty frames you're gonna help me fill. They are calling our bluff, and quite frankly, Brookstone is not the man to bring it all together. Russell probably thinks our harassment case is dead in the water, and they have us in a confidentiality pigeonhole, because all the stuff that was said today cannot be repeated in court. We'll go after wrongful discharge, all right, retaliation, breach of contract and fair dealing."

"What does all this mean?" Rebecca asked, reeling from the information, but relieved to be out of Burke's presence and out from under his influence.

A fire blazed in Connie's eyes. "It means they didn't use the steps they put in place. There was no leash for this guy, Burke. Then, when they thought you were going to blow the whistle, they got rid of you with no cause. We're done here, and we're filing in court. We've got a real case to prepare. We're leaving the dance."

Chapter 28

They had been dating in the traditional sense for nearly a week, enjoying meals and brief outings together. She canceled the noise in his life that said he should be doing more, probing more, promoting himself more, studying more. They didn't avoid, but rather tiptoed around, tense subjects, like her case and his election.

They were lounging once again in his living room, barring everything else from their existence. He was coming to find out that she was quite the homebody, but this was not her home. She was making a case about moving back to her home. She had the gravest expression on her face. He wasn't making the connection between it and the optimism she was spewing. This time she didn't have reservations about them dating long distance, so he didn't bother her with reservations of his own.

"Remember you said I can stay here as long as I like? I can't with a clear conscience keep you from your space any longer, especially if I will be running back and forth to Salisbury to prepare my case."

"The time has come, huh?" Will said, trying his best not to crowd her with his hopes, to be a big boy.

He had first realized that something was up when he noticed that her hygiene products no longer took up residence around the hallway sink when he went to the bathroom earlier. He pretended he hadn't seen her suitcase out and open in his bedroom. She had retrieved her ballet slippers, and he instantly regretted not asking her to dance the way she was designed to—divinely. He could call some buddies of his to have that wall of mirrors and a ballet bar installed in less than two days, if it would make her stay.

"I don't know how I can go back. Your bed is way cozier, and you get better water pressure in your shower than I do in mine," Rebecca said.

"But—" Will began.

"That's just it," she said, interrupting him. "I don't know how to finish that sentence, and the more I talk, the harder it is."

Will knew what she meant. Something was missing from their narrative. He suspected he knew what would complete it, but was it the right time? They stared at one another. "I guess I should help you to the car with your stuff."

Will decided to occupy himself by moving his car while she finished packing and bringing her bags out. He had her trapped in. *God, what is going on?* he thought. Just then he heard a voice, reminding him again that he wasn't very brave. He rushed inside without moving his car to tell her how he really felt, only to find her rushing in his direction without her bags. He let her go first.

"I don't want to leave here," Rebecca assured him, facing him now. "You know, all I knew was fear and frustration after going back to Salisbury after the funeral. I didn't have a single day of freedom, like I've known here."

"You know we'd have to be married to stay here together."

She smiled shyly, slowly nodding her head in full acknowledgement. "I know."

Will balanced surprise and shock, which threatened to topple him over. "Do you know I was set to ask you—"

"I know," she said again.

"I don't want to be made to feel like I've coerced you in some way or tried to get you to do something we shouldn't or to feel something you don't," he told her, rambling.

Rebecca glided closer to him and palmed his face. "I know, I know. I know you are tired of waiting on me."

"No . . . but, yeah, kind of." He smiled. "So are you saying you feel the same way I do?"

Rebecca shook her head.

"Are you gonna accept my ring?"

"Are you gonna propose?" She laughed. "Gosh, I must be past you now. Isn't that how it traditionally goes? Do you even have a ring?"

Will had to laugh at himself also. He was messing up royally, but on reflection, he realized that he had never been so nervous. He walked away from her to reach for the ring and remove it from its hiding spot. When he brought it back and revealed it, he could say he had sufficiently turned the tables. She delighted in this, his ultimate gesture. Everything else was a formality except for their feelings at that precise moment, feelings that were both overdue and overwhelming.

Chapter 29

They made many decisions while standing in Will's living room. He wanted to have the wedding as soon as possible, which realistically would be a week after getting the marriage license. She wanted it to be a small ceremony, with just a few family and friends and none of the formality that being a leader of a church could entail. They wanted the focus to truly be on them. They hugged and kissed, then both got down on their knees, at his suggestion, asking God to bless their decision and impending union. Then he asked her to leave.

It was the second time he attempted to kick her out. She was a woman on the verge of being someone's wife; she needed her mom or the next best thing. She was going to her sister's, where she hoped to stay until the wedding. She didn't call ahead, yet she fully expected Gail to bear the weight of the surprise she carried on her ring finger.

Rebecca drove along Zion Hill Road, the road on which her childhood home was nestled. When she reached the house, she parked in the driveway, climbed out of the car, and took one suitcase out of the trunk. Wheeling it behind her, she walked to the front door. She knocked and waited and knocked again.

"Sis, I'm—" Rebecca began.

"You're here, Lord Jesus. You're here in Easton now," Gail said, flustered.

Rebecca couldn't contain her happiness or the truth. "I've actually been in Easton for about a week and a half now."

"Excuse me?" Gail said, still blocking the doorway.

"I'm sorry for not calling first, but can you let me in?" Rebecca was tired of holding her luggage and holding her secret in.

"Ah, wait a minute." She turned to shout something over her shoulder. "Milo, it's Rebecca. Here for a visit."

Only then did Rebecca notice her sister's disheveled appearance. Never had she seen her sister in a shirt that wasn't buttoned up correctly or tucked in perfectly around her petite frame.

"Oh my God, were the two of you having sex?" Rebecca inquired. "In the common guest area, no less? Is that what married people do?"

Rebecca giggled when she saw her sister's face flush. Gail shushed her, but it was no use. The thought of her and Will enjoying each other in that way set off multi-colored fireworks of anticipation, excitement, and joy. Just when Gail finally gave her the all clear to enter the house, Rebecca's phone rang, letting her know she had received a text message.

I miss you already.

"He's such a sweet geek," Rebecca said, feeling her face flush as well as Gail escorted her to the great room.

"Who?"

Rebecca wiggled her finger, trying to get her half-carat diamond to shine brilliantly in the light for Gail to see. "Your brother, and soon-to-be brother-in-law."

They both squealed and hugged and rocked back and forth. "I knew you were a smart girl. I just kept praying you wouldn't lose this good man, waiting for things to be one hundred percent perfect. That almost makes up for you being in town and not telling me. I'm going to get the both of you for not calling or coming to visit."

Gail called out to her husband, who had scrambled somewhere, to join them but he didn't appear. When another text came through on Rebecca's phone, Gail went in search of her husband.

> That ring is a summons.

She thought that was strange message, until she remembered her track record. He thought she might skip out on him. She wished she could erase traces of her past that were selfish and inconsistent. She texted him back.

> I won't change my mind. This ring means trusting on both our parts. Security. Devotion. Love.

Those very words were incorporated into their vows exactly one week and one day later, on Valentine's Day. She and Gail had found the perfect gown for her. It was strapless and short, with a delicate detachable train that was long and cascading in the back. She caught a reflection of herself as she got ready in the hours leading up to the ceremony and thought that she could see what Will must see when he looked at her—her true self, a beautiful, intelligent, and mature woman worthy of being happy. That image started to fade a bit when she thought of the role she'd play in his life. A good wife for Will would have to make a good first lady. She wondered, if only briefly, on her wedding day about the wife of Will's competitor. Will didn't talk much about her, telling Rebecca only that she was pregnant. Would marrying put Will at an advantage or a disadvantage in terms of securing his future at Grace Apostle? Rebecca brushed those thoughts away, like the wisps of loose hair that fell from underneath her headpiece.

The timetable for this wedding was disproportionate to their journey. They couldn't have pulled it off any faster had they flown to Vegas. They sat down just once with Pastor Cutler for counseling before he pronounced them man and wife in front of a modest crowd in an elaborately decorated forum. Cutler's kids formed a makeshift chorale and performed during the ceremony. They rented a banquet room on the neighboring campus of Salisbury University for a reception dinner for their invited guests. Everyone else would find out through a subsequent announcement that would run in the local paper and the church bulletin.

Now Rebecca was trying on the name Donovan for size, Rebecca Lucas Donovan. To think, she carried the title Mrs. Donovan that her mother had always wanted, and just months ago, she had thought Will's dad, the man missing from the festivities on her wedding day, could have also been her father. Will was not fast to include his father in the ceremony, maybe for that reason. She didn't question him as to why. That was a conversation for another day. She did, however, call her future father in-law to invite him, to which he simply replied, "Congratulations." Rebecca couldn't help but think he was more enthusiastic when he said the same thing to her at her high school graduation.

Married. Finally, her husband gave her a choice of local destinations for a brief honeymoon, but she preferred to go to the home nestled off the road that she had come to love so much. He was a traditionalist in the way he opened the door and carried her over the threshold. She couldn't explain it, but the house looked different somehow now that she rightfully belonged there.

She practically jumped out of his arms once they were inside so that she could set up his surprise. They hadn't had their first dance.

"What are you up to?" Will asked, loosening his bow tie around his neck and the cuff links at his wrists while watching her carefully as she tried to work his sound system.

"You're not the only one with a playlist," she announced as she searched for a particular song, one that she was sure he had programmed somewhere.

"No Ordinary Love," by Sade, started playing too loudly at first, so she adjusted the volume so that it complimented their mellow mood. He smiled and took her by the hand in no time.

They swayed in time to what would forever be their song. He gave her the look that Rebecca was coming to know, and then leaned in to her in a special way, which meant he desired her lips. Once he had tasted them, without warning, he hoisted her up again, this time putting her over his shoulder like a sack of potatoes. She yelped and playfully tapped him on his back. He headed off toward the back but backtracked to the kitchen. She thought he might be hungry again, until she saw him place his parents' special occasion wine from their twentieth anniversary and two glasses in an empty ice bucket, all of which he managed with one hand while holding her across the rear with the other.

He was hungry, all right, or so his eyes communicated to her once he put her down in their recently redecorated bedroom. His coverlet had been replaced by crisp white sheets and a comforter, which was folded back, showing off red rose petals, which had been strewn about. Candles were everywhere, and Will looked around for a lighter. Rebecca spotted a box next to his chair, which contained his lava lamps and a note, which she brought over to him to see. It was from Gail, and he read it aloud. "Remove these permanently. Your new wife doesn't need to know you sleep with a night-light." For some reason that was hilarious to both of them, and they laughed until tears streamed down their cheeks.

"Aw, Rebi and Will went off and got married, oooooh," Rebecca said, throwing her hand over her mouth, as if she was actually tattling on herself.

"That's right. Little Willie done grown up and got himself a wife."

"Is this crazy, or what?" Rebecca asked, as if the magnitude of the whole thing had just occurred to her.

"I don't feel crazy. This is amazing . . . a dream." Will abandoned his search for a lighter and popped the cork on the bottle and poured two glasses of the vintage wine.

She reached for his arm and took hold of it, and he pulled away until his wrist, hand, and then even his fingertips were out of her grasp. He stood away from her at the edge of their bed. His eyes narrowed to take her all in. She understood hot and passionate, but his silence and extra consideration were smoldering and sexy, too, though unnerving. He was showing her a new way to passion, and she wanted to plant a flag on what he had previously termed amazing.

"Do something. Say something," she said after about a minute had passed, no longer able to stand it. She was bound by a corset and garters under her wedding gown and couldn't wait to be released.

"Your nickname shall now and forevermore be Gigi. Forget Rebi, Weary, and all the other names I've called you in the past." he finally said. His voice was thick and his manner brusque with desire.

"Gigi?"

"That's right. You're God's gift, so excuse me if I take my time unwrapping my present."

With that, they slowly approached one another, kissed, toasted, and did their dance, repeatedly and in no particular order.

Chapter 30

Will spent the better part of the week after the wedding making Rebecca the main ingredient in his sustenance. His every touch was to display first to her and then himself that she was his. She was more than accommodating to her new husband, easily learning his love language and making herself available every time he reached for her physically and emotionally. She had him feeling that he didn't need much more than what was between their front and back doors.

He did want one more thing. As much as he wanted to stay closed up and away from the world in order to build their home together, making it reminiscent of the farmhouse she grew up in, and take care of her, the Lord was not going to let them live in hiding. One Sunday had already come and gone since the wedding. He needed a word, not necessarily a church service.

He nudged his wife, slumbering next to him, and serenaded her with a verse from a familiar song. "Wake up, everybody. No more sleeping in bed."

She rolled on her back to face him, brushing the hair from her face, and mouthed, "Good morning."

"C'mon. It's Sunday morning. This is how it goes down in the Donovan household on the Lord's day. Let's rise and shine," Will said like the drill sergeant he was not. They had set no type of routine and hadn't even discussed whether or not they would infringe on Danny Glass's time as interim pastor by making an appearance as a couple. He had passed along their wedding announcement and a wedding picture to Sister Tyler, the church receptionist, for the weekly bulletin. He was interested to see if those items would be approved or intercepted, or if they would somehow make their way to the *Society Pages.*

Rebecca rose easily. "If we're going to church, I need to call Gail. I left my good pumps over at her house."

Will grabbed her before she could get out of bed. With his lips planted on her shoulder as he made his way up to her neck, he said, "I could be convinced to skip another Sunday. I'm not the charge minister. I am still on my break and, technically, still on my honeymoon."

Rebecca smiled while feebly pushing him off. "Oh no, you're not going to put that off on me. If someone asks you why you weren't in church, you are not going to throw me under the bus. What do you want to do?"

That was a good question. He was not barred from church during Danny's probationary period, but for some reason, he was not ready to go to Grace Apostle's services. "I got an idea. Let's check out the infamous forum at Dogwood Community Church."

She conceded to his wish, anxious to see the kids and Pastor Cutler, whom they had not visited since the wedding. He thought he detected just a hint of disappointment in her face, though. He figured he'd make it worth her while with a brunch afterward. They got on their way immediately to make it by the 11:00 a.m. start time.

"We could swing past your apartment to get the last bit of stuff you said you wanted," Will casually proposed as he drove. "Did you call the storage places?"

"My lease is up in four months," Rebecca said.

"Which means?"

"Which means I have time," she snapped back. "Like I said, I have four months left. Two months are already paid up front."

Will was getting a little irritated. "Convenient for you," he mumbled.

Apparently, he didn't mumble as softly as he thought he had, because she retorted, "Like running down here is for you."

He slowed the car in an attempt to get where she was coming from. "Huh?"

"Nothing," she stated.

"It's apparent you don't want to give up your apartment. However, I don't know why you would need it or why we should continue to pay the rent when neither one of us has a job right now. To me, it just gives you a place to run. That's all I'm saying."

"Oh my God, can we not," Rebecca pleaded spastically. "I mean, can I just live with the illusion that everything is perfect in my world for a few more weeks after my wedding, or, at least until the trial starts."

He alternated looks at the road and his wife. He could promise her nothing at this point. They hadn't confronted his dad. They hadn't confronted their church. Will thought about the temporary worry-free happiness that they were able to grab for themselves and wondered if it existed for them outside of their home.

They arrived at the church after sharing a brief period of silence. It was certainly noisy inside of Dogwood Community Church. It sounded as if someone was doing a drum solo when they arrived. There was a mixed group of familiar kids and new faces filling the chairs in a circle in the center of the forum floor. Ethan was nearby, propped on a stool behind a keyboard, as if he was the leader of the house band, with Marcus going at it on the drums.

Pastor Cutler was in the middle of all this. He was dressed in all black, except for his trademark white priest's collar. He rose, along with a few others, to greet Will and Rebecca when they came in and to offer them a seat. Will carried his Bible and low expectations of anything that resembled a true worship service to the seat at the right of Pastor Cutler, and Rebecca pointed to indicate to him that she would be joining Trixie at the wide end of the oblong circle. *The two women must have genuinely formed a bond,* Will thought as he watched his wife bend over to give the often cantankerous college-aged woman a hug. Trixie reached out for Rebecca's ringed hand to check it when Rebecca pulled out of their embrace.

"Welcome, welcome," Pastor Cutler said to the couple, while signaling to Ethan to wrap up his renderings. "This is an awesome segue with our guests joining us. I guess I can hardly call them guests anymore. Who wants to start our forum discussion? What do you all want to talk about this week?"

"Hypocrites," Trixie called out boldly.

Will immediately thought of the Bible verse that said the wisdom of the Lord was without hypocrisy and set out to find it in his Bible, although the chapter and verse escaped him.

"Okay," Pastor Cutler said above the commentary the kids were used to issuing whenever one of them shared with the group. "Are you talking about those in our lives that profess to love God but do the opposite?"

She shrugged, as if she was in a game of charades and could offer no more clues. "Yeah, those too."

Ethan was the first to reply. "Who can really know who is a hypocrite or not? I've been called all kinds of things, but what really gets me is when someone tries to figure out whether I'm a Christian or not."

"Oh, you can tell," another kid said, chiming in.

"Who can say whether I feel God or not? Who can tell me what's in my heart?" Ethan said passionately, pointing to his own chest. "Tell me that."

"Do you feel God?" Trixie questioned. There were some snickers, but she was serious.

"Yes, yes, I do," Ethan said, rolling his eyes. He was standing and was defensive.

"No offense to you, Ethan." Trixie stood as well to claim her space in the conversation. "I'm putting myself on blast. I'm trying to carry the cross like my nana told me when I went away to school, but I'm confused about why I'm here and if I'll make it. I deal with craziness on the daily. Y'all just don't know. You aren't the only one who is misunderstood."

In a moment of seriousness, Bruce came over to hug Trixie, who was reluctant at first to be embraced. "I got your back, sista. Don't let them girls get to you."

Others responded in kind, with expressions of support for Trixie and Ethan.

Will was half listening as he flipped from verse to verse, searching for a particular passage so that he could introduce meat into their diet of opinions, which he felt they should have started with. He kept thinking about his competitor, Danny Glass, and the possible hypocrisy he was keeping hidden. From his dad's indiscretions and marred legacy to the scandal rag left repeatedly on the church's doorstep, and to Veronica showing up, he was ready to blow his lid over double standards.

"Anyone else want to share before I comment," Cutler asked, pausing. "If not, I'm going to concede to my fellow theologian here first. He looks like he's about to burst over here. Take heed from this man. He came armed with his Word."

Will was caught off guard, but his hand marked the page that he had decided to read aloud without considering its relevance. "Even so ye also outwardly appear righteous unto men, but within ye are full of hypocrisy and iniquity."

Everyone stared at Will as if they expected him to expound on the passage. He was lost and didn't know why. He coughed on his pride, despising this conversation format. He wasn't expected to be fully armed when speaking off the cuff, or was he?

"Okay, I think that verse shows us that if an unrighteous man has a heart full of hypocrisy, then we who have felt God and have yielded our lives to His will should have a heart filled with the opposite. Like Keith hinted at earlier, it should be hard *not* to notice you've felt God or spent time with Him in your prayer, because you're a little more patient and loving toward people. We're set apart because we take what the world gives us, which is cruelty and hypocrisy sometimes, and respond with love or charity. It's called bearing fruit," Pastor Cutler explained.

Will tried to redeem himself. "Yeah, 'the fruit of the Spirit is love, joy, peace, long-suffering, gentleness, goodness, faith, meekness, temperance.' Galatians five, twenty-two and twenty-three."

He wanted to tell them more, such as that some people plagued by darkness might not be able to see their light or truly understand them. That didn't mean they should stop shining it. He wanted to share that he also was misunderstood.

"That will fill ya. Thanks, Minister Will," Pastor Cutler said. "You don't have to be shy. We can all benefit from this knowledge. I suggest you all write that one down and commit to reading it this week, especially when you're being misunderstood. Check your understanding of these characteristics and make sure you're displaying them. Wow, that felt like the perfect wrap-up. We usually begin and end with free expression to start our week. Anyone else have something on their heart that they want to share?"

There was a pause, and some kids' eyes brightened with the possibility of being released from their discussion early. Then Rebecca stood. Will was interested in what she wanted to share.

"Mrs. Donovan, by all means, sweetie," Pastor Cutler said, nudging Will in the arm, as if to say, "Take notice."

"I, too, have been struggling with being understood. Minister Will, my husband, taught me a while back that praise opens the door for any kind of breakthrough. Sometimes, even when my circumstances seem to go south, I still want to praise Him with my whole heart. See, I am a dancer. I call what I do dance therapy. It's as if I am tapping, knocking, beating, really, at the door, saying, 'God, let me in.'" She looked in Will's direction. "Honey, you may have to help me with this song. How many people know the song 'Imagine Me,' by Kirk Franklin?"

Before Will could place the melody, Trixie started humming it. Ethan then resumed his tinkering on the keyboard. Out of the blue someone produced the radio version on their iPhone. Will thought it was a great song to have on tap. He watched his wife, who had worried earlier about the appropriate pumps to wear, kick off her shoes and take to the center of the circle and begin to dance. Her choreography included a succession of repeated movements that had her looking like she was tethered to a puppeteer. Trixie and, of course, Bruce-Bruce tried to pick up the choreography. Rebecca stopped her own dance to help them. Standing in front of them like a conductor, she signaled to them to continue the movements once they got them down.

Then Rebecca escaped into her own dance. She was like the prima ballerina, the soloist. She became a banner for the freedom that flew over you when you were able to paint your own reflection. She danced with every muscle and bone, from her cheekbone to those of her little toe. Will felt the indecision and eventual joy you could feel when you let go of the expectations others tried to put upon you. It was all illustrated so beautifully. Rebecca pantomimed a mirror, and she gracefully posed before it, then hid herself from its reflection. She moved around the entire circle with her pretend mirror, forcing them all to take a look. In the end, she covered her face with the rush of the Holy Spirit, while the others, including her backup dancers, applauded her. Will rose from his seat and joined in on her ovation.

He was proud, but in some small way he was a bit peeved as Pastor Cutler raved on and on about her after the forum was dismissed. His smile was wearing thin. He watched her interact with Trixie again, apparently letting the young woman punch her number into her cell phone and vice versa. She then gave Trixie a hearty hug and seemed to pass something over to her. Will waited until they were in the car to broach the subject.

"Are you all right?" she asked, noticing his disposition, as they sat in the car.

"Yeah. Why?"

"I don't know. You just didn't seem like yourself in there," she said, studying his profile.

"I'm good. I'm usually serious when I'm in worship—if you can call what we just did that. Except you, now, you ministered, worshipped, and some more. It was absolutely beautiful. You did your thing. I'm just scratching my head, wondering what you gave Trixie before we left."

"There were some things we discussed the first time we met that have intensified for her on campus. She's got a little chip on her shoulder because of it," Rebecca said, clearly trying to keep the young woman's confidence by not revealing too many details.

"A little chip?" Will smirked.

She tapped him. "Anyway, I gave her a key to my apartment to have until things cool off a bit."

"What?" Will asked. "I don't think that's wise. I don't think that's wise at all."

"Why would you take objection to that? We were just arguing about that on the way down here. I thought that would be a solution to the problem when it presented itself. And I sort of remember someone ministering to me and offering me a respite not too long ago."

"Yeah, but I know you, Rebi. What do you know about her, or anyone else down there, for that matter?"

She shrugged away the insecurities he tried to pass her way. "I don't know. I was just there to listen to her that day. My heart went out to her. That's how I know about what she's going through, and Bruce-Bruce, Ethan, all of them, and about, you know, Cutler losing his wife to cancer around about this same time two years ago."

He felt his intelligence quotient dropping. He couldn't hide his ignorance. She caught on due to his silence.

"You didn't know?" She pursed her lips. "That's why he doesn't preach. I guess he can't see doing traditional ministry without her."

It was almost too much for Will that he had spent all this time there and had not realized his friend was hurting still.

"That has nothing to do with Trixie being an irresponsible college student, and you kissing your security deposit good-bye by handing her your keys without even consulting your husband."

She sighed heavily. "It's only until semester's end. She doesn't have a car on campus, so she'll mainly be camping out there on the weekends. Plus, I'll be up here checking on her every time I come to Salisbury."

"Oh, so you're like Harriet Tubman, making return trips, leading folks to freedom." Will couldn't make himself stop. How could he forget her trips to Salisbury for the trial? Something else he knew about only secondhand.

"Excuse me, Pastor Donovan. Isn't that what ministry is all about? Freeing people? It seems to me that you are throwing me unnecessary shade for some reason. I didn't know that with you, it matters who we're freeing and who is doing the freeing," Rebecca said, squeezing her eyes shut with her fingers, as if his comments had just brought on a tension headache.

Deny, deny, deny, Will thought. "I was kidding. Harriet Tubman . . . seriously, that was a joke."

"Well, obviously, I don't know you very well. I don't know when you're serious, when you're just kidding, and when *we're* going to our home church, where you claim you want to be the pastor."

There was nothing more that he could say. It occurred to him that she knew him very well, indeed, maybe even more than he knew himself.

Chapter 31

Rebecca was out shopping with Gail to replace what her sister termed her "less than saintlike Sunday attire." She admitted she loved her short and slim-fitting styles, but she was willing to add some classic pieces to be seen in around church. She was, after all, the potential first lady of Grace Apostle. Boutique shopping had never been her thing, but the boutiques were far less crowded than the malls.

"Tell me honestly, Gail," Rebecca said, putting a nautical blue suit jacket up to her bosom at the mirror. "Is it crazy at all for you that your sister married your brother?"

"It's crazy that I even have a sister or a brother after all this time," Gail said, not bothering to look up.

"What do you tell people?"

"Seriously, it's our truth to tell or not. I'm from a generation where you don't ask about people's business. Most folks know I am Pastor Donovan's daughter. Okay, that's all they get. You know me. I come to church with praise on my lips, but I will be quick to tell someone, they can't earn a degree in my business, so stop studying me."

Rebecca laughed. "Seriously, a lot of my hang-ups are still about people knowing."

"We were raised together, so you feel more like a sister to me. Brother, brother-in law, in a close-knit family there is not that much of a difference between the two. I don't know. It's you, me, Will and Milo, and then there's dad."

"And then there's dad," Rebecca repeated with a heavy sigh at the end.

That stopped Gail's progress through the racks. "I don't know what's going on between your husband and his father, but they've got to make it right."

"You know what it's about. Somehow I feel his hang-ups are the same as mine—your parents and their affair. Never in a million years did I believe I would be marrying Will and his dad would not be there to do the ceremony at Grace Apostle Methodist Church. Neither one of us was willing to wait until that rift was mended to make that a reality, though. Is that wrong?"

Gail just shook her head. "I don't know. Milo and I had discussed hosting a family dinner either at our house or dad's, if it'll make him more comfortable."

"Like an intervention?" Rebecca asked. *What a first family.* Rebecca began to think about the distance Will seemed to be putting between the two of them since last Sunday at Dogwood. Everything was an irritation to him, her case, her apartment, just plain her. So she had been finding refuge down at her old dance school, sitting in on classes. The dance school's owner, Jolee, was trying to convince her to teach a liturgical class. "I may need you to intervene in my relationship already. He's got some stuff about him that I can't quite figure out. I was set to bail on him last week."

Gail shooed her. "It should take an act of God or insanity to make you even mention bailing on your husband so soon."

Rebecca showed Gail a dress that she was interested in, and got an almost instant thumbs- down from her. "The other day I sat down next to him on the couch, like I normally do when he's staring into the Bible, to ask him straight up why he's weirding out on me. I mean, he used to call me Weary. I asked him if he has grown weary of me already, and you know what he did? What he told me? He patted me on the bum, asked me to give him some space, and told me to just hold him down. That's his new phrase now. 'Hold me down.' What does that even mean?"

Gail moved on to another rack, amassing more things to try on herself than for Rebecca to try on. "Girl, sisters have been holding their men down from the beginning of time. It simply means bear with him. He's going through a lot—church, dad, you—so bear with him, have his back, don't sound crazy around here, talking about bailing on him. Gosh, you need a mentor. The both of you do. What first lady says that to her husband?"

Rebecca spun around so fast, she almost got caught up in her purse. "It seems mighty one-sided. He can shut down everywhere except the bedroom? Following his lead, I'm just making my first appearance at Grace Apostle after I happened to marry the pastor-to-be. I'm so over the eggshells and the kid gloves. Who are we protecting, really?"

"He's just trying to be diplomatic, that's all. Trying to separate what you guys have from what people think they know about the entire family. Even dad's been sitting in the congregation. I can give or take Danny Glass, to tell the truth, but his father, honey, I used to have the biggest crush on him. Junior is overrated, and I think he knows it. He doesn't need a separation from his daddy. He needs to keep the ties. I believe the bulk of the people are waiting for Daddy Glass to make an appearance either beside his son or through him."

Gail had her selections for Rebecca and the ones for herself spread out in front of her, as if she was still deliberating. "Sunday, Sunday after next, Palm Sunday," she said, pointing at suits on the end cap, where they were standing. Then, pointing at the one white and navy blue suit Rebecca was holding, she said, "And Resurrection Sunday."

Rebecca was ready to make the bulk purchase without even trying anything on. "I'm going to need the check from my share of the well inheritance left by our mother to the both of us, because first lady garb isn't cheap and I don't have a job."

Gail didn't miss a beat. "Now, tell me about this trial with your former employer, which I don't know anything about. You're over there, carrying your own burdens, like you're husband. Will mentioned it when I spoke with him two days ago. Then he immediately tried to backpedal out of the conversation, like he doesn't know what's going on. You got him trained well."

Rebecca stopped to shake her head. "He really doesn't know. That job is in my past, and I don't want to mix it with my present or future. That's a conversation for another day, sis. Can we go?"

Gail put one hand up in the air. "Hey, me and Mr. Milo don't have any kids. You're grown, right? If you say you don't want to talk about it and don't need any support from me, I believe you. Hopefully, you know how to do your own damage control, because if it's something that gives those few folks at Grace Apostle ammunition to use against your husband, you're really going to wish you hadn't complained about supporting him. Knowing my brother the way I do, he won't have a problem if you need him to hold *you* down."

Guilt weighed on Rebecca, and she was forced to look at her wedding ring. *That's right, devotion.* As long as that ring was on her finger, it was an indefinite summons to hold her man down.

Chapter 32

Will had his girl; now he wanted his title. He wanted the opportunity to introduce his bride properly to the congregation at Grace Apostle. He didn't intend on being a spectacle in service, but he wasn't willing to wait until he possessed the pulpit again to make a final plea for votes. He left their home early with the hopes of testing the waters in Sunday school and setting everything up with Danny Glass. He was encouraged to see so many warm and supportive faces in the adult class. Many others were curious to see the misses, including Sister Eve Bunter.

"How's your mom?" Will asked her after the class.

"She'll survive. It was just cataract surgery, but she ain't likely to forgive or forget how you went off and got married and didn't tell anyone. I took her the bulletin, and all she could say was that she has known you all your natural-born life. Mama and Ms. Beasley both say they don't know about you. We wondered why we didn't rank an invitation."

"It was small and intimate. C'mon now. Tell Mama it's not like the Bunters to be unforgiving," Will said, managing to get in those words in the midst of her rant. Sister Bunter's mom, Claire, was not one whom you wanted to wrong. She was the matriarch of four generations, and together they had to be close to holding two thirds of the vote at Grace Apostle right there.

Sister Bunter rolled her eyes. "I didn't think it was like the Donovans to keep secrets, but you find out all kinds of things when you're scouting for a new pastor."

Will wondered which "things" she was referring to. "I hope to smooth things over with everyone later on today, in the service. Then you can go home and tell Mama I'm sorry," Will conceded before he excused himself. *Sorry for living my life or thinking that as pastor, I can have a life outside of this church.*

As he headed back to the office, Will thought again about what his father had said. Was Rebecca going to dig in with him? Rebecca was to meet him in the back office, where they'd hang out until the end of the 11:00 a.m. service, which was similar to what Danny had done when he was first introduced to the congregation. That was the plan, anyway.

Will sat in the office, listening to the service, which was piped in through their archaic intercom system. His tie was loosened and his suit jacket was hanging on a nearby hook. He was seeing if he could identify who he could hear. It was youth Sunday, and as many kids as possible were used in the service. The Glass children, Megan and Tyler, had just finished reading the scripture. Will allowed his mind to drift to his own future offspring, who would be attending their church and school.

Although he knew Veronica might be present today, he hadn't expected her to knock and call out his name at the outer office door. He contemplated hiding for a second but decided to face the awkwardness head-on. He was still behind the desk when she peeked her head in. She wore a billowy yellow dress, which was different from the more structured business suits he remembered her wearing in the past.

Will's voice almost caught in his throat. "Hey, I'm surprised to see you here."

"It hasn't been that long since I used to hang out with you until you were ready to join everyone in the sanctuary, has it?"

"How did you know I was back here today?"

"Does it matter? It's obvious I knew you were back here if I called your name, right?"

She was calm, although she was batting her eyes excessively, so he decided he would remain calm also. He didn't have time to question her again. It was best to let her get out what it was that she had come there to say.

"After your sabbatical the past two weeks, I wanted to see firsthand if you were better this week."

Will gave her a quizzical look. "I wasn't out because I was sick. It was Minister Glass's turn to preach, so I took a break."

"A break? I know you got married, Will, to that . . . to *your friend*. You got married." Veronica repeated the word *married* and her eyes widened, as if she was still in disbelief. "I doubt she'll make your existence exceptional, but can you even say she makes you better?"

Will didn't answer right away. He was thinking how egotistical and immature he and Veronica both had been to think that they could achieve exceptionality. It was an ideal that had them playing a role and living a lie. Then he thought of his relationship with Rebecca, the realist. Loving her was so much easier, although the way for them as a couple was made harder by people like Veronica and her cronies.

"Look, Veronica, I'm sorry if finding out about my wedding was hurtful to you in any way, but quite frankly, Rebecca and I made the decision to follow our hearts. So in that way, we *are* better. She'll be joining me here in a minute, so I'd rather not continue this conversation."

This time her eyes narrowed. "So what was that visit about, huh? Have you told your wife about that?"

"That visit was about closure." His speech was slow and measured to drive home his point. He thanked God that Veronica was too prim and proper to act a fool, but he wished she'd get to the point and leave.

She smirked and shook her head. Then she extended her hand across the desk for him to shake. "Well, congratulations. The native son snuck off and got married, but I guess you're ready to tell the world. So, I guess I should be leaving to avoid any further . . . unpleasantness."

Will stood to accept her concession of defeat graciously. They shook hands, but her hand lingered in his, and the familiarity of her touch made him slow to pull his hand away. They were about the same height, which made it hard to escape her glare as well. He heard the voice of Danny Glass on the intercom as he started his sermon, and remembered a snippet of their conversation from the other day, when he warned Will that he needed someone to run interference for him. He agreed with that notion now.

"I guess I should be joining the party inside the sanctuary," Will said.

"Not like that, you don't," Veronica said, circling the desk to meet him on the other side. "I may not be your woman anymore, but I can't let you walk in like that."

She began tightening his tie around his neck. He tried to sidestep her to retrieve his suit jacket from the hook. *What is she doing?* He figured the only way to get her to leave was to leave himself. He could meet Rebecca at the door, in the hallway, anywhere but locked inside the office with his ex-girlfriend.

Without warning her hand became like a shoehorn, smoothing his shirttails within his waistband. "Oops, wait. Tuck it in, sweetie."

It was then that Rebecca walked in. His heart stopped, and the next second it started back up again, and she was gone.

Chapter 33

Rebecca took off running. Then she thought of the very scene in so many television shows and movies that she despised, the scene where someone was caught in the act of cheating and the faithful, innocent partner fled in distress. She was certainly in distress, but she was determined she wasn't going to be the only one.

She saw a woman pass across her field of vision in the doorway leading to the hallway, but she couldn't be concerned about that. She searched around quickly for something to arm herself with. The voices she heard were elevated, and she felt the force of energy like a rushing wind, like someone rushing toward her. It was as if her rational mind had blacked out. She picked up a vase of fake flowers from a side table and separated the plastic petals from the heavy glass.

"Rebi, honey, c'mon, now. Listen to me. You can't believe that anything was going on back there in the office," Will said, stopping short, then reaching out for her.

"Oh yeah, I believe the hand that I saw down your pants, and I believe it took you too long to come after me, 'cause look what I found," Rebecca said, ditching the flowers and taking a pitcher's aim with the vase.

Veronica came out of the inner office at the tail end of Rebecca's statement. Her smug expression evaporated quite considerably when she took in the scene. She kept her distance.

"She was just . . . I was . . ." Will alternated between looking at Veronica and at Rebecca, as if one of them was going to help him out with his explanation.

Rebecca kept the vase moving from hand to hand, partly because it was heavy and partly because she wanted to keep her husband at bay. Tears were streaming down her face full force. How could this be happening?

"You weren't even going to tell me she was in town until I heard her voice on the answering machine. Why? Huh?" She was shouting now, regardless of the open door.

Veronica stepped out from the shadows. "You don't like it so much when the tables are turned, do you?"

Will and Rebecca both started shouting at Veronica. Then there was a third voice.

"I'd shut up if I were you," Rebecca said, charging Veronica until Will caught hold of her around her middle. She still managed to raise the vase above her head.

"Why don't you just leave!" Will exclaimed over his shoulder at his ex-girlfriend in the midst of the tussle.

"Is everything okay?" asked a midsize woman with an extra-large belly, clearly pregnant, partially closing the door to give their very public display some privacy. "You may want to keep your voices down."

"You call this first lady material?" Veronica said, emboldened now that Will was holding Rebecca. "What makes you think you can move to the front of the line and take my life? Let's just see if it fits you."

Rebecca took her best shot, hurling the vase, which shattered to the right of Veronica's feet. Veronica hopped back on her patent leather heels. Unarmed and unencumbered, Rebecca tried to squirm out of her husband's hold, but he wouldn't let go. He was whispering things in her ear, but her hysterics wouldn't allow her to hear him.

"Just go," the woman with the pregnant belly ordered Veronica, trying to march her toward the door.

Veronica just kept on coming, stepping gingerly on the broken glass. "Wait, could that be? Your ring looks like the exact design I picked out when me and your husband went window- shopping over a year ago. Talk about lazy! I guess it's time for another installment of Lay-Z in my news column."

Rebecca felt faint. She waited until Will dragged her over to the couch to escape from his grasp. She could hold out only a stiff arm to him. After Veronica's comment she had no energy to fight or run. Veronica had won. She had officially cracked Rebecca's armor.

"Who do I need to get to make you leave here like the other day? The deacons, the ushers, the mothers' board?" The pregnant woman aimed her comments at Veronica. "I'm ready to try nine-one-one emergency, but as sure as my pregnant behind, you're getting out of here. Respect this couple, respect yourself, for God's sake, respect Sunday morning, and leave on your own accord." The woman stood there pointing the way to the exit.

Veronica took one last look at Will before proclaiming, "You ministers are a joke." She threw open the door and left.

Will and the waddling woman walked through the door, possibly to see to it that Veronica exited without causing any further disturbance. When they both returned, Rebecca reached for the sympathetic hand of her mama shero, not that of her husband.

"You can go too," Rebecca said to Will.

Will tugged at his earlobe. "Maybe we should postpone . . . I could go see if Gail is in the sanctuary."

No one was listening today, Rebecca thought.

"Yeah, go to service, sit in the pulpit, and pray at the altar. I don't care. Just go and leave me alone!" Rebecca shouted.

"I'll take care of her. Let me talk to her," the woman said to a still lingering Will.

Seeing her husband remorseful filled her with dread. Watching him walk away was worse.

Chapter 34

"I'm Marie, by the way," the woman said, closing the door to the pastor's study completely before returning to the couch. "Marie Glass."

Rebecca cupped her forehead in her hand, knowing she had just bought a bolt of bullets for the competitor's wife. She didn't even want to own up to who she was. "And I am Camilla Parker Bowles. You know, the woman Prince Charles married after Princess Di."

Rebecca explained her pun while filling Marie in on her, Veronica, and Will's history. She shocked herself by admitting that she had known and loved Will since childhood. They had parted ways, and Will had begun the relationship with his ex-girlfriend in college. When Rebecca returned to Easton for her mother's funeral, she and Will just deepened their admiration, respect, and love for one another, but Veronica was in the picture. Even when Veronica and Will broke up, Rebecca was perceived as the other woman.

"You've got to know your husband doesn't want this woman. Someone once told me that God can create destiny and permanency, and people can create a circumstance and happenstance, which is what Ms. Thing was trying to do today. She writes those unflattering parodies about this church for the *Society Pages,* calling it a news column. Please, your husband doesn't want her," Marie said, stretching her legs forward to take some of the pressure off her back as she repositioned herself.

Rebecca sighed with relief as she moved over on the couch to allow Marie more room. "What are these parodies?"

As soon as she seemed to get comfortable, Marie was up again. She went through the office door and came back with a paper. "Girl, you haven't seen this? This is the latest. All the articles are anonymous, anonymously evil."

Rebecca read the article, the one entitled "Discarded," that the paper was folded back to. She started to get angry all over again. "She doesn't seem to be a fan of either of our husbands."

Marie huffed, "Or a fan of both. Maybe it's the power or the title, but some women go after the preachers. Then there are some preachers, like mine, who don't give them much of a chase."

Rebecca had questions but didn't know if it was appropriate to ask. Marie had put herself out there, and Lord knows, Rebecca's business was top news today. "So where does that leave you as a preacher's wife?"

"It leaves me as a watchdog," Marie responded.

Rebecca watched her adjust her position again and wondered if it had to do with her baby belly this time.

"How can you be a watchdog and pregnant, Marie? It's not fair."

"It's what I have to do. It's my life." They took an unwritten oath with their eyes to keep each other's confidences at that moment. "Danny has a reputation at I Am the Way. Old girlfriends, Gospel groupies, hangers-on, you name it. Each time I would confront him, he'd convince me it was just a temporary lapse of judgment. I played the good wife until I started playing the watchdog. I went to Pop Glass and told him about it, told him everything, like he didn't already know. He blessed my soul, because he sat Danny down and gave him his walking papers. Now we're here."

"How many times?" Rebecca asked, trying to remember Will's sermon on forgiveness and how many times you were expected to forgive someone.

"At least three, one for each of my pregnancies. I guess you can call them my presents. When I'd get him to admit it, I'd get all his time and attention, until it blew over. Each time I'd believe he was trying to change," she said numbly. "He's a decent man, my man, with a weakness."

Rebecca didn't figure Will as a philanderer and wondered what she would do if he was. This explained so much. Their family wasn't the only one trying to make itself over in this ministry.

"What did you mean when you said you tried to throw Veronica out before?"

"She's been snooping around here for the past two weeks, trying to scout out your husband, but finding mine. Being the watchdog that I am, I asked her to leave one day. Got Deacon Contee to do the dirty work. I didn't want Danny to get any ideas. You know, I thought he would take a break from ministry. I love my pops, but that's all he taught Danny while he was growing up—ministry making and brand building. He's even got an application in at a smaller church in Trappe, where we're staying also."

To think that Marie had to deal with all that was overwhelming for Rebecca. She thought about her situation as she looked down on her hand-me-down ring. "My husband told me this ring is a summons."

Marie smiled and stared straight at Rebecca. "Your husband is a smart man to say that, because the marriage bond certainly is. You've got to be present and participate and be diligent to fortify your relationship in prayer. You've got to be willing to fight over it like you were today and not walk away. You'll make a great first lady."

"I accepted this ring the second time Will tried to flash it at me, and now to find out it was intended for someone else . . ." Rebecca couldn't finish her thought.

"But it ended up on your finger," Marie said quickly. "That's not circumstantial, happenstance. It's destiny."

Rebecca wiped her face, asking herself if she believed what she had just heard. She could hear the organ playing over the intercom. She figured the service was almost over, and wanted to get ahead of the crowd. She stood. "Thanks, Marie. You are a lifesaver. I'm going to get out of here unnoticed. I'm sure we'll meet again. I'm not quite sure of the context, but God does."

"Where will you go?" Marie asked, also standing and smoothing out the wrinkles in her clothing.

"Anywhere but here," Rebecca said.

When she said "Anywhere," she meant outside the city limits. She still had an apartment, and although she didn't go home to get her extra key, she proceeded to the apartment in hopes of getting in contact with Trixie. She had the young woman's dorm room phone number, cell phone number, and suite address. In some way they would cross paths.

She decided to try her apartment since she couldn't get Trixie on the phone. Like her, maybe Trixie needed to take a breather from her day-to-day existence. She knocked on her own apartment door and was greeted by a very stunned young woman. Trixie was silent after she welcomed Rebecca inside. Rebecca immediately became curious. She checked the condition of her place on the surface. The first thing she noticed was although there weren't a lot, Trixie had enough candles and incense burning to hold a séance. Then she looked at the young woman, who was wrapped in a swatch of material meant to be a skirt that could barely pass as a tube top.

"Was I interrupting anything?" Rebecca asked.

"No, Ms. Rebi. I was just studying."

Rebecca squared her shoulders and directed her glare at Trixie. "Studying? Is your little friend coming over or something?"

Trixie shrugged her shoulders, as if she didn't know.

"Why don't I just wait to see if he shows up," Rebecca said, turning one of the living room chairs toward the door before sitting down. "You must think I'm a fool. I'm a pastor's wife. I cannot condone this foolishness. If you're looking for a sin shack, you've come to the wrong place."

"But I love him, Ms. Rebi," Trixie said, all at once becoming upset.

"What are the waterworks for, then? The tears show me you're conflicted about what he wants from you and what you've been taught. I'm going to pray for you, for real. I want to hear from Pastor Cutler that your butt is in the forum on a regular basis. Bring your friend too. If he loves you, he'll go and see what you're being taught. Now, go on over there and blow out those candles and pack your things, so your little friend can take you back to campus without my key."

Rebecca felt eerily like Madame. She now knew what her mother must have felt like when she shipped Rebecca away to Salisbury for college and beyond after catching her with a guy in a parked car. Rebecca figured if she couldn't take part in the girl's deliverance, she certainly wouldn't be a part of her destruction. Trixie didn't need any enabling. She thought about how she owed her husband an "I told you so," but only after he sweated it out home alone for a while. *The only ones who will be residing here will be me and the Lord.*

Chapter 35

Will knew where his wife would be. Two days had passed, and she hadn't come home, nor had he gone to claim her. His life was in utter turmoil without her. He wondered how he had become so reliant on her presence in the three short weeks since they had been married. He was in Salisbury also, but he had to make a pit stop before convincing her they couldn't spend another night apart.

He drove to Dogwood Community Church, desperate to take Pastor Cutler up on his promise to provide postmarital counseling if needed. He found Pastor Cutler in the back office. There were no kids to be found. Will had never heard the place so quiet.

"Where is everybody?" Will asked.

"There were a sparse few. I sent them back to the campus. After spring break, I'm thinking about opening just two or three times a week, unless a certain somebody wants to come help me full-time," Pastor Cutler said, wiping his weary eyes before replacing his glasses.

"Oh no. One congregation, one church is quite enough," Will said.

Will wanted to ask why he was considering cutting back his hours, but his friend's sadness was so palpable. He remembered what Rebecca had shared with him about Pastor Cutler's wife, Sandy. He wondered if, in his selfish desire to be mentored, he had overlooked the signs of Pastor Cutler's depression before. He decided to put off discussing what was on his mind about his marriage and instead somehow encourage his friend.

"This is a perfect place to pray. It's so quiet back here, out of earshot of the racket the kids can make," Will said, facing him now, attempting to chip away at his wall of despondency. "You've got to know Sandy would tell you that church is not about her. It's so much bigger than you and me, bigger than what the two of you established together. We can't claim it for ourselves. We can't hamper its growth. C'mon, man. You think God wants you to stop preaching, teaching, and counseling 'cause He called Sandy home to glory?"

Pastor Cutler's eyes were cloudy, but he was seeing something as he stared straight ahead. "I preached and taught under the obedience of my call, and nothing I said from the pulpit stopped me from free-falling when she left this earth two years ago on this very day."

"I know. When my mom died, my dad and I had to get out of the muck of death, before it sucked us up too. If you get sucked up, then not only did we lose Sandy, but we will have lost Monty too. Wallowing in it won't help. I pray even now that the Lord fills those spaces for you. Service helps. I've seen how it fulfills you. You can't give that up. Promise me."

Will stretched out his hand for Pastor Cutler to grab, and when he did, Will pulled him into an embrace, lending his shoulder for his friend to cry on.

"Thanks for that, my friend, honestly," Pastor Cutler said, swiping at his eyes with his hands and then wiping hands on his pant legs as he stood. He pulled the blinds to let some sun in and gazed outside. "I know you didn't come for this, but did you see the beginning of buds on Sandy's roses? I almost forgot about them, stuck in the back here."

"Buds? Really?" Will asked, although he doubted it. He didn't want to get up and look, knowing his face would give it away. The hips or knobs on a rosebush could be deceiving, but he wasn't siphoning off any hope. "See? A new beginning."

"Speaking of new beginnings, how's Rebi?"

There was no way to ease into his present woes. He began to explain to Pastor Cutler all that had transpired since the wedding, with its tie-ins to the past. He was almost embarrassed to admit that he hadn't taken his new bride to the church he claimed to love and wanted to lead. He concluded with their mini separation, although he didn't quite call it that.

"It's simple. Your wife wants to be loved in the open. You're not having an affair. She wants her own ring and a public display of affection beyond your wedding day. What woman doesn't?" He smirked. "She's tired of smelling your armpits, and you should be tired of smelling hers."

Will dared to ask, "What does that mean?"

"I'm rusty at this. I beg your pardon, but when I told you to go find her, I should have told you to go find yourself first. A man who would give up a woman so easily must have been hurting himself. I should have recognized that. So, what do you do? You followed the advice of an old man like me, and you hunted her down and got married as a crutch."

Will wanted his mentor to get away from the window immediately and explain himself. "You're losing me."

"You have to learn to walk side by side, and not use the other's arm as a prop. You're so used to coming to one another's aid as friends. You're a minister. She's a dancer. You two should be soaring, but you are still walking with a limp."

Will wanted more than anything to heal; he just didn't know the origin of his pain. This time, Will went to the window. He looked beyond the bushes to the soil beneath them and wondered to himself when it had last rained.

"Why are we so willing as Christians to stay in dry situations?" he said, thinking aloud about his old relationship with Veronica, and the relationship Madame entered into and endured with his dad.

"In marriage, Will, a little tending goes a long way," Pastor Cutler said confidently.

"What if she's left . . . temporarily, I mean. Rebecca is back at her apartment for a while, figuring out whether she can take the life of a preacher's wife."

"That's what you pray about. Although, if she doesn't want to come back, I don't know if God is gonna make her. Human will has its place."

Will's jaw dropped. He was expecting more of Pastor Cutler's optimism, not uncertainty. "C'mon, man. You admitted you got me into this, so help me fix it. I'm begging you."

Pastor Cutler suggested to Will that to save his marriage, he should get to the point of being vulnerable. "Give her a pointed illustration. Women respond to honesty, so you have to see it in your mind, feel it, and take her there so she can understand you. For me it was white-water rafting. I'm a fairly good swimmer, but I remember being scared to death going with my cousins when I was about fifteen. So, I took Sandy there, just four weeks after her diagnosis. She had started chemo, because her doctor wanted to take an aggressive approach. That, too, had me scared to death."

Pastor Cutler's eyes shone with the light he had when he was helping someone. Will had to sit for this, knowing this tidbit could very well be what he had been coming here for all this time.

"This particular canyon run was a bear. It had so many dips and curves. That part was fun, but the speed was uncontrollable both back then and the day I took Sandy. Fortunately, or not, we skimmed past a mini waterfall and got stuck. I kid you not, but what seemed like a geyser full of water flooded our boat. It was more than I bargained for. When we finally reached land and were drying off, I was crying like a baby."

Pastor Cutler told Will that he had to admit to Sandy after their trip down the rapids that one of his worst fears was drowning. He also shared with her that learning about her diagnosis had put him in a boat he could not control, one that was traveling faster than expected and potentially taking them both under.

Will saw the sadness return to his eyes for a brief moment. "What did she say to you?"

"She said, 'Monty, you and God have been my constant traveling companions. I can't help but ride it out and enjoy the company.'"

Oddly, that brought a smile to Pastor Cutler's face, and Will knew what else would as well. He walked with Pastor Cutler to their garden. There he pretended that every rose hip and thorn latch was a bud ready to blossom. He prayed that God would bring the blooms and dry his friend's tears before he ended up drowning in them.

Chapter 36

Some men brought flowers, candy, or jewelry when making up with their wives or girlfriends; he brought coffee. He knocked on the door, with the hope of never having to knock on that door again. His first job was to convince her to come home; his second was to convince her to get rid of her honeycomb hideout.

"I have a hard time sleeping without you," Will said as an introduction. He handed her the coffee, which she seemed happy to accept. He was glad to see the ring was still on her finger.

"You miss me in your bed? How original. I didn't have to get married to hear that one." She fanned her free hand out in front of her, as if to halt her frustration.

He could have cursed the look of disappointment in her eyes and the fact that he had helped to put it there. "To me, the beauty of our relationship is not so much its romantic or sexual aspects, but its sacred aspect. Gosh, you know, I love you in every way possible. I'd rather cancel the whole notion of being pastor if you're not beside me, and I'm sorry if I've been acting contrary to that."

Rebecca sniffed and cast her eyes upward. "It just hurt, that's all. I was geared up that day of the church service. Thought I was finally going to get that affirmation, that confirmation that I was ready for this thing called ministry. I've been thinking . . . been praying, actually. I know I give up too easily. I want to believe that there is a spot for us, if not at Grace Apostle, then somewhere."

"Cutler wants me to take over for him at Dogwood," Will said.

They both shook their heads before she spoke. "I'm sure we could both help him out, but Cutler is uniquely suited for that assignment. We've got to know our roles. I might have overstepped mine. The night I got here, I found Trixie setting up a rendezvous with some knuckleheaded boy. I've got a lot to learn, *a lot* to learn."

Will saw her contemplating the matter and wanted to put her at ease. "Don't we all. It's all or nothing, baby. I'm prepared to tell the congregation that the Sunday after next. They will respect you and our entire family, or they can leave. That's exactly what Veronica did."

"Will, I don't believe you and—"

"Well, I checked. I wanted to make sure there were no further episodes of times past. She has packed up at the Pritchett place and gone back to where she came from."

Will paused once he made that clear. He could tell that she had been dancing before he arrived. She might as well be Jennifer Beals from *Flashdance,* because her blouse hung loose and off her shoulder and her sweatpants fit over a leotard. She had a gorgeous form, and even when she was sweaty and caught off guard, he still wanted her. He hoped they were making up right now.

"Can I take you out?" Will asked.

Once again Will had to ask her whether she trusted him enough to go with him without necessarily knowing where. Will didn't entirely trust that he'd be able to pull off Pastor Cutler's experiment, but it was worth a shot. There were so many things he wanted to share with his wife, things that he felt she needed to know, before taking on ministry with him.

They headed in the direction of their home but turned off and drove into the town of Hurlock. Will remembered a FOR SALE sign he had seen on a commercial farm there on his way to another Perdue Farms site when he was training his replacement. This farm was known for selling fruit in season and giving kids wagon rides and a choice of pumpkins in the fall. Pastor Cutler had said to think about a time when he was most vulnerable. A distinct memory of being on a farm like this came to mind.

"Remember going on a field trip like this when we were at Grace Apostle?"

"Yeah, and guys and girls pairing up and kissing with reckless abandon in the fields," she said, closing her sweater, which hung loosely around her, to combat the wind. "I always wanted to be kissed like that."

Out in the open, Will thought.

"Weren't we hanging together on one of those trips?"

"Uh, yeah, but you weren't up for any kissing. That was what was so interesting and frustrating about you. It was not at all where your head was at. I think you had a notebook out and were taking notes. You were such a geek."

"I guess I missed out. The owner was telling us the dimensions, because unlike other corn mazes in the area, he had cut a perfect square," Will noted.

She rolled her eyes at him. "Who cares? We were out of the classroom, free to roam free."

Will brought the car to a stop across the street from the farm's main entrance, and they climbed out. Their feet crunched on the ground beneath them as they made their way onto the abandoned property. She was adventurous, and Will thanked God for that. There was a corn maze cut out up ahead. Although they were coming upon the season to plant again, the owners had left before plowing the field. Will pointed at what he thought could be the entrance to the maze, and like fools, they rushed in.

It was unusually spacious inside the maze. Fallen cornstalks and straw carpeted the inside. Rebecca sprang ahead, doing a graceful leap over a heap of debris. She couldn't resist spinning around as he studied the rows of stalks that separated one section of the maze from another. They were forced to turn left in one spot but made the decision to go right at another.

"Honey," Will called out to her when he couldn't see her. "Stay back with me."

"I can really reenact *The Sound of Music* in here," she said from around a bend ahead of him.

He quickened his pace while calling out, "I thought we were supposed to be walking this thing together."

"You're too slow," she called, sounding farther away than he expected. "You got to catch up."

Will went left into a dead end. He did a one-eighty and wondered whether he was traveling back toward the start of the maze. Each turn and crossroads got him more and more confused. He felt dumb. With all his intellect and wisdom, he couldn't get himself out of this maze. He felt exactly the way he did over fifteen years ago—fearful.

"Rebecca," he shouted out of frustration, and then he heard her giggles.

He dropped to the ground and sat on the straw, resigned himself to staying there until she came looking for him. This was crazy. He was thirty-two years old, but he was feeling like a boy a third his age and was near tears. What was this? He decided to do as Pastor

Cutler had suggested and simply feel the emotion. He breathed in both the experience of then and now. Then it all made sense.

Rebecca crept up on him quietly, as if she were wearing her ballerina slippers instead of her boots. She was startled to see him on the ground. "What happened? Where were you?"

"Where were *you?* I was right here. I couldn't go anywhere," Will tried to explain. "I kept trying to tell you to stay back."

She stared at him like someone who was having fun and thought all along he was feeling the same way, only to find out in her joyous state that he had been in trouble. She was concerned, but it was a selfish concern. "I have been to the end and back again."

"What if I said it wasn't about you? It's not about a chase." He knew it was going to come out wrong when he said it.

"What if you tell me what it is all about then, 'cause I'm tired of guessing with you," she said, flinging herself beside him on the ground. "What's going on? Why are we here?"

"In high school the same thing happened. We all ran in, and folks left me. I remember being hot and sneezing repeatedly. I didn't have my allergy medicine and thought I would have an allergic reaction."

"You've got allergies? Isn't that something you think your wife should know?" Rebecca asked.

Will grabbed his head in his hands to slow down his thoughts. "Oh my God, I'm stifling you. If I don't get it together, get your head out from under my arm, I'm going to stunt your growth, for real. Jesus!"

She mirrored his position and his fear as well. "Dude, I don't understand you."

Before he tried again to explain, he stopped to feel the fear. "I can't lead," leapt from his mouth.

"Huh?"

"Just like I can't get myself out of here, I'm afraid I won't be able to lead. I get lost sometimes . . . me. I don't know what direction to go in with the ministry. I have at least half the congregation depending on me, but what if I dramatically flip the script to follow the move of Christ instead of what they are used to? Will they stay with me then?"

Rebecca swallowed hard. "Everyone feels that way at some point. Why is that such a scary proposition to you?"

"The other half or third or quarter wants me out on my butt like my dad. I'm afraid that percentage is right. I can preach—it's a no-brainer—but so can Danny Glass."

She grabbed at his arm, propped now on his knee, and he extended his hand for her to hold. "You're an amazing preacher, though."

"Preaching and leading are two different things," he was fast to say.

They were silent for a while, alternating looks at each other and at the sun above. The afternoon sun was doing very little to warm the ground beneath them, though. Will knew that soon they'd have to move on, but had they learned their lesson?

"It's a known fact that men don't like to ask for directions. Ask for help, Will. You've got your dad. Make things right between the two of you. He can help you at every turn, but you have to make clear to him that it's your chance to lead. You will lead. Remember I told you the day after our wedding that being the First Lady scared me – that ministry scared me. You told me that ministry was simply living before people in the most authentic and God-ordained way. Life is like this maze. I imagine God's watching us like mice in experiment. He set us free to run our course. He knows we can do it, and he's rooting for us, baby."

He pulled her up off the ground with him by her arm. "And I got you, right?"

"How did Pastor Cutler put it at the wedding? I am your helpmate."

He stopped dusting off the seat of his pants. "That's another thing. I am supposed to lead in this marriage. I just pray you don't leave me in my indecision. That's why I need you to give up your apartment after the trial. I don't want to make it any easier for you to run."

"Haven't I just about proven I'd follow you anywhere?" Rebecca said, fanning her hand out to indicate their surroundings. "I'm here to stay."

"Good. Now, get me out of here," he commanded.

She huddled next to him, basking in his body heat, and turned his attention upward with her hand. "I find a focal point way up high. It may be in front of me going in and in back of me going out."

Will didn't know if she was pointing to a high tree limb or the water tower high above, but he chose God. God was his focal point. She stepped out from under his arm and allowed him to lead them out.

Once they were at the end of the maze, he took her hand and planted little kisses around her wedding ring. "This is still a summons. I'm the sheriff who has been ordered to take you in."

"That's all well and good, Mr. Sheriff, but you're going to owe me another one of these, let's say, in ten years."

"So when we get back, can I see some of your moves?" he asked, flirting.

"It depends on what kind of moves you're talking about," she countered with a coy look, "'cause right now I really don't feel like dancing."

Will looked at his wife, then at their car across the way, then back at his wife. "Let's go."

But she was backing away from his grasp and heading toward the entrance to the maze again. She called to him, "Now that you can navigate the maze, let's see if you can redeem yourself with me in terms of that high school field trip. Set this maze on fire."

His heart raced with the notion of what she was up to. He watched her dip back into the maze, a lone finger peeking out from behind some cornstalks, beckoning him to follow. He kept thinking he couldn't wait to get her home, but then he realized that like she had said earlier, he'd follow her anywhere. He scanned the property for any other visitors, tugged at his earlobe, and set off on the chase.

Chapter 37

Will wondered now how he could do this without his father. His family had to come together for the sake of his campaign, but he and his father needed to come together for the future of their relationship. They needed a jump start. When he heard that Gail and Milo had arranged this family dinner for later on that day to do just that, Will felt it was only fitting that he, Rebecca, and his dad have a conversation beforehand.

"Well, hello, Rebecca, son," Pastor Donovan said.

After they crossed the threshold of Pastor Donovan's house, Rebecca excused herself and carried grocery bags, their contribution for the dinner, to the kitchen.

"Good. I needed to talk to you, Will. The gleaners at church are usually collected and the money divided between benevolence and the local food bank. It's long since been a tradition. You're the only one to make sure that still happens."

"Wait, Dad. I just got married and all you can talk about is church?" Will made sure Rebecca was out of earshot.

"Oh, am I supposed to respond to what I wasn't told and was hardly invited to?"

"Rebecca said she called you with the details of the ceremony."

"Rebi did. You didn't. I didn't know that I had done or said something so wrong to you that I would be kicked off the guest list, but I guess I did."

"Admit your wrong, honey," came the voice of Rebecca from the kitchen.

They both smiled, which helped to lighten the mood. Will had been so offended by his dad's comments about him and Rebecca remaining friends that he hadn't thought how much it would hurt him and his dad by not having him present at the wedding. He was mostly still ticked off about his father's affair. He didn't want to get into that all over again, not with Rebecca listening in.

Will lowered his voice. "I guess I should have thought about honoring you with your rightful place at the wedding. I'm sorry for that, but don't take it out on my wife."

His dad looked at him with what looked like a new respect. "Your wife. My son has got a wife. I've got to get used to that."

"Did someone call my name?" Rebecca said from the door frame. She was determined to be a part of this conversation.

His dad chuckled. "If you aren't Ava Lucas's daughter, I don't know who is." He reached his hand out to Rebecca, and she came over quickly and grabbed it as she stood over him.

The light in his eyes and the mention of Madame's name made for an awkward silence, though. They never could get him to speak about his adulterous affair before. They were all family now, and the secrets were what was tearing them apart. Will just didn't know how to ask for the information he needed to start his own healing—their healing.

"Ava actually was a reflection of me in many ways, cynical but in charge, but Will's mom was every bit of what I hoped to be. I honestly did love them both," Pastor Donovan revealed.

"And you balanced them both with your ministry? I still struggle to think about where Mom was when all this took place. Where was I?" Will felt emotional asking the questions in his mind before he finally voiced them. "Oh my God, the ice cream."

Will remembered his dad always going on ice cream runs. He used to love escaping from the kitchen table, if he had finished his dinner, and going with his dad to the supermarket when he was younger. When his mom got sick, his dad's runs for ice cream still remained a constant.

"Ice cream was just ice, cream, sugar, and a little salt, son. Ice cream was ice cream then."

Will looked up at his wife, who had dropped his dad's hand and was now sitting on the arm of Will's chair. He wondered if she had the same questions. "It started taking you longer and longer to go fetch a pint. There is no need to lie to me, Dad. When did ice cream become sherbet? And did Mom know?"

His dad had an odd expression, which Will tried to read. He thought about his mom, so gracious and kind, and knew at that moment that while she was dying, his mom had somehow given him the green light to be with his first love. Will had to cover his eyes to hide the tears.

"Ask Rebecca how stubborn her mother was. We weren't together while you both were young children. Actually, Ava despised me for a long while after we broke up, before I met your mom. Let me tell you, when Ava held a grudge, Ava held a grudge. Watch out for this one here," Pastor Donovan said, pointing in Rebecca's direction.

"Hey," Rebecca said in mock defense. "I was on your side."

"So why don't you defend yourself, put everyone of us at ease, if you didn't cheat all that time they were accusing you of cheating?" Will asked.

"It doesn't matter. All sin is weighted the same in the eyes of the Lord and is multiplied times ten in the eyes of church folk. We weren't completely innocent," his dad replied, defending himself. Then he turned his attention to Rebecca with fresh tears of his own. "I couldn't have gotten through my wife's death without your mom. She was my comfort. We grew close again, and in some ways I felt I took advantage of her. I definitely didn't give her what she truly wanted. That's why when I look at the two of you—happy, together, bold enough to get married despite what anyone says—I'm both proud and ashamed."

Not since his mom's funeral had Will seen his dad weep the way he did that afternoon. He wondered how much more or less he wept for Madame Ava in secret.

Will looked at his wife by his side during the dinner, which was served once Gail and Milo arrived, and thanked God for the lesson of loving her in the open. They talked about future gatherings at each other's houses during all the holidays to come.

The conversation eventually turned to Grace Apostle and the family presentation and sermon that both candidates would do on Easter Sunday.

"I know the future first lady is going to dance as part of the presentation," Gail said.

Pastor Donovan smiled at Gail. "You know, I was thinking just that."

"I was telling Rebi we had her pegged as the woman with the alabaster box. Remember we talked about that, Dad? I think CeCe Winans has a song by that name, 'Alabaster Box,'" Will added.

"I like 'Take Me to the King,' by that woman who plays on *Meet the Browns*. She can sing. I know that would be simply beautiful," Pastor Donovan said.

They did not stop to consider what Rebecca thought until she butted in. "Excuse me, all of you, especially the two Donovan men. Can we all agree that my gift is not a gimmick? You don't see me trying to tell either of you how to preach. My friend Marie Glass informed me that we have a forty-five-minute presentation, including the Word. I was figuring I could speak too. I do speak." She paused for a moment. "Since you've thought about my dance, have you thought about your title or topic?" Rebecca asked, putting Will on the spot. His dad was chuckling.

He had thought about his topic, and all they had been through. "The stigma stops here."

Rebecca smirked. "Well, then, give me some space and leave my part of the presentation up to me."

Will just shook his head. He thought about what Pastor Cutler had said. Now that they were learning to walk side by side, he had to allow her to soar.

Chapter 38

Preparing her wrongful dismissal case, which was grounded in harassment and cover-up, was like a game of Chutes and Ladders. Some doors could be opened, and others sent them hurling back to the beginning. The EEOC had finally done its own investigation and had determined that there was enough evidence for a civil trial. Rebecca and Connie were informally interviewing people who would cooperate and corroborate the story they were trying to tell as witnesses. With a court date set for the beginning of Holy Week, Rebecca and her counsel still had frames to fill.

Virtually every call to Sanz, Mitchum, and Clarke put her in contact with Celeste. Sometimes Rebecca was able to disguise her voice so that Celeste wouldn't know who was calling, but one day Rebecca called at the end of the receptionist's shift to talk directly to her.

"If this isn't the woman who dared to take on the firm. You've got your nerve calling here," Celeste said, her way of warning Rebecca not to ask or expect much of her. "Talking about biting the hand that fed you."

"C'mon, Celeste. You know more about what goes on than anyone else there. I was railroaded into doing this, and you know it."

"I know you asked for a lot and did very little," Celeste said loudly, but then brought her tone down when she continued. "I know you are the type of woman who prances around with a little air about you and then tries to take down all the other black people at the firm."

Rebecca felt she could say the same to Celeste, but it didn't prevent the wound of her coworker's words. Then she remembered she was no longer accountable for what others saw in her when she knew what she was about. "I'm sorry you feel that way. I don't know what I've done to you personally, but I'm sorry if I offended you. After my leave, I honestly did just want to do my job."

"Yeah, right. Burke couldn't hardly say hello to anyone else without you showing up. You fell for the angel line like so many, and you probably believed he used it just with you. That was his open line of credit with every female in the building."

Rebecca wondered if Celeste knew how much she had helped her with that call. She wasn't the only one. She reported back to Connie, and they set about hunting down a possible cohort of women that Burke had similarly handled like candy in a dish. The new paralegals came to mind, as well as Ms. Humphries, who seemed to know a little more about Kenny Burke beyond their counterclaim.

Finally, they struck gold with her fellow paralegal, Bethany, who was now a new mom. She was willing to attest to the fact that Burke was indeed a supreme jerk. On one or more occasions he had used sexist slurs with her. When asked by a client why Bethany was filling in while Rebecca was on leave, Burke had commented that he had them all, blondes, brunettes, and that the client, who was male, should take his pick. According to Bethany, one female client had even complained about Burke's mouth and attitude to HR.

"Fortunately for us, all the damaging testimony about your flirtatious and otherwise fraternizing behavior cannot be revealed in these proceedings, but that makes Burke a fading character. If he's our anchor, we need everything that sticks to him to also stick to the firm," Connie observed at a strategy session for just the two of them.

Rebecca was at her wit's end. They had Burke the jerk, Bethany the believable, Calhoun and his card, and Connie thought that might not be enough. Rebecca was so over it that she couldn't recall all the details of her time spent at the firm. This case wasn't a federal grand jury investigation, was it?

Connie was looking for a central thread that tied them all together. At the eleventh hour Rebecca awoke with the final thread and frame. Celeste had mentioned that charm was Burke's line of credit, but Rebecca clearly remembered that he and one of the partners' grandsons, Skip Clarke, had blown through a company expense account for tee times, tequila, and whatever else they needed to get clients to come aboard. Rebecca was sure that was traceable. Connie was quite intrigued about Skip as a potential witness. She explained that his involvement implicated the whole firm. He was the face of the partners.

Rebecca felt the chips could fall where they may. The case had taken her away from her home and her husband. She spent the next week at her apartment, preparing for the case by day and preparing a dance piece to share at church by night. She chose words that would convince both the court and the congregation that she was worthy to be heard. She was concerned with the appeal of both.

The night before the trial was to begin, she went back home. She asked her husband, who was all of a sudden keen on the idea of letting her walk on her own, if he'd accompany her to court. She didn't think she needed a character witness, but a character supporter always helped. He paraphrased a couple of stories from the

Bible that spoke to the battle being fought and won by God. When they awoke, Will brought a newspaper article to the breakfast table. She didn't want to read another thing and thought it might be about her, since a small story had run in the *Salisbury Times* about the pending case.

This article was about the current U.S. president, who ran for and won reelection. The columnist spoke about the opposing party, which continued to blame him for not cleaning up his predecessor's past mistakes and to discredit his record from his first term as president. Had he made enough of a difference? Rebecca had grown tired of reading and preferred to concentrate on other things.

When they were in the car on their way to court, Will asked, "What did you think of the article? Kind of reminds you of us, right?"

"Nope. Not at all. I failed to see the correlation," Rebecca said, trying to hide how nervous she truly was from her husband.

"There are a lot of people who would like to see the man fail, but incrementally, he's getting things done, and he even got reelected, despite staunch opposition. Did you see the title?"

"No," Rebecca said.

"I cut it out for you and me. I'm going to use it in my sermon," Will said, reaching into his suit jacket. He handed her the folded headline, which read: THE POLITICS ARE LINING UP FOR A SUCCESSFUL SECOND TERM. She prayed silently that they were.

Once in court, Rebecca realized that this was more than a dance. It was a ball, and she was the belle. All the players whom she and Connie had framed were present. Connie and Bryan Russell were the perfect matchup. Each line of questioning was like a tug-of-war, and they seemed to bring the case back to an equal footing by the end of day one. She kept telling herself the politics were lining up in her favor.

On day two, Rebecca took the stand. She spoke candidly about her time at Sanz, Mitchum, and Clarke, particularly about that month after her return. She delivered the one line she had practiced and was told by Connie to deliver: I insist.

"When asked to entertain Mr. Calhoun on his yacht, did you attempt to tell Mr. Burke and Mr. Clarke that you were uncomfortable with their proposition?" Connie asked.

"Yes," Rebecca declared.

"What was their response, if any?" Connie said, prompting.

"Mr. Burke and Mr. Calhoun both told me, 'I insist.'"

There were objections from Mr. Russell when Connie made the case that their insistence had registered as a demand with Rebecca.

During the recess, when Rebecca thought she had taken all that she could take, there was a call made to Connie's office. It was Mr. Russell. Connie eagerly put him on speakerphone so that everyone could hear. To the surprise of everyone, except maybe Connie, who had been fearless in court, and God, the firm was willing to sacrifice Burke, Humphries, and quite possibly the second generation Clarke to appease them and to reach a sizable monetary settlement.

It all seemed too easy. The other side offered, and their side agreed. This was the judicial system and politics at their best. What Rebecca had thought would be long, drawn out, and dirty, like the presidential election, had been miraculously quick and easy. The first thing Rebecca did, other than release a sigh from her soul, was reach over to embrace her husband.

As they were crossing back over Courthouse Row, heading to their car, they ran into a dazed and seemingly wandering Kenny Burke. They didn't know if he knew or not that his job was on the compost pile. Given that he had such a brilliant legal mind, Rebecca almost felt sorry for him. Will quickly got in front of Rebecca, who was tense with apprehension.

"You're good, angel. I got to hand it to you. You show up in court with a broad whose guns are blazing from her bosom and a husband . . . the preacher." His glare was squinty as if he was looking directly into the sun and his gaze jumped between Rebecca and Will. "I know now you'll go to extreme lengths to prove you are a good girl."

Before Will could speak on her behalf or lay his hands on Kenny, Rebecca thought about what he had said and how far she had come and said, "No, Kenny. It shows how far God will go to do just that."

Chapter 39

The following article appeared in the Easter edition of the *Society Pages*.

Trial and Error, Trials and Tribulations

A pastor's wife is meant to be an asset to her husband and the church, but not if she has more issues than he does. We've met the candidates for pastor at a local historic church, and now it's time to meet the missuses.

First up is the wife of the native son, formerly known as Lay-Z, who had to be hiding something when he snuck away to marry his childhood friend and classmate, or shall I say playmate to many, Flu-Z. Talk about all in the family. Apparently, the men in his family can't resist the women in hers. The family ties are closer than what is socially acceptable. If you figure out this family tree, will you please let us in on it?

The second competitor has got more game than Jordan and apparently isn't the only guard in the family. His wife intercepts passes and is ready to call a flagrant foul on anyone caught close to her man. I foresee trials and tribulations for this wifey, whose husband has eyes set on more than one pulpit and possibly more than one woman at a time. Since he is a man chased from his father's kingdom, who is fool enough to give him the throne?

Matches made in heaven, I think not. It's as if these pairs should do a wife swap.

The Donovan clan came to church on Easter Sunday with a chip on their shoulders. Once again, Will found two bundles of those papers, which had been left on the corner of the church steps, when he and Rebecca walked up. A few had been siphoned off the top, which made it easier for Rebecca to nab her own. Will carried them into the back and prepared to put an end to the paper's distribution, among other things, today. They were greeted by Deacon Contee, who no doubt was waiting for the arrival of the Glass family, who pulled up to the church five minutes later.

The families were cordial with one another, with Rebecca and Marie sharing a warmer reception than Will and Danny. When the women went into the inner office to hang up their outerwear and talk, Will couldn't help but idly listening in as he held a copy of the *Society Pages.*

"Where are the kids?" Rebecca inquired.

"With their grandparents at I Am the Way, celebrating Easter with the friends they left behind there," Marie told her.

"Have you seen the latest *Society Pages?* Marie, it leaks the fact that Danny is not totally committed here at Grace Apostle and has applied somewhere else as well," Rebecca said with growing concern.

"I know. The leak doesn't trail far from where I poked the hole," Marie said.

"Does Danny know?" Rebecca said, just short of a whisper.

"I guess he'll find out soon enough. It doesn't matter, though. The man thinks he's invincible."

"I don't understand. Why would you put that kind of information out there?"

Marie leaned her girth against the desk. "I asked for a break from ministry. I think he owes me that much. He wants to create one church in two locations, like Pop's dynasty. That's well and good, but I can't be a watchdog in two locations and a mother of three."

Will couldn't believe what he was hearing. The knowledge of everything that was inconsistent about Danny Glass was held by these two women. Why hadn't Rebecca shared with him some of what she knew about his competitor, such as Danny's womanizing? Will had to wonder whether he would have used it against Danny. Then he thought about what Mrs. Glass had witnessed between himself, his wife, and his ex. The woman had realized that healing and loving support ranked higher than competition. They had chosen to minister to one another.

Deacon Contee was calling them all together, ready to execute his plan for the service, which would include presentations and a final church-wide vote. Will was coming to realize that like himself, Contee wasn't in control, and he definitely wasn't calling the shots when it came to worship.

"What I think we will do is take each family out one by one. That way each candidate can deliver their sermonette and any other message they want to share. The Glass family can go first, and then I'll be back for Minister and Mrs. Donovan. Is that all right with everyone?"

Will looked around before speaking. "This is the celebration of the Resurrection of our Lord and Savior. This is like a preachers' Super Bowl. Deacon Contee, you've overstepped your authority again, thinking you can order worship service. I want the Word and the revelations this day will bring. You just worry about the vote."

"I don't mind sharing the pulpit," Danny said, chiming in, extending a hand for Will to shake.

"Or the front pew," Rebecca said. "It would be good to have a girlfriend to sit next to."

Deacon Contee looked around, stunned, as if he could sniff out a conspiracy but wasn't ready to name it. "I guess I'll be back to get you all at the beginning of the processional. Is there anything else?"

"Yes, take these," Marie said, bending toward the pile of papers Will had brought in, but then thinking better of the decision. "Have the ushers pass this paper out. If folks are determined to digest this trash, let them get their fill of it. I think it's high time both of you spoke out against the accusations found inside. If it's lies, call it lies, but call it what it is."

Will stared at her strangely, much like Deacon Contee and her husband did, but no one disagreed. In actuality, Veronica's column was the perfect tie-in to Will's sermon.

The Glass family presented themselves before the congregation with grace and humility. They were polished. Danny didn't touch the scandal rag controversy and its depictions of his family. Will wondered if he had read it or had just chosen to ignore it. Mrs. Glass ended their presentation by thanking the congregants for the hospitality that her family had been shown and by expressing the hope that they would be welcome if Danny Glass was elected to preach and teach from the pulpit or if they simply visited in the pews. It felt eerily like a good-bye.

Then it was Will's turn. He carried the love and support of his family with him to the sacred desk.

"I have the esteemed pleasure of being in the presence of the Lord today, my father, Pastor Emeritus William Henry Donovan Sr., my fellow laborer, Danny Glass Jr., my sister and brother-in-law, Gail and Milo Green, and a woman who has changed my world. Many may know her as my best friend and confidant growing up, but now I have the privilege to call her my wife. Some say we snuck off and got married, but if you were to ask us, we'd say that it has been a journey. That goes with anything you need to perfect, to get right. I got this one right. Please show your love and respect for Rebecca Lucas Donovan."

He paused and waited for the applause of all who were assembled as Rebecca stood from her place in the front pew and waved. His dad, Gail, and Marie Glass led the charge.

"She's going to speak to you all and share from her heart at the end of my message."

His talk, entitled "The Stigma Stops Here," spoke to the banishment of judgment once the Lord showed up in a person's life. He mentioned Joseph protecting Mary from public ridicule when he realized she carried God's gift, the leper, and even the woman with an issue of blood, who became uniquely changed when He showed up. Nothing was more powerful than the accusations, the trial, and the eventual hanging on the cross of Jesus, who died for every stigma in our lives.

"How many of you read the *Society Pages?*" Will asked.

A precious few responded, some before they had thought better of it. Will smiled good-naturedly, as only he could do when he was setting up his point. "We've passed them out for your convenience. Turn to the article on page two. One writer of this periodical has found it necessary to poke fun at this church and our desire to pass down the legacy to our next leader. It has a place, but not in the church. I think I'm depicted as the character named Lay-Z, trying to live in the shadow of my dad. Some of you feel this way about me. Some of you have told me.

"Fans of this paper should say good-bye to the notion of picking up their copy at church. Tell the writers, producers, and manufacturers, especially the paper girls and paperboys who deliver it. The columnist makes a point of placing a label, a stigma, if you will, on something from which God has removed a stigma. How many people know that when He removes the stigma off of you, whatever it was that people called you, or you called yourself, it doesn't stick anymore?"

Forty-five minutes was just enough time to shame the devil. Once again Will left them with something to think about and grow upon. He was coming to understand that that was his niche, his ministry trademark. He had to let Rebecca do her thing before the benediction, the close of worship, and the official vote. He called out to her to join him in the pulpit .

"Hello, Grace Apostle," Rebecca said, adjusting her tone to the microphone. "Some may know me, may have known my mother, which can be both a blessing and a curse. Like my husband indicated, I carried a stigma for a good while. Even recently I was caught up in a harassment case and trial with my old job. I was like, 'Lord, why?' I had just gotten married. I didn't need and didn't want to dredge up my past. Where I may be ashamed of my past, I'm not ashamed of the Gospel. God saved me. He delivered me. Even in my trial, he exonerated me, vindicated me."

Will could hear her sigh deeply into the microphone as he stood near her shoulder and whispered words of encouragement in her ear.

She continued, "I won't claim to know everything about the Word of God. Maybe that's why God put me with this man. What Will has taught me is that I embody the Scriptures. We are all a walking verse. You might not see me in the Bible, but can you find yourself? I just want to impart that my family is not here to intimidate you, do you wrong, or hold a grudge. I, personally, am here to seek the Lord, help some people in the process, and hold my husband down."

She left the microphone abruptly. Will caught her before she descended the ramp and kissed her right there on the pulpit platform.

"Amen," Will said. "Don't hate. Just call me blessed. I want to be mindful of the time. Those of us who were present at the anniversary know my wife is also an anointed dancer. She shared brief expressions with you just now, and the rest can be shared through the ministry of dance."

Rebecca walked down the ramp on his cue to an awaiting Gail, who draped her in a robe of royal blue. Rebecca wore the same color as Trixie and another woman from her old dance school, whom she brought to the church to minister with her. She stationed herself in the middle of the aisle, with the other women on opposite sides of her.

The words and the music started with no precursor. The three of them started to move together. The song's first line went, "I've been changed, freed, healed, delivered."

Most agreed with the songwriter and the choreography of the song as they stood where they were, clapping and singing along. Rebecca almost demanded it of them, as she broke away from the group and clapped her hands over her head to the a cappella breakdown of the song's title and refrain, "I Won't Go Back."

When the song was finally over, it felt like they had knocked on the door of heaven for God to let them in. It was time for the anonymous church-wide vote. The ballots were printed in the church bulletin, and trustees held baskets in which to collect them. Deacon Contee, in his last act as the selection committee chairperson, called the candidates to the front from the floor-level microphone. Will met Rebecca, who was flushed and was still reeling from her performance, on the floor level. When they looked for the Glass family to join them, they realized that they had left.

Deacon Contee looked at Will, as if he knew their whereabouts, but Will only shrugged. He approached a confused Will and Rebecca after giving the official signal for the vote to commence. He pointed the way to the side aisle so that they could exit.

Once in the hallway, Deacon Contee asked, "Where is Minister Glass?"

Will shrugged again as he followed Contee, who was walking briskly to the back. "He left the pulpit with you. I thought it was just to remove his robe and refresh himself after he preached."

"He did, but then he asked me to signal for his wife." Contee rushed inside the outer office to search for clues as to the Glass family's whereabouts, while Will and Rebecca remained outside in the hallway.

"That must have been after I got up to speak," Rebecca observed once he returned.

Crestfallen, Deacon Contee let his gaze wander up the back hallway toward the door. Will almost felt sorry for the deacon, who was locked in place, as if he had bet all his money on the wrong horse. "Tell me they haven't gone."

"I can't speak to the integrity of your candidate. I'm here. I've been here. I come from this," Will said, more to himself than to Deacon Contee. He was a little shocked when his own voice seemed to break with emotion.

Will felt Rebecca's hand curl up inside his. He turned to look at her and grabbed her other hand in the process.

"You know what that means?" he said. "We did it, baby. If the Glass family has bowed out, we've won."

She beamed.

Will looked from his wife to Deacon Contee, who reluctantly shook his head in confirmation while staring at his cell phone. He passed the phone to Rebecca, who held it up for Will to see. It was a text from Danny, stating that he was withdrawing his application for the position as pastor at Grace Apostle Methodist Church.

"But it's by default. I don't want it by default. I've got to know for sure that the people I'm leading think I'm competent," Will said.

This time they followed Will's trail from the back of the church to the front entrance of the sanctuary. As they walked by, they saw the trustees huddled over a table of ballots, counting, in one of the side offices. Will did not interfere. He stopped short of the sanctuary door, where he, Rebecca, and Deacon Contee could see that the crowd was restless, like a class with no teacher, awaiting a leader.

"What do you want me to do, Pastor?" Contee asked.

Will wanted to dismiss him permanently, but he saw the deacon for who he was, loyal but misguided. "Supervise the vote, and I'll take care of the people."

Will took a look through the glass in the door one last time. He remembered feeling not too long ago as if this congregation was not his people. Even now, the crowd had thinned out considerably since the service. His dad and Rebecca had reminded him that he wouldn't win everyone over. He took Rebecca's hand this time, and they entered the sanctuary. Will saw a familiar face up ahead, and when he reached that aisle seat, he dropped Rebecca's hand to pull Pastor Cutler into a full embrace. The handful of claps that erupted at that moment eventually turned into a rousing standing ovation.

"You all must know something I don't," Will declared once he reached the pulpit with Rebecca, who stood off to the side, still in her liturgical robe. "With all seriousness, Minister Danny Glass sent word that he is withdrawing his candidacy at this time."

There were some gasps and murmurs, but Will continued. "With respect to the process, we will wait for the official vote. In the meantime, I recall that when my dad was pastor, he would get several invitations from people in the congregation to join them for Easter dinner. I'm just saying."

By the time the results of the actual vote came in, Will and Rebecca had at least four invitations to Easter dinner, and he fully intended to make his rounds and honor those invitations as his first act as pastor.

He pulled Rebecca close to him. "I hope you're ready to dig in."

Readers' Guide Questions

1. Who is your favorite antagonist? Deacon Contee, Kenny Burke, Danny Glass, or Veronica Deeds? And why?

2. What does Rebecca's apartment represent? Why was she reluctant to give it up, and why was Will so adamant about her giving it up?

3. Will and Rebecca soon realized they couldn't continue to live together without being married. What is the danger of platonic friends living together the way they did?

4. How did Pastor Cutler and Marie Glass serve as mentors to Will and Rebecca's early ministry?

5. Discuss the dynamic of the Glass family. Do you believe it is the first lady's role to play watchdog and protect her husband from Gospel groupies and hangers-on?

6. The *Society Pages* articles struck a chord with Will, his father, and the Glass family. Discuss the truths and accusations in each article printed about Grace Apostle's search for a new leader.

7. Discuss the hand-me-down ring Will gave Rebecca when he proposed to her. Would you have similar difficulties accepting an engagement ring if you found out what Rebecca found out? Does Will owe her a new one?

8. What did Pastor Donovan mean when he said that seeing Will and Rebecca married made him both proud and ashamed?

9. Discuss Will's corn maze admission. What did Rebecca learn about her husband from that experience?

10. What did Rebecca mean when she said to Burke that God went to great lengths to prove she was a good girl?

ABOUT THE AUTHOR

A multi-published author, dynamic speaker, teacher, wife, and mother, Sherryle Kiser Jackson hails from Prince George's County in Maryland. Trained at former Salisbury State University, now simply, Salisbury University, she's a teacher by profession, but a writer by pure passion. Her writing style encapsulates honest commentary on her life with Christ. She strives to be a fresh voice in Christian iction. She's the author of five other novels, and she's also the host of the Write Away Weekend, an intensive writers' residency held in Fort Washington, Maryland during the first weekend in October.

URBAN CHRISTIAN HIS GLORY BOOK CLUB!

www.uchisglorybookclub.net

UC His Glory Book Club is the spirit-inspired brainchild of Joylynn Ross, an author and the acquisitions editor at Urban Christian, and Kendra Norman-Bellamy, an author for Urban Christian. It is an online book club that hosts authors of Urban Christian. We welcome as members all men and women who have a passion for reading Christian-based fiction.

UC His Glory Book Club pledges its commitment to providing support, positive feedback, encouragement, and a forum whereby members can openly discuss and review the literary works of Urban Christian authors.

There is no membership fee associated with UC His Glory Book Club; however, we do ask that you support the authors by purchasing their works, encouraging them, providing book reviews, and, of course, offering your prayers. We also ask that you respect our beliefs and follow the guidelines of the book club. We hope to receive your valuable input, opinions, and reviews that build up, rather than tear down, our authors.

WHAT WE BELIEVE:

—We believe that Jesus is the Christ, Son of the Living God.

—We believe that the Bible is the true, living Word of God.

—We believe that all Urban Christian authors should use their God-given writing abilities to honor God and share the message of the written word that God has given to each of them uniquely.

—We believe in supporting Urban Christian authors in their literary endeavors by reading their titles, purchasing them, and sharing them with our online community.

—We believe that everything we do in our literary arena should be done in a manner that will lead to God being glorified and honored.

We look forward to online fellowship with you. Please visit us often at www.uchisglorybookclub.net.

Many Blessing to You!
Shelia E. Lipsey,
President, UC His Glory Book Club

Notes